THE
LAST
BOY
IN HIS
CLASS

GEOFF GREEN

You can only keep a lip buttoned for so long

The Last Boy In His Class
By Geoff Green

ISBN
979-8-316160945 (Paperback)
Published by Geoff Green
www.geoffgreen.co.uk

Also by Geoff Green

NON-FICTION

Paying for the Past

FICTION

The Sand Hide
Cold Friends
The Prisoner of Brenda Brown
The 22nd Floor
The Door to Her Father (unpublished)

CHAPTER ONE

The boy's unexpected words, 'you'll pay for that, Father', had more of an effect on George Brownlow than he dared admit. Was that a threat – from his own son – a child?

Following the day George broke his wife's jaw, he'd held back on his church visits for some considerable time. And Florence wouldn't be going anywhere near the confessional until the jaw had healed sufficiently for her to be able to speak.

His anticipated declaration of physical abuse, followed by the same priest hearing Florence's side of the story, would prove unbearable for George Brownlow. His fall from a tenuous grace was something he could never have imagined; they'd been married for twenty years and managed, by hook or by crook, to avoid anything but the mildest of fallings out. So where had this come from? He was trying to recall the words that had triggered some deep psychological button – unrelated to anything he could fathom – and induced such anger.

He couldn't admit to the event. Not yet.

Florence Brownlow's jaw had been broken in three places and the operation, involving titanium plates and screws, was lengthy.

A surgical slit had to be made in her cheek and teeth removed to get at the difficult fracture site. Months were needed to allow for healing and therapy. She was on soft food for the duration. She looked different too. And her voice had altered from a soft motherly purr to a croakier, harsher version as if she'd just survived strangulation. Alex wasn't sure if the change in speech was due to the operation or the psychological effects of the unexpected whack from his father.

Her recovery period wasn't wasted. She spent considerable time on the phone telling Vera, in graphic detail, what had happened; and sleepless nights worrying that she'd no longer be attractive. Florence made it clear that Vera was not to visit her in hospital, or while she was going through the early stages of convalescence. 'Please trust me, Vera. I really want to see you again, but I need a little more time, for all sorts of reasons.'

Vera noticed a difference in Florence's voice, a particular frailty, not the woman she knew. She understood the need for caution, and certainly didn't want to embarrass Florence or risk bumping into George or Alex until she'd got her head round the situation. However bad things were, physical scarring would never affect their relationship.

She wanted to kill George.

Florence was also planning the best way of ending the marriage. Not wavering at all, just working out how to accomplish it, figuring out the least painful way of taking a boy away from his father with as little emotional scarring as possible.

But Alex, a mature thirteen-year-old, had no illusions and was already his own man, independent, reliable, resourceful, and honest. He'd spotted the latent brutality developing in his parents' relationship long before it had manifested in physical abuse. Their long silences had been the most disturbing effect. Minds working overtime, creating scenarios outside any fathomable prediction. Stewing up trouble, it now seemed.

During the 1980s on the outskirts of London, some educational establishments had yet to modernise.

Old wooden desks and the faint aroma of lavender polish lingered. The lift-up pine lids revealed a redundant storage space, little used nowadays because if anything was left in them, it would soon disappear. Inkwells were redundant too. The school owners hoped that keeping things as they were from the last century would encourage the present incumbents to work with the same dedication. But the pupils who used them originally were long dead, their expected legacy of commitment and discipline gone to seed.

Greg Smart didn't like Alex Brownlow. Smart wasn't alone, many of the class and teaching staff didn't take to him, despite Alex being reliable with passable social skills. Coming close to the middle of the class in most subjects made it difficult for mates to ridicule or envy him academically.

Outside school? Ditto. Any stranger watching Alex's daily routine unfold would be hard pushed to guess why he was so disliked. He wasn't lacking intelligence, emotional or otherwise, he wasn't ugly or racist, didn't smell, didn't bully, and wasn't a wimp. He looked fit, gaining height and muscle fast. Alex's hair parted naturally, a well-groomed look which contradicted his true nature and gave his serious face dignity. The reason people found him so difficult was simple. He spoke the truth.

But getting on with everyone, regardless of age or position, compels people to lie, it's how the civilised world manages to rub along. It can seem mighty tough if they don't.

If there was a contract to be signed, a kind of Ten Commandments of how to live with as little falling out as possible, to make lots of friends and influence people, lying would be close to the top of the list. Doesn't sound good, does it? But the alternative is worse. When we start to believe our own lies and spend time sculpting them to sound like the truth, we're lost…

When he was quite a bit younger, Father kept telling him to button his lip. Why? Because Alexander had a view on everything

and was unafraid to share it. An unhelpful trait when parents and
their friends discussed topics of the day.

By the time he was halfway through primary school, he
realised that if he wanted to be an honest person, buttoning a lip
was counterproductive. Mum and Dad were fine examples, and
look how they'd turned out. It was obvious, they couldn't even be
honest with each other. Conversations and body language were
nothing more than defensive, ineffective ways of keeping the
peace. But underneath that façade, a volcano bubbled. They'd
been buttoning lips for far too long.

Alexander was well into his first year as a teenager when the
volcano erupted. He'd sensed an impending doom, like a
premonition, and recalled the scene in detail, a quirky talent he'd
been gifted from as far back as he could remember.

Their house on Arnold Street had been built sixty years ago,
but the Brownlows had done little to keep it up to date since they
moved in.

Mum was bent over the sink, head hung loose, hair damp with
steam from the weekly wash. There was an odd change in her
breathing; a musical note seemed to form with each exhalation as
if she was humming an unrecognisable tune. A cobweb in the far
corner of the kitchen moved as a small spider travelled across it to
spin more of a home. Steam rose from the old clay sink, the
wooden clock ticked away on the kitchen shelf and the spider's
web stirred from a sudden draught. The smell of recently burnt
toast emanated… He felt tense without quite knowing why.

The morning sun lit the creases in her frown and aged her
further. The past year had been tougher than usual for Florence
Brownlow. Much tougher. She was a pale, short woman with dry
ginger-peppered hair and tired blue eyes in need of a
handkerchief. She worked part time at the bakery, longer hours
than she would have liked but the hourly rate was poor. So, what
was she to do?

Father, a stout man with bushy eyebrows and thin tight lips, came in with a thunderous face. He was unable to find his glasses and for the first time anyone could remember, he was late for work at Oakland's Joinery. His job as a foreman demanded precision and reliability – nit-picking, his wife secretly called it. Qualities he was proud of. But patience was not one of them.

An unspoken tension filled the room, both parents on edge. Alexander guessed they'd had words and a sleepless night; they both looked tired. More than tired, exhausted. Alex picked at his toast before dropping it onto the floor, marmalade side down. Both parents looked but, unusually for such an event, said nothing, the tension palpable. He watched Father whispering to Mother, sensing it was an accusation of some sort, something spiteful it seemed, words that didn't reach the boy's ears. She visibly stiffened and with a sudden flash of movement, struck Father a fierce blow. He held his face where her fist had landed and felt for the trickle of blood before returning the punch as hard as he could. Her jaw let out a mighty crack. She collapsed to the floor. Father kicked her before screaming in rage and turning toward Alexander, his face blank as if he were now the observer, not the assailant. George Brownlow no longer resembled his father.

'You'll pay for that, Father,' said Alex, aware of his sudden boldness.

Alex was ignorant of his parents' intimate life; buttoned lips were never helpful. But Father John, the Catholic priest was fully aware. Mother and Father had discovered Catholicism late in life. Or rather, they'd discovered the confessional late in life, instigated by an old black-and-white film they'd watched on telly, *I Confess*, starring Montgomery Clift, about a priest listening to admissions of terrible acts but sworn to secrecy.

His parents had been baptised as Catholics and as luck would have it, total devotion wasn't necessary, baptism turned out to be all that was required to access the confessional and spill the beans. The only place in the world where they told the truth. They weren't bad people, they'd attempted to live an honest life, but their relationship couldn't take it. Why? Because speaking truth in a relationship required occasional conflict and disagreement, something neither could manage without hostility looming. Anxious to get along, they eventually found the perfect answer: lie to keep the peace whenever necessary but tell all in the confessional. That wonderful release of tension, and forgiveness, was so heady. Secrecy assured.

Initially things improved, but they soon got used to the routine bursts of penitence. Things came to a boil more quickly as they found that truth outside the confessional was *against their religion.* Lies kept you safe.

Alex lay thinking one night. The house was silent, as it usually was after his parents' meeting with the priest. Wouldn't it be wonderful if a parent could slip into the priest's side of the confessional incognito; mother one week, father the next? One could spout the truth without restriction and the other would have to listen to every damn word – and keep their mouths shut.

Father had gradually been drawn in by more than his weekly declarations. While waiting for the priest he'd admired the architecture, the vaulted roofs, the pillars, the sheer height of the towering structure where men in medieval garb had worked high up on wooden scaffold tied with rope, pulleys hauling huge lumps of masonry day after day. There must have been deaths. He wondered what sort of cement they used, for a bond that lasted centuries. These churches and cathedrals were something a man worked on his whole life, and probably passed the job on to be finished by a son. George Brownlow became reflective in this atmosphere and more critical of his life and his marriage.

And his son.

Mrs Brownlow didn't spend her church waiting time in the same way. She thought of her extraordinary son; he'd hardly needed bringing up at all. Parenthood seemed superfluous. Alex had potty-trained himself, started to read before he went to nursery, and insisted on tying his shoelaces and combing his hair at a ridiculously early age. He didn't do well at school, not from lack of intelligence, more a lack of interest. He liked observing others, a subject he found far more fascinating than anything he'd been taught at school. A people watcher.

The Brownlows had more to confess as each month passed. Both were convinced that the priests – there were more than one lately – wearied, as if their lengthening list of confessions had become so burdensome that ecclesiastical work shifts had to be arranged. Priests weren't exactly queuing up to listen to the Brownlows. In fact George could have sworn that on at least two occasions, he could hear the rumbling snort of a man waking from a heavy sleep.

CHAPTER TWO

Alex was having his favourite lesson. And the lesson with the most desirable seating arrangements; Friday afternoon, English in the oldest classroom, sitting two rows behind but to the right of Mary, the girl he was going to marry. Her innocent profile in the morning sun made his heart skip a beat. She didn't know it yet, but no rush, he needed a few more years under his belt and love needs time to be absorbed subliminally through the ether. He wouldn't send her notes or behave in a flirtatious way, as he knew from observing others that girls were put off by the too direct approach. Especially thirteen-year-olds; something to do with hormones and cheesy lads, boys unable to express themselves without coarse emphasis or unwelcome physical contact.

If she'd had any idea that their love was destined to last a lifetime, it might prove a bit overwhelming at this stage. But he hadn't missed her expression when their eyes met, a pinking of cheeks accompanying the moment. His and hers, especially when he smiled warmly, and took an inordinate amount of time rearranging his bag before leaving the classroom.

'Who do you fancy then, Alex?' asked his pal Eddie.

'It's not like that, Eddie, fancy seems a bit silly, like choosing the best horse or dog in a race.'

Eddie thought that choosing a girl was exactly like that. 'Okay, well who's the girl you like most in the class? There must be one! Never seen you chatting anyone up. Not gay, are you?' he asked, walking along the edge of a kerb with his arms out for balance. 'You don't look gay,' he added, without taking his eye off the task.

'Gay is not a look, Eddie, it's something in you that's genetic or maybe a choice for some people, I don't know. But I'm not gay and I've already met the girl I'm going to marry.'

Eddie missed his footing and tripped awkwardly off the kerbstone, ricking his ankle, and shouting a few obscenities as he recovered. He limped for a bit. 'You made me do that,' he said, a grin spreading as he thought about Alex's ridiculous revelation. 'That's not possible. You don't know enough about girls until you've left school. Not to fall in love with anyway,' he said. 'You have to try things out and get some experience otherwise you won't be able to make babies.'

Alex laughed hysterically. Eddie was the same age as him, but surely it hadn't taken this long to figure out the basics of birds and bees. 'Do you have a special girl, Eddie?' he asked, skirting the path his pal seemed to be going down.

'Bella,' he said without elaboration.

Bella was a bit of a mystery. Silent, studious, exotic with long eyelashes, super-white teeth and skin the colour of honey. Boys ogled her because she'd developed rather more quickly than the other girls. Alex suspected she'd be the choice for most boys in the class – for all the wrong reasons as far as he could tell.

When Alex told his father *he'd pay* for putting Mother in hospital, he didn't quite know how or when that was going to happen, except that it was inevitable. The outcome seemed obvious now; Mother would get Father to pack his bags, or she would leave and take Alex with her. Divorce would follow, that was for sure. Any court in the land, once presented with the detail of father's attack, Mother's protracted surgery, the long recovery and mental scarring, would grant the divorce quickly. Abusive men were dealt with more swiftly these days, especially when photographic evidence and a witness (Alex) made the case as strong as it could get. Father had never been an ideal parent, more of a silent one with a few harsh directives peppering the relationship in an attempt to mould Alex into his vision of an upright human being, a silent buttoned-up one preferably.

'You saw what happened, son,' said his mother, a statement that sounded like a question.

Alex nodded.

'We won't be staying together. Your father and me. Once a man strikes the first blow it can only get worse. I've heard all about this stuff. He was so vicious, wasn't he?' she asked, looking for confirmation. 'Look at me. He's changed my face and my voice. My ribs still ache, they were damaged too,' she stressed, pulling up her jumper to reveal faded bruises along the exposed ribcage.

Alex nodded again, aware that there was nothing he could add to Mother's reasonable analysis. He wondered if she'd contacted the priest once she was able to speak. Father John might not have easily recognised the voice next to him in the confessional, but he would soon pick up on the situation. His advice would probably be to keep the marriage going, 'for the child's sake at least. Give your husband a chance', he would say. 'It was the first time he'd hit you, wasn't it? Perhaps find it in your heart to forgive him. Think about it. We all need at least one chance when we make a mistake, do we not? And think of all the happy times you've had together'. Alex struggled to visualise those little rays of sunshine.

The scene in church and Father John's words of comfort were close to what Alex had imagined. At the end of his advice Mother stiffened, her face reddened, and she left the confessional with a swish of her plastic raincoat.

CHAPTER THREE

Alex was preparing mentally for the move which, given the insurmountable family rift, now seemed inevitable. Hopefully he'd still be going to the same school, still be close to Mary. If not, he'd find other ways of seeing her. The upside was that Mother liked him being at that school. It had suited them all, he could bus in easily, it didn't interfere with the family routine, didn't need to be picked up or dropped off and he'd never missed a single day. So, it made sense for him to stay there.

Alex sat scratching at uneven knots in the old wooden table, waiting for his father to appear. Mugs of tea in place. Scene set. Mother was gazing out of the window at nothing in particular, it was a time for silence. He checked the spider's web in the corner of the kitchen. It had grown somewhat, as had the situation between his parents. The ticking clock continued its rhythmic beat, like a mechanical heart.

George Brownlow, unshaven and baggy-eyed, only managed a polite nod at his son as he took a seat at the table. Alex's words 'You'll pay for that, Father' had interrupted his sleep regularly since the event. He had a feeling that this was it, payback time. Son and father waited for Florence to turn away from the window.

She sighed heavily as she did so, and moved slowly toward the remaining chair.

'Well, George, I guess you know why we're having this little gathering,' she said, glancing at Alex by way of inclusion. Husband and wife were at opposite ends, mugs of tea steaming in front of them, hands out of sight twitching and contorting into various stages of anxiety. George nodded again.

'Being sorry will not change a thing,' she said, aware that George had yet to make any serious attempt at contrition. 'Look at me! Listen to my voice.' George nodded glumly but didn't offer anything in the way of defence. 'How could I ever look in a mirror again without reliving what you did to me. Tell me, George?' she said, her eyes bloodshot and piercing. She didn't expect an answer.

George shuffled and glanced at his son, expecting...he wasn't quite sure what. Alex decided that the much-despised *buttoned lip* was appropriate at this particular moment.

'So, this is how it's going to go.' She stood, placing her hands flat on the table, twitching over. 'We're going to sell the house...' She paused, letting the first blow sink in. 'In the meantime, you will move out.'

George felt a sudden spasm of fear. He started to sit more upright, the chair creaked. He wanted to say something, but nothing came out. His mouth was dry, he needed a drink. He knew there was no coming back from this. His wife's views regarding even a hint of aggression had been made clear from the start. She'd seen programmes, been to various women's meetings and swapped notes with God knows who. Buttoned lips had worked so well over the years. Silence was often said to be golden, but it wouldn't save him now.

'How will I get to see Alex? What about my work? What will everyone say?' George's voice pitched higher with each futile question. 'Our neighbours and friends think we're a good family. We rub along despite what happens in our lives. That's what everyone does. It always worked for us too.'

The bloodshot piercing eyes focussed on him again. 'You may be missing the point. It always works until you nearly kill your partner. Then, for some strange reason, George, it doesn't, and will never work again. For obvious fucking reasons!'

Alex had never heard his Mother swear. Yet he didn't find it distressing, in fact it was good to hear a bit of honest speaking. And if father moved out, Alex would remain at the local school and be able to continue his 'love affair' with Mary.

George reflected on the situation. Given Florence's threat to expose him to the world at large if he didn't do the right thing, he had no choice. He wouldn't waste time fighting it, wouldn't labour the fact that he'd worked his butt off to keep them in the manner to which they'd become accustomed, hadn't hit her before, though he'd been tempted a few times. His gut instinct had been right all along, she was a *one strike and you're out* kind of a woman. Hence the tactical silence that had sustained their marriage for so long.

He wasn't going to argue over the boy either. He'd always thought Alex had been transported from some distant planet. He bore no resemblance to either parent, in looks or nature, and his perpetual questioning of everything was hard to keep up with, bloody annoying in fact. He was a good lad, in the normal sense of the word, keen to learn, polite, clean and tidy, low maintenance in every respect, but remote. George wasn't going to miss him that much, consoling himself with the fact that the boy didn't really seem to need a father.

Tears filled his eyes and ran down his burning cheeks, a mixture of rage and exacerbation of a developing heart problem. If she'd buttoned her lip, everything would have been okay.

Florence felt a great weight had been lifted. Admitting to her affair was the best thing she could have done. The timing might have been better, but it just slipped out, the pressure had built up for far too long. Even the presence of Alex at the table didn't stop her.

News of her *coming out* might have been a step too far.

But George knew who it was and had often thought Vera Harris to be that way inclined. She was a loner. Never saw her with a man, and not often with a woman for that matter. She was a writer as well as a lecturer, apparently, though he'd never read any of her books, but Florence had. He remembered her enthusing about a launch where Ms Harris was the key speaker. Despite not being a fast reader, she'd read the book in two days. Florence didn't do dewy-eyed, but she'd come close that weekend. That must have been the start of it all.

Father John wondered how much longer he'd have to wait before George Brownlow turned up for confession. He'd known about Florence Brownlow's attraction to Vera Harris for some time, recent confessions left him in no doubt as to the intensity of their developing passion. Her confessions had been full of the appropriate regret and guilt interspersed with a childlike enthusiasm to… *let it all hang out*, was a good way of describing it.

Although she was a lifelong dedicated Catholic, Vera Harris's confessions were not so guilt-ridden. But they were confessions of a sin at least. Mainly to do with atypical bedroom issues rather than the breaking-up of a marriage. She was a writer, able to articulate well, often sounding as if she was writing a blurb for a book rather than purging pent-up misdemeanours. Father John had been duly entertained. He was not asked for advice in either case, he just needed to listen.

George crossed the street when he saw Father John exit the shopping centre. He was on his way to the church but for obvious reasons wanted any conversation with the priest to be in the darkness of the confessional. How much easier that was, when neither had to look each other in the eye. They were long past the stage of confessional anonymity. Stepping into the enclosed darkness, he anticipated Father John saying, 'Good morning, George. How's the wife?' Which never happened of course. The greeting would not have troubled him.

To George, the act of contrition and penance was a ridiculous pantomime. He'd written his offering on a scrap of paper, ready for each occasion. *'O my God, because you are so good, I am very sorry that I have sinned against you; and I promise that with the help of your grace, I will not sin again. Amen.'*

The words sounded false, even though he was deeply disturbed by what he'd done to Florence. He was tempted to justify his outburst, blame Florence for striking the first blow, rattle on about his wife's affair with Ms Harris, which would have been a big mistake. Not the time or the place.

He knelt in the church after his confession and repeated the prayer given to him by the priest but hadn't felt the lightness he was meant to, only the unwelcome flashes of his brutal attack and his wife rolling around in the sheets with Vera Harris.

CHAPTER FOUR

Most of the kids in Alex's class copied the best part of each other's work. It was the reason they all ended up with similar outcomes. The old maxim, *copying from one is plagiarism, copying from many is research,* seemed a perfectly reasonable approach to exam success for most.

Adults tell us that schooldays are the best times of our lives. *I hope not,* thought Alex. He'd never seen such a depressed, mean-spirited bunch of youngsters. Following the first term of unease and disquiet, groups started to form, and he sensed trouble was on the way. They hung their shirts out after school, he tucked his in. That small act alone isolated him further. He was not cool. Not in the gang. Not cocking a snook at authority. A traitor, it seemed. To him it was all a bit ridiculous and childish.

Home wasn't getting any easier either, as Florence and Alex prepared for life without Father; hers by choice and his because he was a dependent child who couldn't do anything about the situation. But understood, exactly, why the marriage was over.

Florence gave George a few weeks' grace, to reorganise his

affairs and pack his bags. She set an exact date for him to be gone, during which time he was to stay away from the marital bedroom. The spare room had never been decorated during the time they'd lived there. George Brownlow now had more than enough time to examine the results as he lay half-awake on top of the narrow single bed. A water stain from an old leak had spread like a brown mushroom across the ceiling. Wallpaper split and curled from the same intrusive water damage. Paint peeled around the windowpanes. He felt ashamed that he'd let Alex sleep here for most of his young life while it was in such a state. What sort of a father was he?

Now fully awake, he heard banging from outside and squinted through parted curtains at the bright day. His wife was taking a cup of tea out to a heavily built guy with a *For Sale* sign which he was hammering into the garden alongside the gatepost. The man looked up, saw George peering, and gave him a thumbs up, which George, for obvious reasons, decided against returning.

The awful truth was becoming a reality, the mental anguish and uncertainty developing physical characteristics. People would be calling, talking about what they'd do with the house if it were theirs. What walls they would knock down, where the new kitchen and ensuite would be best placed, building rockeries where there never had been, converting the garage into some sort of studio where bored children could play games away from the parents whose only desire was to have a peaceful life.

That same afternoon the first viewers arrived. Florence offered tea. George disappeared down to the pub. Alex wanted to hear what people said as they invaded his house and his space. A mixture of sadness, fear, and excitement swept through him. This was the only home he'd ever known.

'We could knock this through,' said a well-dressed woman, waving her hand at somewhere in space as she entered the small lounge.

'Easy-peasy. I could do that,' said her scruffy husband, who looked like he'd just come off a building site. He tapped the wall as if searching for a hidden compartment. 'Only breezeblock. An afternoon would do it.' He seemed to address this to Florence as if she might be taking some part in his future plan.

His wife had already started to ascend the staircase. 'Careful on the stairs, Albert,' she said, for no obvious reason; Albert was not an invalid, and the stairs were rock solid.

Florence wasn't stupid. She knew these remarks were part of a bargaining ploy. The potential buyer had already created an atmosphere of dissatisfaction that could only be mollified by a substantial reduction in price.

'Ah. The tiny third bedroom. Always a problem getting any furniture to fit,' said the woman, running her fingers along the top of a drawer unit, checking for dust. 'Perfect for an ensuite.'

Albert was still tapping walls downstairs. The agent stood behind him, rapt, as if he might be learning something new about testing the quality of houses.

The woman intimated she needed to look no further. She huffed and peered out of the window, scanning the paved front garden and street beyond with a critical eye. 'What are the neighbours like?' she asked, not really expecting the truth. They'd been around the block a few times, she and Albert. People were inclined to paint a rosy picture when they wanted to sell a house.

'Keep themselves to themselves,' said Florence, hoping she wouldn't be asked about kids, omitting any reference to party nights.

'Everyone knows the seller hikes the price and expects to bargain,' said the woman, having already worked out exactly what she was going to do with the place and how much profit she'd make. A few thousand off would make a nice difference. She decided to pitch for five. 'Can we assume you're open to reasonable offers?' she asked.

'Depends,' said Florence. 'It's a fair asking price already, property is going up in the area and there's quite a bit of interest.'

'You may be right, but these potential buyers have not seen the place yet, have they?' she said, head bobbing, critical eyes flitting from ceiling to floor, not expecting an answer. A moment's silence followed, a tactician's pause, expecting Florence to see the transaction in a different light. 'They'll have their own places to sell or mortgages to arrange. It can take forever. We'll pay cash if you knock a little bit off. Shall we say five thousand?'

'There's other offers to consider,' said Florence, not affronted by the woman's aggressive tone – she'd pitched things high anyway. 'I'll let you know when we've given everyone a fair chance, I'll need to discuss things with my husband before coming to any sort of decision.'

'Take it or leave it. I'm a busy woman...I've got other properties to look at, this may be your only chance,' she said.

The downstairs tapping had ceased. Albert had found his cursory examination conclusive, his wife would do the haggling. He stepped out to the small front garden, pulled a small notebook from his pocket and added a few thoughts.

When they'd gone, Florence put the kettle on and took a packet of chocolate digestives from the larder. Alex was already sitting at the kitchen table thinking about the recent visitors. 'What do you think, Ma? Do you want to know what I think?' He often asked two questions at once and Florence knew it was best to leave a moment's silence which would soon be filled with whatever her son had to say first, before she took the floor.

She filled the teapot and spread half a dozen biscuits on a small plate. Two disappeared before she had time to pour the tea.

'She's not a nice person,' he started, his summary of the arm-waving woman who appeared rude and mercenary. 'I wouldn't deal with anyone I didn't like, especially if it involved money. Her husband seemed okay, but she was the boss.'

'It's not a matter of like, Alex, it's a matter of business. If someone comes up with a decent offer and cash, we'll take it.'

Alex shrugged. 'She'll be trouble, Ma. Just think of how rude she was. She'll probably try more tactics to knock down the price once you give her the nod.'

'What tactics?'

'Solicitors and searches, all that stuff. They'll find flaws in the house you didn't know you had, and she'll expect compensation.'

'How come you know so much about the property market?' she asked, grinning while she poured the tea and snapped a chocolate digestive in two.

'I've seen documentaries, you have to be careful. The minute that woman came through the door things didn't feel right. All that silly arm-waving. What was that all about?' He took a third biscuit and dunked it in his tea, waiting for a response.

It was getting late. The streetlights were due on in an hour. The knock at the door and a ring of the bell made them both jump. No one used the tarnished brass knocker. It was hardly recognisable high up against dark paintwork. Father had forgotten his key. Disturbing the household by ringing and knocking usually meant he'd had too much to drink. Not often, but unsettling for that very reason.

CHAPTER FIVE

Father slumped in a kitchen chair. He was wet. Alex could see he was angry but a thoughtful angry, not an anger about to unleash havoc.

'Tea?' asked Florence, already getting a fresh mug out and pouring.

Father looked up, slightly less tight-lipped as it was placed in front of him, but said nothing. A ritual so deeply embedded, a nuclear war could not disrupt it. No one seemed to have a word ready for this moment. Alex looked from parent to parent, his eyes searching for something which might lead to dialogue. He found nothing; no enquiry from Father about the first potential buyers, no asking Alex about his schoolwork – which he was never that interested in, but it was what normal families did. Something George and Florence had tried so hard to be – but never to their mutual satisfaction – not even a comment about the rain running down his face from the sudden downpour.

'We have to talk in front of the boy,' said Florence.

'No need on my account, not while Dad's been drinking anyway,' suggested Alex, aware that they'd only use their *'don't forget we're talking to a child'* voices. They had other voices too; the one they used to speak to each other in the garden when the neighbours might be listening, the one they used for shop assistants, the special voice for friends they wanted to hang on to, or people they needed to impress.

His parents had never been *bright-eyed and bushy-tailed*, (his grandma's favourite, but often misattributed, quote) but their eyes were now dull, almost lifeless. Time for someone to leave. He knew about his ma's girlfriend, Vera Harris, she'd given a couple of lectures at his school, to pupils interested in the written word, particularly those tempted to enrol in creative writing courses. There'd been hints about her sexual leanings then and, like all rumours, her reputation had been set in stone by the end of the first term.

Most youngsters don't take long to categorise adults by perceived ethnicity, sexual orientation, and temperament before christening them with less than endearing nicknames.

'The boy knows enough anyway,' said George, taking a tissue from the worktop to wipe his face. 'What were the punters like?' he asked, more a diversion than interest.

Florence was in the driving seat now. 'They want five grand off,' she said.

'Did you accept?'

'Not yet. We didn't like them, did we, Alex? They were only the first. The second lot are coming...' she checked the clock '...in about half an hour.'

'This time of the day?' asked George, making a meal of focussing on the kitchen clock.

'On their way back from work,' said Florence without elaboration.

George, too drunk and depressed to face strangers, went up to the spare room and fell asleep the minute his head touched the pillow. The state of unconsciousness did not stop his brain reliving the moment he'd sabotaged his marriage. In the cold light of day, he realised the relationship had been doomed anyway, the broken jaw speeded up the process. Vera bloody Harris had been *comforting* his wife for God knows how long. Comforting was a little easier to comprehend than to consider anything remotely sexual.

Florence had made it clear that she didn't want sex before marriage. He'd felt rebuffed but admired her for being so straightforward and honest, and did his best to cope – not an easy task for a twenty-one-year-old. She decided to be less than straightforward with the fact that sex after marriage was not desirable either.

His father was right, the boy knew enough. More than enough, if the truth be known. Certainly more than either parent would have suspected, because Alex – disinclined to take anything his parents said at face value these days – watched and listened, looked and learned. Their deceit and lies stood out like a sore thumb to him. But they seemed oblivious to their dishonesty. Not quite as cut and dried as oblivion, more like collaboration.

When he was very young, his parents' tactical silences made sense. They held back on conversations best shared with adults. Then he began to realise those silences were just as much for their benefit as his, a truth missed here and there to bypass ugly confrontations.

Thoughts drifted to that morning.

His biology teacher had described Alex as *rheotaxic,* a fish who swam against the tide. The word needed translating for the benefit of the class who nodded, more or less as one, in agreement.

The corridor had been crowded with students making their way toward classrooms, the opposite direction to where he was going, to meet the educational psychologist. Had he detected some knowing grins along the way, some nudging? Maybe. When he'd passed Mary, his heart skipped an impromptu beat. 'Good luck,' she'd said, smiling. She couldn't possibly have known about his appointment... Perhaps she'd had a similar one. Students were only allowed into Staff Room B1 when discipline or serious issues were on the cards.

A ring at the bell announced the second couple planning to view the property. They were older, less abrasive, seemed less inclined to knock down walls and fit ensuites where they were never intended.

The agent introduced them to Florence, who was slow to reveal that her husband was asleep in the spare room. 'Been working all night,' she declared rather than admit he was too drunk to stand. And the room was a mess.

The couple smiled sympathetically. 'Not a problem,' said the woman, 'We've seen details and a photo of the room in the agent's file. And we can always call back if we need to.'

The couple used their own sign language, gesturing without comment as their eyes scanned each room. They ignored the chipped kitchen sink and the large spider taking its time crossing it. The agent swept ahead, extolling the benefits of having small cosy spaces to live in.

The viewing of upstairs was brief, because the second and main bedrooms and bathroom were visible from the small landing. Plus, George's snoring and shouting was rather disconcerting.

Florence offered tea but they declined on account they had to get back for the dog. They were tired and had more properties to view the next day. The couple checked their watches, encouraging the agent to check his. The sun had almost set, and the streetlights would click on any minute now.

Florence switched on the porch light before walking back to the kitchen. 'Let's have some supper, Alex. I'm not that hungry, but you must be. We can leave Father where he is,' she said, with a scathing upward glance toward the spare room. 'Beans on toast?'

'I'll get it, Ma. You sit down, it's been quite a day, for both of us.'

'Sorry, son, I forgot to ask. How did you get on with Dr Grayling?'

'Not sure what it was all about,' he said, noting the odd twitch in his mother's eye. 'I know you wanted to help but Grayling's got the wrong end of the stick. It's true, my grades are down. But not because you and Dad are splitting up and the house is being sold, they're down because school isn't teaching us what we need to face the world. I want to learn about things they never seem to teach...'

Florence, surprised that the upheaval at home had not made much of an impact, was not in the mood to ask what Alex and these *kids* needed to be taught to face the world. *How can anyone teach experience?*

'Of course, I'm upset about you and Dad. But I'd do the same in your position.' Alex tipped a can of beans into a saucepan and turned the hob up high while he placed some ready-sliced bread into the toaster.

The beans bubbled in no time and the toast popped up with a reassuring ping. He spread some butter liberally onto the four pieces, piling the beans and grated cheese on top. The kettle boiled, gurgling and spitting because it was too full. He poured some of the water into the sink then made two cups of tea from the same bag.

Florence smiled despite herself. He'd rustled up cups of tea and beans on toast in five minutes without batting an eyelid.

'What did you think of the last couple, Ma?'

'Quite nice, easier than the first. A bit embarrassing that your dad was in bed, but I couldn't wake him up, could I? Let's see if they make us a decent offer.'

The boy reflected on his odd interview with the educational psychologist Dr Grayling. Alex's parents had been concerned about his increasing lack of interest in school, his grades having dropped even further. They couldn't attribute it all to the family breakup. Alex felt the arranged therapy session was more to do with his parents' efforts to distract him from the impending split. But the real reason for the downward spiral was his lessening interest in school generally. What he wasn't learning there had a stifling effect on his enquiring mind. He wanted to understand people, what made them tick. About personalities, likes and dislikes, good and evil, problem solving, how to be whatever you wanted to be... He had a trillion questions, but none he'd get answers to. Not at school anyway.

Grayling looked the part with his tweedy jacket, bifocal glasses, and unblinking eyes. The psychologist's questions were aimed at trying to understand how the boy ticked but his approach seemed unnecessarily intrusive to Alex. The guy went through all the school stuff, what subjects Alex seemed to be finding difficult, which ones he liked and his general attitude to school life. Grayling was also aware that the family were going through difficult times. Florence had made a big thing of it when seeking help for her son from the education authorities.

'...Then what are your life views, Alex? Are you racist, worried about the colour of someone's skin or whether they come from a different culture?'

'No, sir.'

'How about religion? I've heard from the Head, that your parents are Catholic and attend church fairly regularly.'

'But you'll never see me going to church, sir,' he said politely.

'Why?'

'Haven't made up my mind about the subject. From what I can gather, all religions seem to be following variations of the same story. Even fighting over those differences in some parts of the world. It's confusing.'

This eloquence from a kid! Grayling sniffed, unable to work out why this opinionated youngster hadn't been encouraged to attend church with his parents. He was thirteen years old for God's sake!

'So, race or religion doesn't bother you at all. Do you have an opinion on sexual inclination, whether someone is gay, lesbian, or something in between?'

'I don't know enough about the subject, sir,' he admitted, despite Eddie's attempt to educate him about *queers and straights* while he'd puffed away on a fag. Eddie's take on life seemed even less convincing amongst billowing clouds of choking blue smoke. 'Does it really matter, Dr Grayling?'

Grayling shuffled his notes without answering. 'What about games, sports; football, rugby, cricket, tennis…tiddlywinks?' he said, an attempt to inject humour.

'I like watching games but don't care who's playing. I'm not a team person, sir.'

'What then?' he asked, a little irritation in his voice.

'I guess you could call me a work in progress, sir. I'm undecided about most things.'

The session ended in what could only be described as stalemate. Grayling had never come across a pupil like Alex before. *Work in progress* seemed a sophisticated summing-up. He was in no doubt that Alex would find his own path in life – but not through formal education.

There was an almighty thump from upstairs. A body. George must have fallen out of bed. Alex and Florence held their breath, stared up at the ceiling, but said nothing. The silence was broken when they heard him clomping around, walking along to the bathroom, and slamming the door. He was okay, or so it seemed.

CHAPTER SIX

The couple who'd wanted to redesign the house came back with a better offer and Florence accepted. George was not consulted.

Alex tried to steer her away from doing business with 'that woman' but his ma had been worn down by Father's continued presence in the house. His toing's and froing's from work, the trying to miss each other by adjusting schedules, wake-up times, mealtimes, and sleep patterns. Plus, there was no chain involved regarding the sale of the house, the deal was cash up front with one stipulation; that the place would be vacated on the day of completion so that the new owners could start knocking down walls and putting their unique stamp on the house.

Not until all the money is in the bank, thought Florence. She'd see how the deposit panned out, how quickly money was transferred, and whether the cheeky buyer felt moved to add a few more conditions before the transaction was completed. Alex's words of warning about this woman had made her cautious. Despite his youth, Florence knew he had pretty good instincts.

Alex was ready for school. He took a quick look in the hall mirror and adjusted his tie before looking closer to determine his state of readiness. A shadow crossed the frosted glass panel of the front door. The letter box clattered, and a brown envelope was hurriedly pushed through. Alex struggled with the temperamental door lock, trying to catch who'd delivered it, but they were already in the passenger seat of a grey car and pulling away.

Brown envelopes, from his limited experience, were usually trouble, official and a cause of concern, but this was different. No text type font. *Florence Brownlow* was written in beautiful script, created by someone who had time and an interest in calligraphy. A romantic feel, something Shakespeare might have written for Romeo to pass on to Juliet. *Vera Harris*, he guessed. If she'd wanted secrecy, she should have printed it on a computer or scribbled the name in pencil. He was pleased that his father hadn't picked it up, it might have started another round of marital shenanigans. He loved that word, *shenanigans*, and applied it to many situations. Not sure where he first heard it, probably from Eddie.

Florence had heard the commotion and met Alex halfway down the hall. He handed the letter over. She stuffed it into her pinafore pocket without reading the envelope. 'Have a good day, son,' she uttered, a little pink around the cheeks, and not from the washing-up, he guessed.

Ma's hurried action and noticeable blush made Alex wonder about just how intimate his mother's relationship with Vera Harris might be. He was more intrigued than disturbed and couldn't quite suppress a smile as he thought of the latest biology lesson. He'd been sitting next to Eddie, a perverse beacon of knowledge on most things. The lesson was headed, *An Introduction to Entomology and Ornithology* – words chosen by a teacher who wanted to *stretch young minds*, fully aware that twelve-year-olds would be turning to their dictionaries for explanation. Eddie had already looked the title up so's he'd be ahead of the game. He nudged his pal. Birds and bees? No way. 'This is how adults fanny around when they want to tell us about sex,' he chuckled, elbowing Alex sharply in the ribs.

Alex already knew about the birds and bees. He'd got quite a bit taller, developed extra muscle – unrelated to an increase in exercise – and noted a change in his voice and other bodily parts, he'd looked it up. It was all about puberty and what to expect from the unavoidable changes. But he didn't want to ruin Eddie's superior take on the subject. Or reveal too much about what the process might be doing to him.

He thought of Mary and wondered if she was thrilled or disappointed about the dramatic changes rampaging through their young bodies. He'd heard that girls experienced symptoms earlier and that they were better equipped to deal with them, emotionally and physically. Not all girls, but most. Boys talked a lot about sex, often bragging about ridiculous imaginary conquests. Hard to believe any of it, coming from sniggering lads in school trousers with runny noses and shirts hanging out.

George's thoughts were of a more mature nature, imagining his wife and Vera Harris expressing their love in the most intimate way possible. The escalating images had the effect of accentuating his fear. But Harris wouldn't dare call round while he was still living there. Would she? He needed to keep a closer eye on the place, suspecting that Florence and Alex might move out and leave him stranded while he was down the pub. So, he had to say a brief farewell to the Goldsmith Arms. For the short amount of time left, he decided that his imbibing would best be done in the shabby confines of the spare room at home. Only two weeks left before his deadline for moving out. Where was he going to go?

Word had got round once the ambulance had turned up, and the neighbours taken a front row place on the pavement when Florence was wheeled out. Speculation circulated. Neither George nor Alex were allowed in the ambulance so the boy, shaking with emotion, had waved while George stood at the front door afraid to go out should he be set upon. He needn't have worried so prematurely, everyone thought that Florence had fallen or had some accident, never suspecting that her mild-mannered husband had nearly killed her.

Florence felt like a born-again virgin. The anxiety, knotted stomach and uncertainty preceding a first sexual encounter had re-entered her life. She hadn't had *proper sex* with Vera Harris, not yet, but they'd kissed and fondled and understood that a full-on affair was inevitable.

Vera was aware, it was obvious, that Florence had no experience of sex with women. She'd tread carefully, particularly as the deteriorating situation with George must have left Florence extra vulnerable and clutching at emotional straws to fill the void. In her mind, she considered them unqualified equals: She'd never had a man and Florence had never had a woman.

Their first kiss had been a surprise. She'd seen Vera Harris around, their paths had crossed. They'd passed each other at the church, either entering or exiting for a bit of peace or the confessional. Neither had bumped into each other at a service. Alex had mentioned Ms Harris in the context of an occasional lecture at school.

Florence had been sitting outside a high street café on a sunny day. She'd been shopping and sat deep in thought staring out toward the small green patch where kids were playing ball. Vera, on leaving the bank, spotted Florence, and noted the faraway look, the vulnerable posture. She could have walked on unnoticed but felt drawn to make a friendly gesture.

She looked both ways as she hurriedly crossed the street, missing a cyclist by inches. The guy waved his fist and shouted. Vera mentally thought of a single finger response, but let it go. *Why no bells these days?*

'Looks like that coffee's gone cold. I'm just about to get one, would you like another?' she asked, adjusting a neighbouring chair. 'Can I join you?'

The tall studious looking woman, shadowed by the bright

sunlight, waited for a response. It took Florence a moment to place Vera Harris. 'That'd be lovely, thank you,' she said, fumbling for her purse.

'On me,' said Vera, waving a loyalty card. 'All free,' she smiled.

Once she'd returned from placing the order, Vera sat, checked her diary and, without preamble, asked Florence how things were at home.

Florence knew that she gave occasional lectures to her son's class. He liked Ms Harris and found her unorthodox approach to his taste. She told interesting stories instead of pouring out facts. 'I'm a bit worried about Alex and his grades,' she started.

'Every mother's worry. I can't speak generally because I'm not on the staff, but Alex is very bright during my lectures, doesn't ask questions, but he does take lots of notes and writes the occasional good essay,' said Vera enthusiastically.

Florence smiled weakly, not mollified by Vera's sole opinion. 'George doesn't seem to be bothered about the detail as long as his son goes to school and does his homework. George isn't so interested in such detail. Do you find that, with husbands, Vera?'

'I'm not married, thank God,' she replied, without elaboration.

'Maybe we've been married too long, all three of us seem to have grown apart a bit,' said Florence. 'The gap between us has widened over the past few years especially as Alex now seems more grown up than his father...and they're the same height now,' she laughed.

Vera didn't care so much about the son; she was more interested in the obvious marital stalemate. Bordering on predatory, some might say.

She placed a hand on top of Florence's, who thought it felt nice, comforting and not at all strange. She looked pointedly down at their hands touching. Vera, uncertain now, moved hers gently away.

Florence couldn't work out why she wanted that moment to last longer.

Coffees arrived and Vera thanked the barista. 'Alex is a bright spark,' she started, eager to go where she was being guided. 'He's talked about – he's an enigma. Much too clever for that school, but he must see the process through. In the end he'll realise the advantages of surviving a hostile environment at a young age.'

'What hostile environment?'

'Other kids. Staff. Those who find individuality too much of a challenge. Especially when someone dares to state the bald truth and ruffles feathers…' Vera stopped there; she'd gone too far, too soon.

Florence dropped her gaze and fiddled with her spoon before stirring her coffee vigorously, the buttoned lips of her married life suddenly remembered. A tear formed and she wiped it quickly away with the back of her sleeve.

Vera checked her watch. 'Sorry, Flo, I need to go. Lecture time. If you ever need to talk, here's my number,' she said, pulling a business card from her bag and handing it to her. 'Do you mind me calling you Flo? It really suits you.'

'Not at all,' she said. Mother had hated it –*if I'd wanted you to be called Flo, I'd have christened you Flo!*

Florence wanted to sit a little longer, she hadn't finished her coffee.

Vera stood and took a step toward Florence, who offered her hand to say goodbye. Vera bent low and kissed her. It was so hurried, soft, and totally unexpected that it could easily have been a mistake. But there was no apology and no sign of embarrassment.

Florence went to wipe the moistness away but didn't in case it appeared rude or distasteful. Her lips felt hot, her cheeks were burning, and her legs felt weak. Before she could recover, Vera was gone.

CHAPTER SEVEN

George thought he'd got it right with Florence. Realised from the beginning that the sex issue might be a problem but convinced himself that once they were married, they'd sort things out. He wasn't unreasonable or sexually demanding. At a young age, he'd sought advice about sex. Many sources suggested that it was advisable – backed up by scientific evidence apparently – to delay gratification, and that if you did, things would turn out for the best in a long-term relationship. He remembered thinking at the time, it must have been tricky, collecting all that evidence.

It hadn't taken him long to realise that Florence was in a different category, sexually. Although delaying gratification for him was considered a temporary but necessary setback, for her it was a welcome escape.

The wedding night did not go well.

All those repressed sexual urges had built up a head of steam in George. The much awaited moment was over almost before it began. His finest hour only lasted a minute.

Florence – secretly relieved he'd thought, on reflection – was understanding and kind following his disastrous attempt. 'Let's shower and I'll make a cup of tea,' she'd said, patting his shoulder as if he'd earned the privilege.

They did make love, but not that often. Usually after a couple of glasses of wine and the insistence on some sort of 'preparation' for Florence. This meant at least fifteen minutes in the bathroom beforehand – longer if she could manage it – at which point the wine and the wait had usually lulled George toward sleep. The preferred state.

That routine had set the bar for any future discussions on intimacy. Then Alex came along. Their sex lives ended that day.

He still couldn't understand the Vera Harris attraction. Despite the lack of sex in their lives, he'd never seen Florence overtly attentive to another man or woman, no intimate touching, prolonged hugs, or misplaced kisses. In fact, she seemed to treat both men and women with the same degree of affection…or non-affection, if there was such a thing. The same with kids and animals. He felt safe from competition, so the suddenness of Florence's betrayal was like being woken with an electric shock.

George realised there was no comeback from the assault. Their safely cocooned existence had entered the realms of domestic abuse. The follow-up by police, medics and social workers, and the self-castigation in a confessional which now felt like a solitary confinement cell, had rubber-stamped his terrible deed. But Florence had saved him from his impending fate. Not exactly offering tea and sympathy, but refusing to bring charges against him, on condition that he got out of her life.

Divorce would follow. Uncontested. And George would be allowed to see Alex, as long as it was mutually agreeable. Which, fortunately, it was.

Although Alex was known for his honesty and truth telling, he wouldn't jump in all guns blazing to say what he thought. He'd think of the best ways to put his case. He was never unkind but couldn't understand why people thought lying to please someone could be beneficial in the long term.

What he wanted to say to his parents would not remain unsaid, but his timing should make sense and allow for a continuing family dialogue. He loved them both and had felt, for some years, that they could not have survived much longer without addressing their *buttoned lip* problem. Ending in such disaster made things difficult. Impossible now. He'd no intention of attempting to build bridges, but he still wanted them in his life.

CHAPTER EIGHT

The bus was crowded that morning. It wasn't the proper school bus, but mostly schoolkids got on. Today was Friday, and the 2B was bursting with extra shoppers on their way to the sales in the city centre. Alex was the last one on and looked for a space. The windows were steamed up and Eddie had managed to draw a smiley face on the glass with his finger. He was in deep conversation but turned to wave as Alex struggled along the length of the coach with his sports bag. Games were something he enjoyed; you didn't have to excel, and they didn't involve filling his brain with information that he was never going to use.

The big bench seat at the back was taken, apart from the centre slot between the unsavoury Greg Smart and Mary, which – providing you weren't too heavily built – you could just about squeeze into. Alex could do that easily but was unprepared for such intimate contact with Mary. Their eyes connected briefly as she smiled and shifted position to make more room. The image remained; that hazel-eyed glance was now fixed permanently in his brain.

The rest of her was always easy to conjure up; petite, freckled cheeks and a mouth which turned up at the corners, so it was impossible for her to look grumpy or overly serious. Her walk, more like a gentle skip it seemed, always made him feel lighter.

It was their first physical contact, but the close warmth of her body felt familiar. The boy to the other side of him, Greg Smart, one of the less liked kids in the school, pushed against Alex forcing him against Mary. Alex pushed back, hoping to win some extra space, but the heavier boy managed to move him even closer.

Mary reached across in front of Alex and tapped Smart on the elbow. 'Don't be such a prick, Greg. Can't you see we're all packed tightly enough as it is?'

She smelled of soap, freshly washed clothes, and femininity. She swore but seemed to emanate a gentle authority. Greg shifted position.

'Thanks, Mary, I should have been stronger,' laughed Alex. 'Hope we didn't hurt you.'

'You didn't have anywhere else to sit,' she replied, still smiling.

Alex felt a sudden increase in temperature... He placed the sports bag at his feet and fiddled absently with the strap.

'How did you get on with your appointment?' she whispered, without mentioning Grayling's name,

'Fine,' he said, casually. 'How did you know about that?'

'There's a routine for his sessions,' she whispered, 'Same day of the week as my meeting with him. He's there the first day of every month – his usual spot for dealing with us problem kids.' She laughed.

Alex was surprised and pleased at the same time. Taken aback to learn that Mary could have done anything that might warrant Grayling's guidance but well pleased that it now added a subtle connection to their developing relationship. He'd no idea whether Mary had anything in her mind, even remotely, like the lifelong connection he'd planned, but time was on their side.

Shoppers left earlier on the route, so the bus became more of a school bus. Everyone spread out. Alex reluctantly moved away from Mary, assuming space was the best tactic for both at the time. To stay pressed so closely without good reason would have been a step too far.

'See you,' she said, as he moved forward and took the seat behind Eddie.

Eddie did one of his indiscreet winks as he turned to look at Alex. 'I reckon you're in there, mate. Couldn't have got closer if you'd been superglued.'

'Why are you always so bloody irritating, Eddie?' he whispered, recalling Mary's hazel eyes and feeling that heat again.

'Daily practice,' said Eddie, holding his belly while chuckling like an onstage comedian.

Greg Smart was first to leave his seat when the bus stopped at the school gates. He swung his kit bag at Alex as he brushed past. Greg was known for his childish retaliation for failed attempts at bullying. Following Mary's intervention, Alex expected something like this and ducked low. Smart's bag collided with the metal seat. There was a sound of broken glass and liquid seeped through his canvas holdall onto his trousers and the decking. 'Fuck you, Brownlow.' A couple of girls laughed but Smart, red-faced and embarrassed by the catastrophe – particularly being laughed at by girls – just scuffed along the deck dragging the damaged bag.

Alex Brownlow, she thought. Their proximity had affected her too. She'd got used to recalling his *bottomless blue* eyes, but it was more to do with the sudden and unexpected close contact. That moment, *their intimacy,* coupled with dramatic hormonal changes and her much anticipated first period, had moved her latent feelings up a notch.

Mother had tried to warn her of these inevitable changes over the past couple of years. One day Mary stepped out of the shower as her ma entered the bathroom with fresh towels. She looked at her daughter's developing breasts and uttered some less than comforting words. 'They're like peas on a drum'. They'd laughed but Mary, worried at the slow pace of her development, was convinced that she'd end up flat-chested like her Ma.

The beginnings of womanhood, she'd reasoned and what this might mean regarding her confused feelings about Alex. She was not so much aroused by sex as interested in the changes that preceded it. But she was yet to learn that arousal and interest are not that far apart.

Mary wondered if there might be a suitable time, away from class, when they could swap notes about their visits to Grayling. She could guess why Alex was there; he was dragging his feet academically, easily distracted, secretly reading, and making notes about whatever his real interests were. She wanted to know more about that! Or he'd gaze out of windows, people watching – especially likely to happen during maths or French lessons.

Her meetings with Grayling were of a different nature altogether. She was bright, and prone to adding her own comments at the bottom of completed exam papers for which, despite her comments, she usually got top marks. She'd been pulled up more than once for what Grayling described as her *questioning the teacher's competence.* She argued her point, unable to comprehend why it was okay for a teacher to write critical remarks when students got things wrong but thirteen-year-olds were not allowed to comment when they felt the teacher was *underperforming.* The second-in-command, deputy headmistress Ms Kinley, thought her atypical notations might be breaching school etiquette.

Mary wasn't quite sure what Grayling's duties were. She knew he was thick with Ms Kinley – not in any sexual way, as far as she could tell, but they *scratched each other's backs.* She was sure that such a professional should be dealing with far more complex problems in his clinic, rather than wasting time monitoring healthy enquiring schoolkids.

It was obvious that teaching staff were overworked and

underpaid, so maybe Grayling was taking some of the responsibility off the Head and his deputy, easing the emotional load by allowing teachers to get on with teaching instead of sorting out what Mary felt were minor concerns. What was his brief?

She visited the library, looked up what Grayling's credentials might authorise him to do for students, and asked the librarian to copy the relevant page.

Educational psychologists are involved in assessing children's strengths and difficulties. They work with schools, helping children by working through others who have direct contact with them and who most impact on their lives. Benefits of this approach include:

- *development of strategies that are practical and can be implemented by teachers and parents.*
- *action by teachers and parents which create environments that bring about positive change in children.*
- *enhanced skills and deeper understanding for the adults involved.*
- *reduction in concern about individual children, as a result of sharing information and agreeing actions and priorities.*

She remembered her last visit to Grayling. The psychologist had been avidly going through papers before he'd even looked up, flipping pages back and forth as if looking through the detailed records of a serious offender.

She was exhausted after her morning exercise class, knees buckling with fatigue, and the long wait for her meeting with the psychologist. 'Good morning, Doctor Grayling. Can I sit here?' she asked, 'sorry, but I've been standing a long time.'

'Please do. Good morning, Mary,' he said, peering momentarily over the top of his glasses while still shuffling files.

She looked around the gloomy room, waiting for him to start the conversation. Light paint showed patches of brown woodwork due to many years of hand rubbing and neglect. She wondered if old schools were ever redecorated. No such thing had occurred during her time here.

'Do you know why you're here this time, Mary?' he said, with an expression associated with the beginnings of a Q&A session; the quizmaster confident and totally in control.

'Not really,' she replied, reluctant to admit that her notations on exam papers were anything other than intelligent responses to the bloody obvious.

'Well let me clarify. You're here because you've been writing your own addenda at the bottom of exam papers. That space is not for you, it is for your teachers. It is they who should be commenting on your work, not you on theirs,' he stated while fiddling distractedly with a tissue, attempting to clean his bifocals.

She knew this was displacement activity. She'd noted it before, especially in adults when they realise that what they were saying might be contentious. Grayling was a psychologist, so he'd understand that free speech was an essential part of growing into a rounded human being. She'd read up on it and found out as much as she could about the man in front of her.

'They weren't meant to be rude or cause trouble, sir. I think the teachers who made a big thing of it might have missed the point. Some of the exam questions were not testing enough, like they'd been set for two classes below us. Some were even misquoting...'

'Let me stop you there, Mary. The point is not that you were criticising exam papers, but more about the language you used to state your case. The two teachers who brought this to our notice felt you were...' he coughed politely; delicacy had overcome him...' questioning their mental faculties.' He chose the next few moments to revisit the polishing of his bifocals.

Mary faked a sneeze to hide a developing snigger. 'I didn't mean to upset anyone, but the school – and I believe you do too, sir – encourages free speech and criticism. I felt my comments might lead to a review of exam papers. Not all of course,' she added quickly, 'just the ones which now seem a little tired and not testing enough for such advanced classes.'

She couldn't be sure, but she'd bet on it, some of the exam papers had been used in previous years.

Grayling knew that Mary would soon be taking her final exams to determine her senior education. Ms Kinley had praised her and was in no doubt that she was destined to go far.

'You're a bright student, Mary. I'd hate to see these...minor points affect your final report. You'll be moving on with your education so don't let anything get in the way. Can I suggest that you no longer add your comments to exam papers but discuss issues with the teacher or teachers concerned.' He dropped his voice to a whisper. 'Then there's nothing in writing to go on your record.'

'Okay,' said Mary, unable to sign off with a positive 'yes'.

CHAPTER NINE

Alex knew what was coming. The results of his final exams had been given out. He and Eddie came joint bottom of the class, but for very different reasons. His mind had been on what he considered *more important things*, while Eddie had decided to go down the route of class clown. Popular but, at the end of the day, uneducated, only interested in making people laugh, including his teachers. No doubt he was a success in that field, but Alex was more concerned about Eddie's future.

He wondered how Mary had fared in her exams. Maybe he'd find out soon. He knew she was intellectually clever so expected a good outcome for her. The only time he got to see her routinely was when the joint English session, Forms A and B together, put them in the same classroom. Next period was due in two days' time.

His parents would be disappointed, but not as disappointed as they might have been. The family breakup, Mother's face being rebuilt – and not looking her best right now – and Vera Harris becoming the new focus of her life would have been distraction enough. Anyway, they knew he wasn't doing well, so not exactly the greatest surprise.

When he arrived home his mother was standing at the kitchen

sink. Alex tapped on the open kitchen door so's he wouldn't make her jump. She was looking out across the lawn at a couple of starlings pecking at the washing line.

'Hello, son, how did school go today?' she asked, in a voice that seemed to come from another room. This happened when she felt tired, some sort of muscle fatigue, a legacy from the jaw surgery that affected the facial muscles and distorted sound and speech.

'You'll be disappointed, Ma. I came bottom of the class,' he said.

Her head drooped as she gripped the sink, her knuckles showing bony white. She sighed heavily, the air in her lungs huffed out in one go. 'We knew your grades had dropped, Alex, but thought you might have made an extra effort on this occasion,' she said, wiping her eyes quickly with the hem of her apron, staring out at the now abandoned clothesline. The starlings had flown, as if the news had disappointed them too.

'Where did your best friend Eddie feature in all this? He's as dumb as they come as far as I remember.'

'Couldn't put a fag paper between us,' said Alex, trying not to smile.

'Fag paper? You're not smoking, are you, Alex? Was he better or worse than you?'

'A tad better. Probably because he makes the teachers laugh. He couldn't have beat me on subjects though,' he said confidently, hoping to salvage a little something from the exchange.

'Father won't be pleased,' she said, as if they were still close, a caring mother and father.

Another few days and Father would be gone. He worried about him from time to time, almost got used to him being an absent father; taking to his room as soon as he got home from work, missing meals and limiting his conversations. He was less worried about his ma; despite what she'd been through she was now in control of her future, or as close as it could get. They'd split the sale of the house, her affair with Vera would continue and she'd still have her son.

Father would have less of a plan. Where would he live? He'd be homeless. How would he explain the situation to his pals and people at work? He was drunk as a skunk for much of the time these days. Just the odd evening of sobriety. And no one to love, or so it seemed.

Father and son should have a special bond, but it never was and never would be. They'd all got used to the status quo. Living separate lives really – almost from the day he was born!

Dad would soon be closing the front door for the last time, yet he hadn't mentioned his plans to anyone. Alex had approached him a couple of times, but alcohol blurred the picture, all he could say was, 'I'm sorting things out, son. I'll let you know where I'll be when I know.' End of.

Neither Mother nor Father had mentioned Vera since 'the day'. Like she was some ghost that had visited in the night, caused chaos, and left the family in ruins. The only glimmer of a sign for Alex was the brown envelope pushed through the letter box, and even then he couldn't be sure it really was from Ms Harris. But he'd put a bet on it.

Florence was getting ready, needed to be prepared. She'd showered for longer than usual, trimmed the untidy fringe that threatened her eyesight, and made up her face with the kit she'd bought from Avon but had never used. Did *lesbians* wear perfume? She couldn't escape the word, it came without warning. She dabbed perfume, eau de cologne 4711, behind her ears, smeared a little on her throat and spent some time examining herself in the mirror. She squinted to focus more closely on the result, rubbing the makeup a little thicker into the more obvious scars left by surgery. The cologne was stronger than she'd expected, it had been some time since she'd used it. A quick rub with a wet flannel did nothing to reduce the effect.

As long as it wasn't too bright in the restaurant, she wouldn't look so bad. She was never a beautiful woman, but neither was

Vera Harris. Did it matter? Not in their case, it was less to do with looks and more to do with chemistry. That inexplicable condition that ties people stronger than blood – and makes them do stupid things.

They'd met several times, hurried furtive associations in out-of-the-way places. Intentions made clear; doubt becoming certainty. Fumbling from her, expert guidance from Vera. She'd felt like a child learning how to tie shoelaces.

But today was the first proper date, her first meal with Vera before... She trembled slightly, the anticipation of being in bed with her newfound love triggering waves of doubt, excitement, and terror.

George had caught a whiff of *eau de* – whatever it was – as he lay in his room. He had a nose for changes in atmosphere, particularly as anything other than domestic products were rare in the Brownlow household. He was fully dressed and sat up to take a swig of the cheap wine he kept on the bedside table. He was going to follow her. He wanted to see for himself just how they behaved, these liberated women who had rejected men in favour of...what, exactly?

He heard her move quietly down the stairs, failing to miss the creaky fourth step. He heard the front door close, and the unusual tap of her new court shoes along the concrete path. The gate squeaked. George looked out through the gap in the curtains before taking the stairs.

His plan was sketchy. Not even a plan really, just an overwhelming desire to do something!

CHAPTER TEN

Alex returned from school late after receiving detention for missing an essay deadline. He unlocked the front door and shouted a warning hello to whoever might be there. He'd explain the detention and the hour-long discussion with Eddie who'd also missed the deadline. But the house was silent. A note on the kitchen worktop told him that Mother was having late lunch with a friend and should be back to get supper. No sound from upstairs. Father's door was closed, as usual, but not a sound from behind it, not even a snort or cough.

He went back downstairs to the kitchen, poured a glass of orange juice, made a jam and peanut butter sandwich, and sat at the table. He felt gloomy. His thoughts turned to adults and love and things associated. A recipe for total gloominess if ever there was one.

He wondered if his parents had ever actually been in love. It was hard to imagine. It never showed – not in all the time he was able to comprehend such emotions. Maybe they'd fallen in and out of love several times and now longed for a previous boy or girlfriend who they'd given up? Perhaps they couldn't find 'the one' and decided to risk giving marriage a go, hoping it would turn out well. Time was not on their side. But there must have been something better than this.

Their long relationship had ended with a thirty-second outburst of terrifying magnitude making a return to normality impossible. No going back. Forgiveness unthinkable. If they'd never really been in love, this was their unexpected ticket out of the contract.

He was ashamed of thinking in such depressive terms but how did you stop your mind running with the obvious?

His parents were married for ten years before he was born. Was he planned, welcome, or just a huge mistake?

George and Florence, in their early fifties now, were named after grandparents or favourite relatives. He couldn't imagine their names suiting anyone younger than fifty. The way he fitted into things never felt right, an intruder, unplanned and in the way.

But there was a brighter side. He was free of the overbearing parents that seemed to plague many of the kids he knew: being pushed to near depression with the pressure of it all; to always be good and do well, pass exams, telling them that school days were the best of their lives (oh no they weren't), take up activities that their parents had failed in, learn to like cricket or chess. And don't drink or smoke – regardless of whether responsible grownups did or not.

His parents had cared a little about his schooling, but only in a superficial way, conversational rather than deep concern. The only strong emotion shown by Mother regarding his schooling was when he announced he was bottom of the class. Tying with Eddie rubbed salt in the wound. Her reaction must have, in some way, been augmented by her current situation, the disappointing results of surgery, the parting of the ways with Father, and her new love affair. Though Mother or Father showing passion did not seem feasible. But what about his ma being a lesbian? It didn't seem as bad as going with another man, two women together did not raise eyebrows in the town and, apart from him...there'd be no unwanted children to complicate things. Ms Harris turning up at his school to lecture occasionally might feel a bit weird, but he was used to weird. Everyone had their quirks; we could all be described as odd if viewed in a certain light.

CHAPTER ELEVEN

Florence picked up a cab at the end of the street. George, having stepped into the front garden, held back as he watched her instruct the driver. He rushed back to get his car, fumbled with the keys but eventually managed to start it and pull out into the traffic, a few vehicles behind her Uber driver. They travelled out of town along country lanes onto the bypass, ending up twenty miles away.

Florence got out, paid the driver, and looked around before entering The Stag's Head pub. Vera hadn't arrived. There were mostly men at the crowded bar but only a few tables taken in the restaurant. It was a good choice. Booths for privacy had been set along one wall, enough to seat four but very comfortable for two. A stag's head was the main dining room feature, surrounded by oak panelling and sprays of artificial flowers in urns or huge stonecast vases.

'Can I help you?' asked a bright girl in a smart suit.

Florence smiled nervously, a moment of hesitation as she tried to remember Vera's surname. 'I think Vera Harris booked for two. Is she here yet?'

'Not quite. She rang to say she'd be ten minutes late. Sends her apologies. Can I take you over to your table?' she asked, leading

Florence to a corner booth. 'Let's get you a drink. What would you like?' she asked, handing her a wine list and menu.

'Gin and tonic please. More tonic than gin,' she said, with a nervous chuckle.

Florence took off her coat, folded it, and placed it next to her on the bench seat while staring blankly at the list of food. She wasn't hungry.

George parked way over on the far end of the large car park, facing the entrance to the pub. Trees overhung and kept the area in shade. He wound down the window and pulled his coat collar up to shield the lower part of his face. He was sweating. He could do with a drink.

He'd wait for a moment, let the two dykes get settled and... and walk into the bar, might be able to tuck himself in a corner and observe. Then what? No idea, he'd wing it.

A grey Peugeot pulled up across the other side of the car park. A tallish woman got out of the passenger seat, kissed the man driving and walked toward the pub. He drove off, waving out of the window. The woman looked bookish, a librarian or teacher or something. She wore a tweedy calf-length skirt and a pale green jumper. Despite the warmth of the day, a thick wool scarf covered her neck and shoulders. She checked her watch and hurried toward the pub.

Must be her, he thought, *fits the bill*. And late too, by the looks of it. He'd give them a few minutes to get settled. Once they started gazing into each other's eyes, they wouldn't notice him sitting in a busy bar. They'd got a lot to catch up on, the house sale, Alex's performance at school, the cuckolded husband. Plans.

The gods were with him. The bar was full. Mostly guys, which helped. Of no interest to those two at all, he thought. They'd be more likely to look away from a male gathering than at it.

From a stool at the darkest end of the bar he could see his wife in the restaurant, tucked into one of the booths more than fifty feet away. She was dressed to the nines, by the looks of it, and Vera bloody Harris sat across from her, touching Florence's hand while looking at the menu. They were smiling, laughing, and talking enthusiastically, like teenagers on a first date.

He watched the waitress take their order. Then Harris left her seat and walked toward him. He turned to his drink and, moving his head away from the approaching woman, fiddled with a drink's coaster. He held his breath, certain she'd have no idea who he was but not confident enough to face her head on. Not yet. There was timing involved. She passed him without comment. He looked up to where she was going and noticed signs for toilets at the end of the bar.

There was no smell of perfume as Harris walked by. Florence had wasted her time with the 'oh de' stuff. Nothing feminine to compete with here. He turned halfway toward Florence, raising a glass to his lips to blur some of his features in case she glanced his way. She didn't. Just sat there opening and closing her handbag. She looked quite attractive. It had been some years since he'd stopped to look at her; really look at her. The poorly lit booth and fresh makeup had transformed her. She looked younger. He had a sudden longing. A feeling, buried deep, tried to surface but was held back by circumstance. The paradoxical moment raised his blood pressure and he saw himself in the bar mirror, red-faced and angry. Older than his years under the harsher downlighting of the well-illuminated display of alcoholic drinks.

He was certain they'd been in love, Florence and him, back in the day, or at least had a deep affection and enough reasons to want marriage and children, to set up home together, *till death do us part.*

'Another one, sir?' asked the barman, as Harris walked back past him, unaware of his presence. He was a total stranger. He nodded a yes at the barman, not daring to speak.

Florence looked up as Vera approached their table and smiled, oblivious to her spying husband.

'You look really good, Flo.'

'Isn't makeup wonderful?' replied Florence. They laughed.

George felt a bit let down. Nothing he saw came close to how he'd imagined the scene to play out. The two women continued to chatter excitedly, running their fingers down the menu, touching hands occasionally. Sipping their drinks, which seemed to take forever. It took them half an hour before they placed their food order. George had already downed three pints, forgetting he'd driven to The Stag's Head and was now well over the limit.

He was surprised to realise, that despite ruminating and plotting this scenario for some time, he did not have a plan which suited the moment. He'd been disarmed by the total lack of anything remotely sexual in the scene before him. It was just like any two girlfriends meeting for a meal. Obviously they would be on their best behaviour in a public place, but even so, he'd expected more.

Their first course arrived. They topped up their drinks and spent some time playing with plates of food. A smart-suited girl, the restaurant manager, asked if everything was alright. It was.

George gave another nod at the barman who obliged with his fourth pint. He was getting hungry. Having already emptied the crisps and peanut bowls next to him, he was tempted to ask for a sandwich but decided it might attract attention. He was getting bored and tired. Had he seen enough? He wanted to observe them together and that's exactly what he'd done. Was he ever planning to confront them? He certainly wanted to kill Vera bloody Harris, but that approach had mellowed to a constant but milder version of hatred. Should he leave now with the information he'd gained stored safely in his troubled mind? He'd seen everything he was going to see. It was time to leave.

He paid his bill, but tiredness, stress and a few beers had taken hold. He slid unceremoniously off the bar stool and smacked his head against a protruding oak moulding on the way down. His neck snapped backward as he crumpled in a heap onto the flagstone floor. The men around him told everyone to clear a space. George lay still, bleeding, unconscious but still breathing.

Florence and Vera, hearing the commotion, went over to see if they could help.

'Please keep back. All taken care of, girls, we've called an ambulance,' said the barman as he replaced the phone. One of the guys checked that George was still alive. A bar assistant appeared with a small first aid kit and attempted to control the blood which had already soaked George's shirt and jacket

Florence went deathly pale. 'My God!' she exclaimed, gripping Vera's arm tightly enough to make her squeal.

'What is it, Flo, you look awful, you're shaking, is it the blood?'

'No. It's my husband…George.'

CHAPTER TWELVE

It was getting late; Alex was starting to worry. No one had contacted him since the note left in the kitchen. He poured himself another cup of tea and reflected on the situation. It was some time since both parents had been out of the house for so long. They wouldn't have been together; he was sure of that.

The phone rang, he hurried to pick it up. 'Hello.'

'Alex? It's Mum...I won't be home yet... Dad's had an accident and he's in hospital. I can't talk now, make yourself something to eat and I'll be home as soon as I can...'

'Is it serious, Ma?'

'The doctors are checking him now. They're doing a CT scan. It's busy and noisy here, difficult to speak...I'm having trouble hearing you. I'll be home soon,' she said, terminating the call with a quick clatter of the phone being hooked into its slot.

He had quite a few questions buzzing around; she must have been out with Dad! An event unthinkable given the situation. What sort of accident? Alex noted that the family car was gone, so maybe he'd driven into something. Was Ma hurt? She didn't sound like it. Was it an attack, was he drunk, a fall maybe?

He could only wait until she came home, or the phone rang with the latest update.

George was barely conscious, lying in his hospital bed, showing signs of confusion and memory loss. His head ached. Two women were staring through an observation window. Staff went through various procedures before taking him down for his scan. One of the faces seemed familiar, recent, but he couldn't be sure. The other, taller, swathed in a huge scarf which partly obliterated her features, was less so. He closed his eyes, tempted to fall asleep again, but the nurse nudged him gently as a porter came in to take him to the radiology department. He felt the bed being jacked up as it morphed into a gurney. The sudden movement made him feel sick, but he managed to control a desire to vomit.

He was trying to remember what had happened. Vague images of drinking in a bar somewhere came and went like brief clips of a blurred film. Was he with someone? Didn't think so.

The gurney virtually flew past Florence and Vera as they watched George being wheeled down the corridor and into the lift. The doors pinged shut and the lift descended to the radiology unit. He hadn't noticed the same two women staring at him in the hospital corridor. The hypnotic effect of fluorescent lights zipping past as he travelled toward the scanning room gripped his attention. The cheery porter insisted on entertaining George with the latest football news. George had never been interested. Certainly not now.

Four pairs of hands shifted him onto the scanner table, as a nurse clamped his head into a special cradle and told him to keep still. Despite his predicament, George felt a sudden calm. His concern and worries left him as if by magic. His anger went AWOL. Recent memories of his son and wife had been erased. Vera Harris had never existed. *And he'd never struck a woman in his life.*

Florence had no idea how she was going to handle the situation. There were regrets, of course. The biggest being that, despite her anxiety, she'd been deprived of an afternoon with Vera Harris. George knocking himself out while spying on them didn't exactly generate compassion. But he was still living at home, in their house, days away from having to leave. Could she even consider kicking him out now? Alex wouldn't be happy. The boy had already accepted the bizarre family situation, like a well-adjusted adult – but this latest development might ensure a more sympathetic attitude toward his father.

Vera held Florence tightly as she held back tears of anger and frustration. 'I'm so sorry, Vera. What a bloody mess! What on earth prompted George to spy on us? It wasn't going to change anything, was it? Our marriage was over, he was about to move out... Seeing us together could only have made things worse.'

'Curiosity killed the cat,' said Vera unhelpfully. 'Or nearly killed it,' she said, smirking sarcastically. They laughed.

'Let's grab a coffee,' said Vera, taking Florence by the hand and leading her toward the Friends of the Hospital cafeteria. Vera queued while Florence found a corner table overlooking the hospital gardens, her mind buzzing with ludicrous solutions.

Coffee in paper cups didn't look inviting but they needed a shot of caffeine. 'Not so bad after the first sip,' said Vera, taking another.

'Don't get too wound up about this yet, Flo. It's only just happened; our minds will be all over the place and not coming up with anything helpful. They'll probably keep him in for a few days anyway in case there's complications. The breathing space will give us time to plan things. I'll do everything I can to make it easy. Will Alex be okay with me being around?' she asked, not expecting to be welcomed with open arms but...

'I really don't know, Vera. There'll be a lot to talk about when I get home. How the hell do I explain all this to a kid? He doesn't know what's going on and when he finds out the details, and how his spying father ended up in emergency...'

'Why not just tell it like it is? I've seen him in school during my occasional lectures. I can tell he's bright. Not oblivious to the adult world. Whatever you do, it won't be easy. Then life isn't, is it, Flo? It's not fair either. We've both learnt that. Or should have done by now.'

The last thing Florence thought of was *telling it like it is* to Alex. Revealing to her son that she was in love with a lesbian and had never felt so alive, seemed…ridiculous.

'Could you drop me back to get our car?' asked Florence. 'George must have left it at The Stag's Head.'

'I'll ring my brother. He dropped me off there. He's not far away.'

'Didn't know you had a brother.'

'There's a lot we don't know about each other. Isn't it exciting?' she said, with fluttering eyelashes, scarf pulled up to cover her nose and mouth.

Florence gave a stiff grin, nodded, but had some difficulty thinking beyond their selfish relationship. It excluded everything and everybody outside their rare moments together.

They drained the remains of their coffee quickly, as if they had a train to catch, and took the stairs back to the ward. The consultant was by George's bed looking through his notes and talking to a nurse.

'Ah, Mrs Brownlow?' he queried, seeing the two women approach.

Florence nodded. 'Yes, that's me,' she admitted, holding the palm of her hand up, in case he confused her with Vera.

'We haven't got the scan results yet but either way we'll need to keep your husband for at least forty-eight hours. We stitched the wound and that will heal nicely. But with head injuries, the real problem is usually about what happens *under the bonnet*; inside the skull, the brain in particular,' he added for clarification. 'George is very confused right now. But, putting it in context, that's not unusual, even when the injuries aren't serious. But we do need to keep him under observation for a little longer.'

The consultant looked at the nurse, who backed him up with a series of nods.

'Why don't you go home and get some rest. We'll ring you as soon as we have news,' he said, snapping his file shut, signalling the end of his visit to George's bedside.

George felt the sensation of people leaving – a mild vacuum – more like a familiar room being emptied than his wife and her lover heading for the door.

CHAPTER THIRTEEN

Florence was going through the list of lies she'd have to tell to get through this. She was practised. Along with her husband George they'd honed their lie lists to perfection. It was the only way they could make the marriage bearable.

Vera had already asked if she wanted to go back to her place for a while.

Florence hadn't answered straight away, there was Alex to think about. He was old enough to stay on his own. Just for one night. If he didn't feel up to it, he could call one of his pals, tell them his dad was in hospital and that his ma wanted to be there in case his condition worsened.

She was certain that Alex would get invited somewhere once he'd made a couple of calls. Eddie sprang to mind. He only lived a few streets away. Not the best influence but they liked each other, and Alex was his own person, not easily led into the childish things Eddie got up to. Plus, Florence had met and liked Eddie's parents. Good solid sociable folk but, unfortunately, with a stand-up comedian for a son.

Her accumulating list of lies was growing fast. If Florence was to write all of them down, she'd have to start another page.

Alex was waiting by the phone, reading about the latest news on computers being introduced to schools. He picked up the second it rang.

'It's Mum, Alex,' she blurted, annoyed that she was finding the call so awkward. 'Father is still unconscious. The consultant's been round, but they want to keep him in for a couple of days. I need to stay for a while. Will you be alright on your own for a bit?'

I'm not a child, Mother, he wanted to say. 'Sure, I'll be fine. Do you want me to come over to the hospital, keep you company?'

'No need. I'm okay, there's loads of people here and there's a comfortable seating area with coffee and stuff,' she said, managing to keep the hint of panic out of her voice. Vera was standing next to her.

'Tell me more about what happened. Are you alright, Ma? Were you in an accident together? Were you going somewhere? What about Dad's injuries...?'

'Hold on a minute, son, it's a long story, we'll talk when I get back. I'm fine but, basically, your father slipped off a stool in a pub and knocked himself out. Too much to drink.'

'Pub? I didn't think you liked booze that much, Ma. Were you drinking with him?'

'Not exactly but I'll tell you the whole story when I get back. It's complicated. Perhaps you could stay with Eddie tonight, then I won't have to worry about you.'

When an adult says *it's complicated* it usually meant they were going to make a meal of whatever it was. His parents often did, and that's why their lives were always difficult, and destined to end so badly.

'The whole night?' he asked. He wasn't fussed about being on his own, but the situation troubled him. The marriage was over, and Father was safely tucked up in a hospital bed for the night. So Alex couldn't think of a good enough reason for his ma not to come home. 'Have you got someone with you, making sure you're okay?'

Florence, momentarily lost for words, turned to Vera and, covering the mouthpiece whispered, 'What shall I say?'

Vera smiled and gave an exaggerated 'search me' shrug.

'Oh…the consultants just called me over, Alex. I'll have to ring you back.' She was now on to page three of her 'lie list'.

'That didn't go too well, did it, Flo?' asked Vera, rewinding her scarf, tossing the end over her shoulder theatrically, to emphasise the point.

They went to take a last look at George before they left. A reflex action, something everyone does when they leave someone to spend time in the unsettling atmosphere of a hospital. He was out of it, mouth gaping, a waxy complexion aging him.

Vera's brother was waiting outside. 'I'm just over there,' he said, pointing to a dark grey Peugeot straddling lines in a parking bay. 'I'll just pay the car park fee and we can go,' he said, before Vera had a chance to introduce Florence.

He came back and gave Vera a hug. Florence received the same warm embrace, taking her completely by surprise. 'I'm Simon. Good to meet you, Flo, sis has told me all about you,' he said, adding. 'Not all about you… of course not.' He said, with a flicker of a wink. He smiled and opened the passenger door.

She might have blushed; the comment certainly made her feel like it.

'How is the old boy? Is he going to be alright, Flo?' Was he talking about someone's grandad?

Two people calling her Flo felt totally odd. And imagining what Vera might have told Simon about their feelings for each other was more than embarrassing.

Vera sat next to her brother and Florence sat in the back of the Peugeot. He didn't light up, but Simon was obviously a smoker, the residue clung to everything. Smokers would be unaware, but the resulting evidence was obvious.

The two women made eye contact via the windscreen mirror, a subtle, intimate sign language which raised Florence's anxiety enough to make her take to looking out of the window at passing shops and traffic.

Simon was silent for most of the journey, just the odd question about how George had ended up in hospital, how her son was doing at school. Vera must have confided in him somewhat. He was polite, but he'd be using the same mirror to monitor the traffic behind – and maybe check on his sister's new woman.

Florence was by no means the only woman in Vera's life.

Simon wasn't a taxi service, but sometimes it felt like it. Vera took advantage because she liked a drink, whilst he rarely indulged. He didn't mind the odd run because he found his sister's mutable love life rather sad and felt a brotherly duty to be on hand, ready for the fallout.

They pulled up outside a mews terrace, somewhere Florence didn't even know existed, along a narrow cobbled street with barely enough room to park without impeding traffic flow. Simon didn't hang around, he let them out of the car, gave them a peck on the cheek and, with his eyes on Florence, said, 'I'll leave you to it.' Florence was relieved, she would have felt awkward twiddling her thumbs while they waited for him to go.

'Follow me. Mind the turn at the top of the stairs,' said Vera. She punched a code into the entry system. The front door clicked open an inch. Vera pushed it further. 'Welcome to my castle,' she said, removing her scarf and coat, hanging them on an old-fashioned wooden rack.

Florence was taken aback. All the rooms led into each other but there were no doors. Apart from what must have been the bath and toilet area, she could see into every part of the flat from the entrance. She trembled slightly on spotting a huge double bed with a padded headboard. Her mind couldn't help creating all sorts of reasons as to why a single woman would need or want a king-size bed.

Florence stared at the black and white prints that appeared to be the favoured framed art decoration. Some looked erotic but she couldn't quite make them out and didn't want to stare for long. That would be rude.

'Aubrey Beardsley,' said Vera. 'Not originals of course.'

Florence didn't like art without colour, but she did spot some beautiful hand-scripted poems, framed in black. Vera's work: like the note that had been posted through Florence's door. 'I like these,' she said, touching a couple gently.

Vera smiled. 'I'll pour us a drink,' she said, walking over to a small cabinet for two glasses and a bottle of gin. She darted into the tiny kitchen, took a bottle of tonic water out of the fridge, and dropped ice cubes into the empty glasses.

Florence wasn't a drinker. No tolerance for it. The gin at the pub restaurant and the single glass of wine before the meal was her limit. But she was not going to spoil the party.

'I noticed in the pub that gin and tonic was your tipple,' said Vera, pouring a generous amount of gin but going easy on the tonic. She handed a glass to Florence and sat opposite, her hypnotic gaze almost too much to bear. 'You can sit here if you want to,' said Vera, patting the sofa next to her. She held back on commenting on whatever cheap cologne Florence was wearing.

Florence almost spilled her drink, negotiating the short distance past an intrusive coffee table.

There was a silence, not awkward, but filled with a myriad of disparate thoughts, swinging from the unnerving present to troubling images of Alex and George. She tried to shut them out, but they continued to sneak in. Before she realised it, her glass was empty. Vera topped it up but had yet to start her own drink, which sat on the coffee table, ice melting fast. She preferred a reasonably clear head on these occasions.

George was having a less sociable evening, unpleasant dreams, and various hospital procedures, emptying bags he was attached to and nurses attempting to wake him up for medication they'd hope he could take by mouth. Not yet.

His dreams were coming and going in short bursts, edited, redacted events, mainly to do with the past; his early days with Florence, his son's propensity to buck the trend. Whenever he woke and stirred in the night, his wife's name escaped him and his son remained an enigma.

The buzz and clatter of hospital life became a kind of tinnitus, an annoying and uncontrollable constant which threatened to drive him nuts.

Eddie couldn't wait for Alex to arrive. His mum had picked up the phone when Alex rang, and on hearing the reason for his call, immediately wanted to look after him. 'I'll send Father out to get you in the car, right away. You poor boy!'

'I can walk, Mrs Burns, it's only a few streets away.'

'You've been through a difficult time, Alex. I don't want you walking the streets alone. Eddie's dad will be there before you can put your coat on.'

When Alex arrived, there was already tea, sandwiches and cakes set out on the chequered tablecloth in the homely kitchen. Eddie had already bitten into one of the muffins, failing to disguise the evidence with a crumpled napkin.

'Tell us what happened, Alex, is it serious?' asked Eddie. 'Was it a car accident? People can die from head injuries…' he said, searching for an example, to illustrate the point, '…even healthy footballers,' he added, looking toward his parents for a confirmatory nod. They shook their heads, raised their eyebrows and sighed heavily. 'Keep quiet for a minute, Eddie, Alex doesn't need more drama than he's got.'

Eddie's parents, Joan and James Burns, sat across from the two boys, waiting for the update.

'Well, Dad's in a coma and Mum's waiting for scan results. When they get the report, they'll know what treatment or operation he needs.'

'What exactly happened to your dad?' chipped in Eddie.

'He got seriously drunk, fell off a stool in the pub and knocked himself out,' said Alex.

The parents didn't quite know how to respond to Alex's direct summary. Father coughed, and mother said, 'Poor boy,' again, reached over to pat his hand and poured herself another cup of tea. Eddie, for once, buttoned his lip. No doubt he'd speculate further once he was alone with his pal.

They all watched television for a bit, some silly game show which failed to interest Alex. He stared blankly at the screen, his mind filling with images of his mother and father who seemed less like real parents by the minute. And now that his dad was in a coma, he didn't think the family's future looked remotely like there'd be better days ahead. He thought of Mary, their brief moments in the odd class...the bus episode which he could still recall in glorious detail. It was about time they managed a bit more time together. Not a date or anything, just a chat. She'd be moving on education-wise, and he'd be wondering what to do next.

Florence felt as if she'd been run over by a truck, unsure whether to blame it on the booze, the sex, or the bizarre family situation in general.

All of the above, probably.

Vera sat on the edge of the bed with her back to Florence, brushing her hair, remembering that Flo would not have done what they did without a substantial amount of alcohol. She knew about alcohol; it gave you the courage to do things that you most definitely wouldn't do without it. They'd never have got past the kissing and petting stage.

'How are you, Flo?'

'I've been better, my lips feel bruised and I'm very sore...down below,' she said, her eyes closed, wondering why she wasn't feeling the anticipated benefits of her afternoon with Vera.

Vera laughed hysterically at the words *down below*! How quaint and so Victorian. 'You haven't had sex for a long time, Flo. A very long time. You were so...tight. When was the last time you had it with George, or anyone, or snogged someone for more than two seconds?'

That was unkind. Florence was embarrassed by the laughter, and the cruel but true summary of her sexual experience. She covered her closed eyes but didn't comment.

'No need to answer, Flo. You probably can't remember much of the afternoon. You'll heal though, I guarantee it. I'll get some cream,' she said, leaving for the ensuite and returning with a small jar. 'Would you like me to rub it in for you? Only joking. I'll leave you to shower and get dressed. You probably need to check in with the hospital and Alex.'

Florence stood naked in the ensuite letting the shower run hot. The smell of another person's body on her own skin was an alien sensation, but not unpleasant. She looked in the mirror, analysing the old scars from George's attack – yes it was an attack – they were fading but she still looked damaged.

From the vigorous passions of the afternoon, she expected some bruising around the lips, but they just looked heavier, pinker, younger.

The mirror steamed up as she stepped into the shower.

CHAPTER FOURTEEN

The grey pebbledash walls of the school building darkened with the onset of thundery showers. Alex didn't mind the rain, but the increasingly sombre look of the building left him feeling a bit down, especially with his forthcoming lessons, algebra and chemistry. If there were any less helpful subjects in the world to be teaching young people, he'd like to know what they were.

It didn't take Eddie long to spread the story of Alex's father around the class and then the whole school. The bus bully, Greg Smart, and his pals, walked around the corridors like robots, their arms outstretched, with stupid expressions and eyes half closed. Presumably this was their version of Frankenstein's monster, or Alex's father in a coma after getting drunk and falling off a stool. But most gave sympathetic looks, and amid the dull day, a beam of sunshine appeared. Mary grabbed his arm, held it, and said how sorry she was to hear about his dad. It was quite close to a hug. In response, Alex covered her hand with his, confirming they'd be bound together for life.

His mother had not been that revealing about his dad's night in hospital except to say that he'd had a comfortable night, was still 'out for the count' and that the results of the CT scan were due soon.

Florence knew exactly how she looked, sitting opposite Alex at teatime. She'd glanced at herself in the hall mirror and decided against applying even more makeup. Alex would spot it. He had a piercing gaze and a sharp eye for such things.

'I'm going back to the hospital after tea. Would you like to come, Alex? Can't guarantee that your father will be pleased to see us,' she said, smiling for the first time that day.

'Have you been biting your lips, Ma, they look sore?'

'All this stress,' she said, touching her mouth to verify the observation.

'Do you want to come or not?' she said, diverting the conversation.

'Only if you need me, Ma. Otherwise, doesn't seem much point when he's not even going to wake up.'

Florence overreacted, showed signs of irritation, but was secretly pleased that Alex didn't want to visit George. She wanted time to think.

Before leaving the mews flat, while waiting for Vera to finish her lecture notes, Florence had spent a bit more time looking at the Beardsley prints and the beautiful samples of her lover's writing. Beardsley was obviously a very disturbed young man, she'd concluded. And Vera, according to her framed letters on the pristine white walls at least, was a romantic. They were love letters, not attributed to anyone but signed by Vera in her faultless script. Florence was puzzled. Their liaison didn't feel anything like romance, it was lust without the trimmings; no words of love, only the climactic physicality that was part of the endgame. In the cold light of day, it didn't seem enough.

Despite all outward signs, George had been living a very full life whilst in his present state. There were things in his past that seemed clearer and more detailed than they'd ever been when he was up and about. He now had enough time to ponder but had some difficulty controlling which memories or thoughts entered his damaged brain.

For some inexplicable reason, he was able to focus on some things and reflect on them in detail. Alex came up frequently, particularly the boy's propensity for being so outspoken and George's desire to be more like him; something he could never admit to.

The problem with lies is that one needs to defend them. He and Florence had developed it into an art form. The trouble was, truth and lies became such a part of everyday life it was impossible to tell them apart. The buttoned lips were, to a large degree, silent lies.

Pleasant memories came up too. The surprise of Alex being born. A great shock as they'd given up on it ever happening. Sex had been infrequent to say the least. But the boy, especially as a baby, was loved by both – until he learned to speak. Then it was as if this little chap became the conscience they'd abandoned. He'd questioned most things and developed opinions beyond his age and his position in the family hierarchy. Thus, George and Florence developed the buttoned lip approach which deprived Alex of any moral or ethical material he might choose to work on – and give them some peace and quiet.

Interspersed with these insights were clips from... He couldn't think what. Old horror films? Dancefloors without men, full of skeletal female couples, holding each other tightly, embracing passionately, kissing – with broken jaws.

George didn't stir let alone speak. He must have given some unconscious sign that he was in distress though, because two nurses came over, mopped his sweaty brow, folded back the upper edge of his sheet and rechecked equipment.

Florence wondered why she'd bothered to come. A phone call would have done. George looked like a cadaver in a TV crime drama where a relative was obliged to identify the body. Yes, it certainly was George, no doubt about that, but not the one she'd married. Was he still breathing? Apparently, according to the flickering monitor and the dribbling catheter.

She walked back to the Friends of the Hospital cafeteria and ordered a coffee. She didn't want to sit there on her own, mulling over her time with Vera. But George's company might be the only alternative right now. She took her drink back to the ward and sat in a chair next to his bed. A nurse came over to tell Florence that the consultant was due on his rounds and might be able to give her an update.

She might as well have stayed in the café because she ended up mulling over Vera anyway. The heated lovemaking in the mews flat had put undue strain on her radical jaw surgery, the same sensitivity that lingered months after the operation. She shuffled in the hard plastic chair, testing the *area down below* for any residual soreness. The cream must have helped.

'Good morning, Mrs Brownlow. You look tired, can we get you anything?'

'No thank you,' she said, raising her half full cardboard cup to demonstrate she'd been catered for.

'I'm Dr Richardson, George's consultant neurologist. We haven't got the scan results yet, we're taking a closer look at things. But the least we can do is give you some idea of what's happening to your husband.'

'Is he going to be alright?' she asked, realising it was a pointless question at this stage.

'I'm going to be straight with you. Always best in the long run. We don't have enough detail to give you a clear picture yet, but here's what you need to know.'

'I'd be most grateful,' she replied, taking a quick sip of her coffee.

'He'll be monitored using what we call the Glasgow Coma Scale or GCS for short. It measures patients' progress, so we'll know if he's improving even though it might not be obvious from the outside. Unlike most injuries, a brain injury doesn't simply heal with time. In my experience – and the literature supports it –

those who sustain a moderate or severe brain injury will never fully recover to be the person they once were and live the life they once lived.'

She didn't want George to have the life he once lived!

'He may be unconscious for a while, it's hard to say for how long at this point.'

'What's the worst-case scenario?' she asked.

'Let me give you some perspective. Sixty to ninety percent of brain injury patients regain consciousness within a year. Recovery is slow and George might have ongoing cognitive and physical difficulties: headaches, dizziness, fatigue, depression, irritability, and memory problems.'

Sounded like most of the symptoms he had before he fell off the bloody stool, she thought.

'A year! That's not good, is it?' she asked, wringing her hands.

'Even with rehabilitation, support and help in the community, survivors and their families are likely to face uncertain and challenging futures.'

Facing uncertain and challenging futures were routine for the Brownlows.

'He'll get good care here. We'll keep you informed,' he concluded, touching Florence's hand in a sympathetic gesture.

She was lucky to catch the bus just as it was about to leave outside the hospital. It was full at ground level, so she went upstairs and found an empty seat halfway along. She was gazing out of the window as they travelled toward town. A figure sitting at the front of the upper deck looked vaguely familiar. She could only see his back, but it was the superior posture that held her thoughts. He turned to look sideways at the passing traffic, and she recognised him immediately. Father John. Probably on hospital visits. She wondered if he'd seen George.

She paled, and slumped in her seat, hoping it would create a less obvious Florence Brownlow. She'd not been to confession for some time and realised there were confessions and confessions. The ones you could tell a priest and those you couldn't. Which was ridiculous! The idea was that you spilled every last bean to a man of the cloth.

She mentally rehearsed being in the confessional asking to be forgiven for all the things that happened with Vera, especially the grand finale at the mews. She could hardly admit them to herself. Every imagined word stuck in her throat.

Will Father John get off the bus before or after her? She had no idea where he lived and was tempted to leave now and catch the next bus to complete her journey.

As if choreographed, she stood up the same time as the priest and they walked toward each other smiling, unable to deploy any other tactic that might save embarrassment.

They both headed for the top of the stairs, she gripped his arm, and he placed a hand over hers. She'd always found this the most comforting of contacts.

'I've seen George,' he said, his face now grim. 'I'm so sorry, Mrs Brownlow...Florence. If you need to talk anytime, you know where we are.'

He didn't mention the confessional and she couldn't.

Vera Harris, on the other hand, took confession the day after the event. She had no such qualms about revealing all to Father John. She knew the guidelines; *unless the priest asks you to clarify, you don't need to confess in graphic detail about your sins.* But it was tempting to elaborate if you had a PhD in English literature from Edinburgh University and believed that Father John was as interested as you in hearing as much detail as possible from someone as eloquent and well-read as she, someone who could make her confession more like the riveting synopsis of an adult novel. And leave the pathetic blustering to those less articulate.

She almost stood up at certain points in her monologue when she needed to highlight moments for impact.

So, when Father John encountered Florence on the bus, his smile hid more than she could ever have imagined. In fact, it could be said that the priest remembered more about the detail of that steamy afternoon than Florence ever would. At the end of the day, he'd eventually put the whole thing in perspective and never doubt the folly, the idiocy, and the sheer stupidity of the human race. Their edited confessions would come back whenever he met either of those involved in the ridiculous triangle, even his visit to George lying impotent in his almost lifeless body, managed to fire off unwanted memories of the Brownlow saga. And, given his sharp brain, poor young Alex would be wondering what the hell he could do to help.

CHAPTER FIFTEEN

Dr Grayling popped in for a quick word with Vera Harris before she started her lecture. They were standing together when pupils entered the classroom for the infrequent lecture with her. The two academics, leaning close, gripping the old oak lectern, speaking in hushed tones, eventually nodding in mutual agreement. Before the end of their brief meeting Harris had taken a lengthy gaze at Alex while Grayling scanned the gathering to observe Mary who hadn't noticed his interest. She was already writing...

'The lecture today will end with a Q&A session. So please listen carefully, take notes, and enjoy the class,' said Harris, approaching the blackboard with a fresh stick of white chalk which she tested with a flourish before writing a quotation.

The difficulty of literature is not to write, but to write what you mean; not to affect your reader, but to affect him precisely as you wish.'

'Anyone know who said that?'

Someone unhelpfully whispered, 'Some old dead guy.'

'I heard that,' said Ms Harris. 'Your answer is not incorrect, but I would have liked something a bit more specific. Anyone?'

No response. She hadn't expected one. She had a knack, a mission some might call it, for asking questions that the class were unlikely to answer.

Alex felt a sinking feeling in his stomach. Not because of the lecture, Harris's were usually interesting, it was more to do with her part in the disruption of family life.

'Robert Louis Stevenson is the answer, the author of *Treasure Island, Kidnapped* and *The Strange Case of Dr Jekyll and Mr Hyde*. Most boys and some girls around your age would have read those novels but I'll tell you something interesting. Many youngsters who first read them didn't really enjoy them. Why? Because they hadn't studied enough or experienced life enough to appreciate what Stevenson was really imparting. The pleasure of these great literary works comes to life when revisited as mature adults.'

The class sighed almost as one. Alex was interested but wondered why Harris was lecturing about these great works to what she'd made quite obvious were immature students.

'And here's my point. If you're interested in literature or writing or letters or poems or being able to communicate at every level, get the best jobs, be articulate, eloquent and succeed in whatever you do – read and write.'

There was a moment of attention.

'Another quote from Stevenson...' The chalk squeaked intermittently as she wrote: *'I kept always two books in my pocket, one to read, one to write in.'*

Harris went on at some length about the writers who admired and were of interest to Stevenson – Proust, Conan Doyle, Henry James, J. M. Barrie, Kipling, Hemingway, Jack London – before offering the floor to Q&A.

The direct looks to Alex and Mary given by Harris and Grayling at the beginning of the class were not about the same things at all. Despite them having been in contact for various reasons. Grayling's eye on Mary was to do with the fall out between two psychologists: Dr Grayling, educational psychologist and Dr Singer, Mary's father, a clinical psychologist.

Vera's interested eye on Alex was about her concern, intrigue and matters regarding the association with his mother, Florence.

'Alright, class. Question time. Let me see hands go up or I'll pick someone to start,' she said, removing the Stevenson quotes from the blackboard with a felt eraser, emitting a cloud of chalk dust.

Alex surprised everyone by putting his hand up first. Mary turned to look at him and smiled. Harris, also taken aback, re-wiped the blackboard despite there being nothing left to remove.

'Yes, Alex.' *This is a first. He never puts his hand up.*

'I hope this doesn't sound too, personal Miss Harris, but do you keep two books... like Stevenson?'

'Yes, I do... Next question,' she asked, pointing to someone at the back of the class.

Alex's hand was still up. Harris looked annoyed. 'Yes, Alex.'

'Could you share a passage or two from your writing and let us know what you're reading right now. It might help us grasp the disciplines you're talking about.'

She smiled, from the mouth only, her face remained stone-like. 'You're asking about something very private, young man. I'm certainly happy to tell you what I'm reading, it's *Breakfast at Tiffany's* by Truman Capote, an American author, but my writing is not for public airing. It's a private journal.

Being addressed as a young man instead of using his name immediately put Alex on the alert. He'd struck a chord, upset her. But he really would like to know what was in her writing book.

'Next,' she said, pointing to the hand still wavering at the back of the class.

The lad checked his notes. 'Stevenson's quote doesn't seem to make sense Miss,' he said, speaking the words, '...*not to affect your reader, but to affect him precisely as you wish.* 'He seems to be saying, don't affect the reader but do it anyway. And, the other quote, '*I kept always two books in my pocket...*' Shouldn't it be, 'I always kept, or keep, two books in my pocket?'

'Valid points, but those quotes were written in the 1880s when the language and the use of it was not the same. If Stevenson had written those quotes today, they would have been constructed differently. But it's not hard to get the sense of what he was saying. Is it?' she asked – as if talking to an idiot, in a tone daring anyone to delve further. She felt tired…too much tension in the air.

Mary's hand shot up. Alex felt it was to support him in the subtlest way possible.

'Yes, Mary?'

'Have you read Jekyll and Hyde, Miss Harris?'

'Yes, have you?'

'Not yet, but I was thinking of it, because it's about someone with two personalities, good and evil, and I just wondered… do you think it's in all of us, this scary good and evil thing?'

'Read it by all means, but If you want to enjoy one of his best and most popular, read *Kidnapped*, purported to be written for young adults,' she said, trying to control a sarcastic expression. She still considered them children. 'It's a short book, so it won't take a lot of effort, and we can discuss it at some point.'

Mary wasn't quite ready to be diverted in her pursuit of an answer. 'I read that Stevenson was a very sick man for most of his life and got the idea of the story from his nightmares.'

'Yes, I knew that.'

'So, was he mentally disturbed in some way?'

'This is an English Literature lecture not a psychology class, Mary. Ask Dr Grayling or your father.'

'I'll ask my father. Dr Grayling wouldn't know, he's taken a different path.'

'What do you mean? They're both in the same profession, aren't they?'

'They decided to follow discrete disciplines, Miss. A bit like an English literature class is different from an English language class.'

Most would have cheered Mary at this point, but they were sensible not to. The atmosphere changed and Alex, mentally punching his fist in the air, was unable to control the broad grin slowly spreading across his face.

'My father is a clinical psychologist,' emphasised Mary. 'He helps individuals with mental health issues. Dr Grayling is an educational psychologist. That's more to do with supporting institutions, teachers, and students to help improve learning.'

'Most informative, Mary. Perhaps you can get your father to read Jekyll and Hyde and report his conclusions back to us!' she snapped, before finishing off the rest of her lecture.

If they'd taken a vote, most of the class would agree that this was the edgiest of Vera Harris's lectures; like watching pupil and academic mentally arm wrestle to win points rather than learn. The tension at the end was palpable.

Vera Harris ought to have cancelled today's lecture. She felt as if the class were against her, and that questions and responses were aimed at catching her out. Wrong choice of author too! When little Miss Clever Clogs started lecturing about psychotherapy and split personalities...

She should definitely have nipped Jekyll and Hyde in the bud.

Alex Brownlow sticking his hand up asking about her journal was not a nice moment either. As if he had some idea what might be in it. He'd always been interested in her lectures but tended to be a listener rather than an active participant.

Had his mother confided in him? *Of course not*, she convinced herself. Perhaps he really was interested in how a scholar kept her diary.

She might need a drink or two to settle herself down a bit.

She wasn't ready to face Florence again, not yet. Novices needed recovery time – both mentally and physically – from their unforgettable experiences with Vera Harris.

CHAPTER SIXTEEN

George was deep into his other life. The images flitting by randomly were not making a great deal of sense much of the time, but some did. Some even seemed to be scenes yet to be part of his life; a grownup son, an estranged wife hovering at the altar with another woman; a new career for George Brownlow, sweeping paths and collecting litter in parks and gardens. He could feel things going on around him, activities. Hustle and bustle. Unseen but obviously there.

Florence had asked the consultant, Dr Richardson, whether George was aware of the outside world. He didn't really know but said that coma patients are unconscious and don't respond to touch, sound, or pain, and can't be woken up. There weren't any signs of the normal sleep-wake cycle.

'What about dreaming?' she'd asked, hoping that George might be having some sort of epiphany during his present state. Father John had used that word, and she liked the sound of it and what it meant.

'No concrete proof,' said Dr Richardson, 'yet many who've recovered report dreams and nightmares and something of the outside world.'

Florence, back at work for her part-time stint at the bakers, wondered if she ought to talk things through with Alex a bit more. They both needed to accept that George, out of their lives for one reason or another, had to be thought of in terms of his future care. Obviously, he was not going to bounce back to the man he was, *thank God*, but they were still bound by marriage, and a tricky separation had been made even trickier by the new situation. He could recover completely or end up a cabbage for the rest of his life. Their savings would not cover the cost of care for long, especially if it turned out to be the 24-hour kind. She wondered if talking it through with Vera might help but realised that Vera hadn't mentioned George in any of their recent conversations. Was that consideration for Flo herself, or a complete lack of interest?

One thing she'd discovered about Vera was how open she was, saying things as soon as they entered her head, spontaneous, no buttoned lips there! She admired that quality and felt the need to start being a bit more honest with herself, with others and particularly Alex. It was time to begin turning her life around.

A visit to Father John might be a good start. A bit of a shock but at least the confessional was sacrosanct. It'd be like an honesty rehearsal programme. It might give her confidence to lead a new life, a life after George.

Father John was trying to connect Florence's confession to Vera Harris's account of the same events. It was like the two didn't know each other, let alone carried on in a serious sexual relationship. As if nineteenth-century censors had refused her full permission to reveal the detail. Not quite the *Lady Chatterley's Lover* furore, but the same censorious panel by the sounds of it. Nevertheless, he realised that the revelations spoken by Florence were a step up in terms of her spiritual and moral evolution. But Vera Harris's version would definitely be the most remembered.

Florence had made some cakes. Well not actually made them with flour, eggs, and stuff at home, she'd made extra at work and popped a few into her bag. They were allowed to get rid of certain products still taking space in the bakery at the end of the day; cakes or bread which dried out too quickly. Chocolate cupcakes, Alex's favourite, came into that category.

Alex smelled them as soon as he opened the front door. He was hungry, loved his cakes but knew that fresh ones at home were usually a prelude to a serious conversation. He remained positive and pecked his ma on the cheek, noting the absence of any indication that she'd been baking. No heat from the oven, nothing dusty on the worktop. Not a problem. Just an observation. He wasn't fussy about where his cakes originated.

'You okay, Ma, any news on Dad?' he asked, matter-of-factly.

'I'm okay. Dad's the same,' *still breathing,* she wanted to add.

Florence turned the kettle on and placed four cupcakes on a floral plate. Alex picked one up and licked the soft chocolate topping before taking a bite.

Florence hesitated, still a little reluctant to broach the sensitive subjects she had in mind. She made tea and stood with her back to the sink while it brewed. 'How was school?'

'Good. We had a lecture with Miss Harris this afternoon, about Robert Louis Stevenson and his books.'

Florence trembled as she poured the tea, using one hand to steady the other. Alex noticed but said nothing.

'Is she a good teacher?' Florence asked. Was this really where she wanted this conversation to go?

'Usually, but she seemed a bit tense today. Everyone noticed.'

'What do you mean, everyone noticed? How could you possibly know that?'

'You could feel it. The atmosphere in the class changed, like someone of authority had walked into the room and made everyone sit up.'

Florence gave an odd grunt.

'Miss Harris was not her usual self. She seemed to get touchy when questions came up, especially when Mary asked about Jekyll and Hyde and split personalities. Mary was interested in one of Stevenson's books,' he added for perspective.

Florence felt decidedly odd. Despite his innocent words it felt as if her son was accusing her, in some perverse way, of having a split personality. Florence stood silently mulling over her analysis for too long. Alex noticed.

'Everyone knows about you and Vera Harris, Mum,' he said, knowing there would never be a good time to bring it up. But with cakes, tea, no father around and a captive audience, it was about as good as it gets. He wanted his ma to move on, tell the truth, share the fallout with him and feel an honest bond develop. Cards on the table. Oh, how he longed for that. And if truth be known – apart from the obvious embarrassment of admitting that she'd changed sides on the sex front – Mother must be longing for it too.

Florence paled and gripped the handle of the cup until it snapped. The tea went everywhere; over her, on the floor, washing across the table like an incoming tide, threatening the plate of cakes. Alex got straight up, moved the remaining muffins out of harm's way and put his arm round her shoulder.

'It's okay, Ma, these things get around.' *She's an adult in a close-knit town. Why doesn't she already know that?* He knew she'd cry.

'How?' she said, face flushed as she watched Alex pick up the broken crockery and pop the fragments into the waste bin.

'Does it really matter now, Ma?' he sighed. 'Miss Harris has a reputation. That's a very difficult thing to keep private if you work in a school. Some of the teachers and office staff are her friends. They pass things on amongst themselves; the walls are thin, and kids are nosey by nature. *And prone to gross exaggeration.* Plus, she's not as buttoned up as you are about things... I didn't mean that in an unkind way, Ma, but you and Dad have never really been open with each other. It's always worried me.'

Alex took some old cloths and a plastic bucket from the utility cupboard and started to wipe the table and mop the floor.

Florence was sitting, playing with her hands, moving a muffin onto her side plate then moving it back. 'So, everyone in the town will know by now?'

Everyone in the town does know, thought Alex. 'News travels fast in this day and age,' he said, emptying the dirty water down the sink and dropping the wet cloths back into the bucket.

'Look, Ma. You and Dad weren't enjoying life, were you? That's an understatement, by the way. It was hard to catch either of you smiling, especially over the last couple of years. You seemed to be having trouble being honest with each other, even over small things. So, when you told Dad about Miss Harris he was bound to flip. Anyone would have done under those circumstances.'

Her face stiffened as if she'd just relived the moment.

'I'd wondered what on earth had got into you, Ma. Instead of discussing it, you just blurted it out at the wrong time and in totally the wrong place… I know what it was like, I was there!'

Florence began to sob uncontrollably. It had never occurred to her that Alex was worried about them. Shame overcame her swiftly, like a storm cloud in a high wind, sweeping across a barren hillside. He put his arm around her and suggested he make another cup of tea.

They both remained silent as he filled the kettle and took a fresh cup off the shelf for Florence. He'd said enough for now. He'd like her to respond but realised that might be a little longer coming.

Florence picked up a muffin and, as a distraction, nibbled the edges leaving a misshapen centre, before starting to speak. A fresh cup of tea now in front of her.

'Just a minute,' said Alex. He ran upstairs to his father's room and took an unopened bottle of whisky from under the bed.

'This might help, Ma. Medicinal as they say. You need a little something to get you through this,' he said, peeling the plastic seal and opening the top. He poured a small amount into a glass and placed it in front of Florence.

'I don't drink whisky. Is that yours, Alex? Have you been hiding it?'

'It's not mine, Ma, obviously. I'll give you two guesses who it belongs to.'

'I didn't know your father drank whisky either.'

'Maybe he didn't. Or maybe it was in case of emergencies,' he smiled ironically. He knew about father's secret storage places.

Florence took a sip and felt the burn as it seemed to travel all the way through her body. She held her throat and took a sip of the cooling tea for relief.

'Here's what I hope we're going to do, Ma. I'm not going to mention Vera Harris again today…'

She took a hurried swig and coughed.

'…but I will do at some point in the future. It's not a secret, everyone knows what lesbians do, it's not a crime. But I'd like to know what happened to you and Dad. You must have been in love once. I'd really like to think you were…' he said, the words tailing off as his emotions rose.

Florence had finished her *medicine*. She pointed at the empty glass. Alex topped it up. The muscles in her face began to soften, her shoulders relaxed a little. She twirled the spirit around like a seasoned drinker, sipped the fresh whisky and placed her hands flat on the table.

'I'm going to tell you a story, Alex. It's mine but I never want it to be yours.'

Alex hoped it was going to be a true one.

CHAPTER SEVENTEEN

'When you fall in love. If you fall in love,' she started. Alex held back on the fact that he was already in love and had been for some time. A lifelong commitment to Mary. But this was his Ma's revelation, not his.

'It's the loveliest feeling in the world. You meet who you think is your soulmate and without any preamble you start telling each other everything. And I mean everything. Pours out like a burst dam. Honesty you never thought possible. In detail. It's easy to maintain until one of you does something the other doesn't like... It may be the smallest thing, magnified in importance because of a bad day, but something that's commented on in a negative way. *'I don't like it when you say or do that.'*

'What happens, so gradually, is that behaviour becomes modified to keep things pleasant. Avoid conflict. You don't want to lose the honesty you had but if your partner seems hurt or offended, you stop saying or doing those tiny, miniscule things. Easy to think it's consideration at first, which in a way it is, but the truth of it is you make so many of these small adjustments that you become a different person. Ten years later your loving relationship is hardly recognisable. More silences, less honesty and it occurs so slowly that it's almost impossible to feel it happening. So, Dad and I tried to make it work, or at least made an effort to make it appear to be working. We tried even harder when you came along.'

'What about intimacy?' asked Alex, his mind flitting from what his mother was telling him to the mind-blowing decision to take up with Vera Harris. Threatening not just her marriage, but her family life, including the relationship with her only child.

'If you mean sex,' she said, emboldened by alcohol, 'I never really enjoyed it.'

'But you never told Dad?' he asked. *Most kids think their parents don't have sex anyway, many can't believe their mums and dads have ever actually 'done it'.*

'He must have known,' she replied, aware that it was a stupid thing to say.

'People tend not to know things by telepathy, Ma, you have to say it.' *Too hard on her?* 'This seems to have been the problem all the way along. Maybe you could both have had professional help, counselling, or something.'

'It wasn't just sex, Alex. We weren't suited at all. Not in any way I can think of. Romance was the first casualty, followed swiftly by a downward spiral in intimacy. We made it work to a point, but it was far from satisfactory. Then it became such a habit; work, watched the telly, ate our food, did our jobs, looked after you a bit. Not much, I agree, but then you didn't seem to need us. You were so capable of living your life from the moment you could walk and talk. We felt a bit redundant.'

'That's how it felt to me too, Ma. Even when I was tiny, you and Dad seemed more like strangers than parents.'

Wet-eyed, she stared at him unblinkingly for a moment. 'Life was so…pointless,' she said, feeling for the hanky in her pocket and beginning another bout of sobbing.

Alex reluctantly poured another whisky. It had loosened her tongue no end, she'd become articulate, more than he could ever have imagined. But he didn't want to have to cart her off to the bedroom drunk. He wouldn't be able to lift her anyway.

'Did you and Dad want me or was it a mistake?' he asked. 'I can take the truth, Ma, really I can. No more lies please. You need to change your life.'

Florence held the fresh glass of whisky, ran her finger around the rim, but seemed uncertain as to whether she'd be able to sustain more alcohol without collapsing. She sat and held the drink but didn't put it to her lips.

Her silence told Alex everything he wanted to know about his parents' attitude toward having a child in the family. He was definitely a mistake. But his ma's silent admission was confirmation rather than revelation.

'I'm so sorry, son,' she said. Which was enough. He believed her.

Alex screwed the cap tight and placed the bottle on the draining board. It had been helpful, but his ma was in no state to further indulge her newly discovered taste for whisky.

'Are you going to see Dad today?' he asked.

'I'll ring,' she said. 'There's no news that he's improved, so he'll still be unconscious. I think I need to lie down for a bit anyway. That whisky!'

Alex was encouraged. Everything his ma had said – *her story* – simply confirmed all he knew about his parents' situation. Put so eloquently by his mother it had exorcised some of the demons. They were living a lie, but the rollercoaster of life had not allowed them to get off and start again. Now, they'd have to.

'Perhaps we wanted love but were never actually *in love* at all,' she sniffed.

Highly likely, it seemed to Alex, who helped his ma half stumble toward the lounge where she fell fast asleep on the overstuffed sofa.

Florence dreamt of her revelations; fast-forwarded her life with George and focussed on her son and Vera Harris. They'd stopped short of talking about her in any detail but given the frankness of their recent conversation, a discussion about his mother, Harris and lesbianism was on the cards. Now that her affair was out in the open, it didn't seem so bad. Nothing much else to reveal. If there was, a drop of whisky might help.

The mews looked like a scene from Dickens' London. The cobbles shone after the rain; a swirling evening mist caused the streetlights to form halos as the figure of Vera Harris, in a hooded cape, hurriedly opened the door to her flat.

She hung her mantle on the hook behind the door and headed straight for the large bureau which served as a combined bar and writing desk. Not quite a bar but certainly a place where she kept her gin and a couple of bottles of wine. She poured herself a shot and added some tonic and ice from the small fridge in the nearby kitchen.

She kicked off her shoes and slumped onto the chesterfield next to an unlit fire. Vera hadn't written a book for some time and was no closer to starting one now. She picked up some scribbled notes, lectures, not stories, and thought of Florence.

She'd made mistakes before, but the jury was out on this one. The woman had certainly been hard work, it took nearly a half bottle of alcohol and some clever persuasion to get her started. She'd hoped that once they were alone and naked, Flo would have been a bit more enthusiastic. But she had to guide her every step of the way, with Flo only showing patchy signs of enthusiasm and spontaneity.

She took a long swig, sucked her teeth as the ice hit, and consoled herself it was early days and that Flo had been a victim of male egotism for most of her life. But Flo should definitely be allowed to make the next move, to even things up, she'd decided. In her experience, a second meeting didn't take long to happen; particularly with someone who'd been starved of affection for so long.

She picked up the sheaf of papers on her desk and took out notes on the Robert Louis Stevenson lecture. It had been an interesting class. They'd got to her. Jekyll and Hyde seemed to resonate somewhat. Kids loved horror but it didn't particularly feel like a kid's response to the story, more like an underlying current of…she didn't know what. It was unusual for her to be ruminating over a lecture once she'd given it. Far too busy planning the follow up.

Perhaps it was because she knew Alex Brownlow was aware of his mother's…impropriety. He did stare at her for a while and put his hand up to ask a question for the first time she could remember. And there was something odd about Mary joining the discussion so soon after the boy.

Or could it be that Dr Grayling's brief conversation before the lesson had affected her attitude as well as theirs? He'd revealed the fact that Alex Brownlow was trailing badly at the bottom of his class and that Mary Singer was rather quick to criticise exam papers and had the cheek to write her own, less than complimentary, comments. Her father's influence, obvious from the way she asked the questions, appeared to steer the class toward a psychologist's point of view rather than the intended literary one. It was Vera Harris's class not Dr bloody Singer's.

She placed the papers back on the bureau and sipped unenthusiastically at her drink. She felt for the cushion behind her back and placed it at the nape of her neck, enjoying the comfortable nestling effect. She gazed around the room. The pictures, the books, the bits and bobs collected from travels; awards for minor literary achievements, certificates, and an unlit log fire which she occasionally felt like lighting for the sole purpose of burning the lot. But there were only moments of such intensity. Vera Harris knew one thing for sure. She was a lonely middle-aged woman. Confirmed, when she got up from her chair and walked over to the full-length mirror.

CHAPTER EIGHTEEN

Alex had got used to the nods and winks around the school and the town, the banal and snide comments about his mother. He didn't retaliate or defend them in any way. He knew from experience that not taking the bait meant that those unkind comments would be short-lived, soon forgotten. There'd always be a residue, but the same philosophy worked either way.

The school secretary gave him a handwritten envelope. Without thinking, he smelt the envelope and knew instantly it was from Mary. He'd picked up her natural scent on the bus when they'd been forced together by Greg Smart. Alex knew he'd never forget it. Perhaps he ought to thank the bully, because without him he'd never have gotten that close. His cautious courting strategy wouldn't have allowed such intimacy so soon.

He was early for class, had some time, so popped into the empty library and sat at a table facing the door, so's he wouldn't be surprised if someone walked in.

He broke the envelope seal with more care than necessary, inching the point of a pencil along the flap hoping to preserve it. The neat letter had been folded in two, and her clear well-formed writing was not a surprise, but its content was.

Dear Alex,

I know you've been having a tough time. The rumours flying round the school are not helpful. I don't want to put you in an awkward position but wondered if you'd like to meet for a chat sometime.

Please don't feel pressured. I'll leave you to think about it.

Love,

Mary

He didn't expect the word *love* at the end of the letter. He hadn't expected the letter! It was more than he could have hoped for. Then he came down to earth, and realised that signing off with 'love' was common. Even people who weren't friends signed off with it. But the fact didn't stop his heart singing.

His head spun as he walked into the classroom and sat down. Biology. Not his favourite subject but this lesson was going to be about the brain, something he was interested in. He nodded politely at others in the class then gazed out of the window waiting for the teacher to arrive.

The conversation with his ma had gone way beyond expectations. When she'd woken up, her memory seemed fuzzy on the detail but there was no doubt that she'd remembered the gist of it, enough to convince them both that 'cats were out of bags' and that their relationship had shifted to another level. Not quite the level reached by recovering alcoholics ready to quit, but the same sentimental scenario without so much reference to sobriety and God. Though he did feel that re-bonding with Father John, and the confessional could only be a good thing. He'd encourage it. *Just be a bit more relaxed and forthcoming, Ma, like you were with the whisky...*

He'd accepted his father's condition. The future looked bleak whatever the outcome. He was probably going to die, and despite having a small percentage of optimism about his father's recovery, the odds were against it. But if he did live – unless the brain damage had altered his personality to a massive degree – Father would prove to be an impossible patient.

The new biology teacher, Mrs Jennifer Mayhew, looked too young to be a teacher and too young to be married. She was a smiley blonde with a ponytail and huge glasses that seemed to bestow extra intelligence. Her loose jumper with sleeves which she kept rolling up past the elbows made her seem even more childlike. One of them.

The class took to her immediately and their interest rose as she removed a life-size model of a human brain from a container and started explaining the different sections and what their functions were. She didn't mind being interrupted by questions, and Alex's interest was piqued by her style of teaching and the freewheeling attitude to the new class dynamics.

It was a jaw-dropping lecture for Alex. He'd no idea that different parts of the brain were so specific in what they governed. That a creative person had a 'different brain' to an academic, that emotions and love had areas that were related to distinct parts of the brain. He thought of his dad's injury and Mary's psychologist father, and Dr Grayling and Jekyll and Hyde, and decided he wanted to pitch his career into that field.

Mrs Mayhew touched briefly on the great philosophers, psychiatrists and psychologists who'd built their successful careers by understanding the brain. Just a few words on each; Freud, Pavlov, Jung, Plato, Aristotle. But enough to cause a flicker of interest amongst the class. This was beyond biology, this was about how people thought and how it affected them in everything they did.

Alex was bursting with energy when he left the class. He could already picture himself as a mature man. Something like Freud or Jung, contemplating in their clinics, helping people solve problems with the use of words.

When he arrived home from school, his ma was catching up on the washing. He noticed a pair of Dad's pyjamas amongst the load. The spider and its home had gone, the windows cleaned. Mother was in distraction mode. He pecked her on the cheek, she smiled but carried on with her task.

'Cup of tea, Ma?'

'No thanks,' she said, 'just had one.' She nodded toward the empty mug on the draining board.

'Just a bit of homework to do, then I'll come back and make another cuppa. Have you got an envelope, Ma?'

'You don't do homework, Alex,' she said, as a frown of mild disbelief appeared, but she knew Alex didn't tell fibs. 'And what would you want an envelope for?'

'I'm writing to a girl at school, Mary. She left me a note and I want to reply.'

'You've never mentioned her before. Is it a secret?'

'Yes,' he said, smiling broadly to take the edge off the seriousness of his mission.

'You mentioned homework as well.'

'Note to Mary, then homework. Biology.'

'Envelopes in the spare room. Dad's room,' she said, without a flicker of change in her voice or the tone of it.

He rushed upstairs, stepped into the room which now seemed so alien, took an envelope from the bedside drawer, and couldn't wait to get out. His breathing laboured for a moment, a mini shock incorporating a thousand images and impressions at once. The atmosphere of a wrecked life, his dad's presence still felt.

In his own room was a table and chair overlooking the back of the street. A place he liked because birds came, and the town's church spire towered in the distance.

He took a fresh piece of lined paper from his school pad and gripped his fountain pen tightly as he concentrated on his composition. He bit gently on his tongue as he wrote. Three drafts later the message approximated something close to a finished letter.

Dear Mary,

Thank you for your kind note and yes, I would very much like to have a chat. You're right, things have been a bit tough but given what's happening at home, it could be worse.

Not sure what the best way to meet up is. Maybe a lemonade or coffee in the town. Or catch the later bus when the school has been emptied. We could talk more privately then.

Hope one of these ideas suits, if not, please feel free to make the best arrangements for you.

Love,

Alex

He hesitated over the *love* signing off. He knew a boy writing it gave quite a different message.

George had been having visitors. Two pals arrived together, one carrying a daily paper; something for George to read.

Their workmate was still in a coma, but it didn't stop them talking in a matey fashion. What else could they do? 'How are you, George? Feeling any better, mate? Not the same without you at work. Girls in the canteen miss you. The boss plans to visit soon,' said one, imagining George twitching in horror at the thought. His silence made it difficult to keep the visit going so they decided to talk about football, mainly to entertain themselves but also to relay the latest news on matches, managers, players, scores, and transfers, to the unconscious patient.

One of the men touched George's hand, a poor substitute for a handshake, and was surprised to feel it warm. Still alive. They left but didn't see the point in leaving the newspaper.

Days later, George's boss arrived with a gift-wrapped box. 'Everyone likes milk chocolate and people who couldn't stomach hospital food were only too pleased to have some,' was how his reasoning went Obviously, George wouldn't be tucking in anytime soon. The boss touched his employee's forehead with the back of his hand, as if assessing the situation in a professional way. Like a senior consultant might, following a full medical assessment and diagnosis. He nodded sagely as if he'd just agreed with a team of experts.

He had good news and bad news, neither of which could be verbalised whilst George was in this state. Bad news first. George would be out of work, regardless of any successful recovery programme. The man would never be well enough to operate the sophisticated and dangerous machinery employed in a joiner's workshop. George Brownlow didn't have the social skills to be 'on the floor' in any managerial capacity.

The good news was, that when George started with the company, he'd been offered and accepted an accident and sickness insurance policy. This would leave him on full pay for six months followed by a negotiable period on half pay. At least Florence would have enough to support herself and Alex in the short term.

'Well, George,' he started, knowing it was impossible to know whether the patient had any sense of his presence at all. 'I'm sorry to see you like this. The old firm misses you. We can't wait for you to come back,' he lied, unable to utter anything other than kindness and optimism for the poor wretch in front of him. He stood for a moment, touched George's head again as if to confirm an earlier diagnosis, and silently left.

Seconds later, he returned to George's bedside and retrieved the chocolates. No point in them going to waste.

CHAPTER NINETEEN

Alex's reply to Mary's letter was the best he could do; the writing not so clever, but he'd pitched the wording about right. They'd decided that taking a later bus would be a good first step to any meaningful conversation. No one from school would be there, and even if there was, it would be hard to make a big deal of it. Two pupils half an hour late could be for any number of reasons: finishing an essay, detention, library, swotting. The bonus for Alex was, that on the bus, he'd be sitting next to Mary. Not quite as close as being forced into position by Greg Smart but near enough.

Mary was at the stop when he arrived. They beamed at each other. Mary waited for a couple of elderly shoppers to get on the bus. He followed her to one of the centre seats, built for two. Hard not to have body parts touching without seeming rude by creating a larger and less friendly space. The bus was almost empty.

It wasn't a warm day, but it felt so right now. She touched his forearm lightly. 'How's your dad, Alex?'

'About the same. The outlook's not looking good. Dad won't be the man he was. No one's really sure how it's going to pan out for him.'

'And what about your mum? Obviously, the rumours aren't

helping, they've probably been blown out of all proportion. Once these stories get out, they tend to stick,' she said, feeling a little unkind but stating the obvious.

'That's not just kids and people rumouring, Mary, it's the truth!' he exclaimed.

She smiled awkwardly; she'd touched a nerve. 'We all know that Ms Vera Harris has a reputation. That's no secret,' she said, leaving out the fact that Ms Harris's relationship with Florence Brownlow, in terms of gossip potential anyway, was a very big deal indeed.

'Generally, I think Ma's doing okay. I gave her some whisky to calm her down and she opened up a bit. I hate to admit it, but it's probably the closest we've ever been...'

The sentence tailed off; he was ashamed to admit to anyone the lifelong lack of intimacy with his parents. And not sure he should have mentioned plying his mother with alcohol to get her to talk. But Mary made him feel safe, she was sensitive to his situation. He could say things. 'Mum and Dad have always felt distant. We'd all got used to it, it's their nature. We can't help that, can we? So, Dad's accident and Mum's relationship with Ms Harris has been a bit of a wakeup call, for all of us.'

He was talking too much and too fast. Was this the kind of thing that should even come up on a first date? Because that's what he hoped this was.

'How about your parents, Mary?' he asked respectfully.

'They're good,' she said guiltily. She didn't want Alex to think she was a goody two shoes with perfect parents. 'You know that my dad's a psychologist, it came up in class, but you may not know that my mum's his secretary. We're a close-knit threesome and discuss most things, including your situation and your poor dad being in hospital. I'm sorry if you think I've gone overboard with the caring routine but being out on your own is not much fun,' she said, aware that having a psychologist for a father was not the easy ride it might seem.

Alex hoped that their first outing would be less about parents and more about…other things, but it was a good start.

'Hope you don't think me rude, Mary, but is this what you had in mind when you sent me that letter?'

'Partly. But when you're a teenage girl, it's difficult to get to know a boy your own age without having something important to start the conversation with. Oh dear, that doesn't sound right.' She blushed a little. 'We've seen each other over the last couple of years, but never had time to speak. Either that or we didn't have the courage.'

He nodded agreement. Feeling a flush starting to emanate, and tempted to undo his school tie, he chose a casual pull at the neck of his collar instead.

'We're both a little outside the class norms,' she continued, 'I could see that your interests were not the ones presented to you at school. It intrigued me because you're…different.' She was getting in deep, her mouth overtaking her brain.

'Thanks for being interested in my mum and dad. That's really kind of you, Mary,' he said, more to help her out of the increasingly tricky situation than anything else.

'My dad, from his experience treating many patients, said that sometimes when people go through such traumatic events, it's helpful to talk. He reckons that if you don't, imagination makes more of it and the resulting stress and anxiety can seriously affect your health.'

'Sure. Absolutely. But, oddly enough, the remoteness from my parents has helped in some ways. They assumed I didn't need them. And that since I could walk and talk, I wanted to look after myself, and pushed them away when they tried to help. They felt redundant. But never said so. Talking about it may have made a difference, but when you're an independent toddler…'

Mary was taken aback. She knew Alex was a strong individual, able to walk into any class with his head held high, despite being shunned because he wasn't one of the boys – and then to stand up to all that sneering, and the vile remarks about at his mother and Ms Harris...

'I heard through the grapevine that you've had a lesson with Jennifer Mayhew, the new biology teacher. She sounds good. What do you think?'

'The class liked her, and I thought she was the best yet. Took a brain out of a box. Not a real one, but as near as damn it, then told us about the different functions. I think we were all eager to know more, me especially. She spoke about people in your dad's field, Freud and all that stuff.'

She laughed. 'Dad would be quite impressed. Could you see it as part of your future, the humanities subjects?'

'Definitely but I'm not sure school is going to be the best place to learn.'

'You've no choice right now but you could speak to Jennifer Mayhew a bit more about the subjects she touched on, she might recommend reading sources and how best to study at home.'

'I do try, in my own way, but it's not easy without some lessons or guidance. And what with Mum and Dad being in such a state.'

Enough of his parents.

'If you need professional support to help you through, someone professional to talk to, my dad has offered his help at any time.'

Alex was lost for words.

The bus arrived at Alex's destination far too soon, and Mary had a few more stops to go. He waved to her as the bus pulled away.

It was a surprise to see Greg Smart lounging against a shop doorway fiddling with a cigarette. He seemed uncertain about whether to light it whilst in full view of the busy street.

'Well fuck me if it isn't Romeo downstairs and Juliet upstairs. Not quite the balcony scene, is it, Brownlow? You must have got further than that by now... You're a dark horse, I must say, but I've got eyes everywhere. From what I can remember – but please correct me if I'm wrong,' Smart continued, 'Shakespeare never wrote any scenes involving a number 27 bus.' He held his stomach theatrically and laughed idiotically at his own joke.

Alex, used to Smart's antagonistic ways by now, smiled at the bully and gave an extra wave at the departing bus. Mary wouldn't have seen the gesture, but it would have irritated Greg Smart no end, because he was his own worst enemy. And Smart thought that being aggressively male and stupidly funny was an attractive trait. Yes, he had mates, but they were only ever going to be happy doing what they did best, irritating other people. Smart might have had a bit more success if he'd been an appealing guy, but he was never out to win the girls with his dress code, or his manner. His expression always looked like a sneer and his eyes never met yours.

Alex wondered whether Smart developed the sneer because of his unpleasant manner or whether he was born with it. Could you train yourself to un-sneer?

CHAPTER TWENTY

Florence's open-hearted chat with Alex had brought on a bout of confidence. Now that they'd discussed 'the elephant in the room', Vera Harris, she felt free to express herself more positively. She'd wondered if seeing Vera again was wise. Too much bruising! There was part of her that wanted to, but it would have to be a bit more on Florence Brownlow's terms, no gin and tonics for a start. If it wasn't going to be a natural progression of genuine intimacy, then there'd be no point carrying on with the relationship. She wanted more than just sex.

The mews telephone rang. *'Vera Harris, please leave a message.'*

'It's Florence, Flo...' She hesitated, unused to answerphones, hoping Vera would pick up. 'Would you give me a call when you get this, please,' she said, adding her number, uncertain as to whether Vera had it.

Florence's phone rang five minutes later. 'Sorry, Flo, I was in the shower. What is it?' asked Vera, surprised and delighted following her fit of depression and loneliness.

Florence wondered if Vera had showered following a hot session with someone else. 'Wondered if you'd like to meet up again?'

You could have knocked Vera down with a feather. She didn't

expect this call quite so soon. It renewed her faith in Ms Vera Harris. So, she was attractive and enigmatic after all?

'Yes, I would,' said Vera. 'We had a good time, didn't we?'

'We did indeed, but can I make a request?'

'What?'

'That we meet and enjoy the experience without alcohol. I want to feel things rather than be dazed by them,' she giggled, realising that Vera might be taking it badly, maybe cramping her style a bit.

Plus, I don't want to end up in A&E. My son noticed the state of me last time and I had to lie big time. Plus, it took me three days to sober up.

Vera took some time contemplating this odd request, unable to understand why anyone would prefer sex without a little drink or two. 'Do you mean both of us?'

'I can't speak for you, Vera. But I'd feel better about the situation if I was clear-headed.'

'Situation? You're hilarious. It's up to you, Flo, but I'll need a little help, even if you don't. Not too much gin though, just enough to...to get me started,' was the rather weak response. From her experience the minimum amount of alcohol necessary for a night of sex should be a shared indulgence or, if not, consumed in quantity by one of the participants.

Florence felt a little insulted. Okay, she was no oil painting and parts of her body had given way to gravity, but she was still in reasonable shape, not too fat, not too thin. A few facial scars. Normal for her age was how she would describe herself. And she felt confident about putting Vera in the same class once they were both free of underwear.

'When?' asked Florence without referring to booze again.

'I'm in London until Saturday so how about Sunday? Would you like to eat out first, or shall I cook something here?'

'That would be great if it's no trouble,'

'It's only trouble if you're fussy or have any of these new-fangled allergies.'

'Don't like tripe.' They both laughed.

'How are you with spaghetti bolognaise?'

'Messy.'

'Great, I'll see you on Sunday, six-thirty. And, Flo...no cologne please,' she finished, putting the phone down quickly to cut off any further discussion about all things fragrant.

Florence almost blushed, she'd never thought of wearing eau de cologne as a faux pas. But then she had no idea about the finer points of courting another woman.

It was hard to concentrate on anything for long without being interrupted by thoughts of George's predicament. The man she married, totally alone, lying in a hospital bed with no one to love. Her heart softened a little as she realised that much of the blame for what happened could be attributed to her. They'd both lost it for the same reason. Love and respect had deserted them both and when they go, who knows what takes over? Nothing pleasant that's for sure. And poor Alex witnessing it all without their apology or explanation. How could there be an explanation when the reasons were so obscured by lies and deceit?

She'd leave the divorce proceedings for now.

George was in the critical care ward, floating above the bed at ceiling height, looking down at his lifeless body. This was something he'd read about but could never quite believe. This was what some so-called experts thought happened when you were about to die, a separation of the spirit from the body. He wasn't sure about spirits either.

Probably from the same article, he remembered that some people also re-entered their body and magically came back to life. For the moment he remained observant from on high with no real thoughts except the desire to reconnect with that sorry-looking human lying on a hospital bed.

Nurses hovered nearby, but they didn't appear clearly in George's view. Their faces blurred, unrecognisable apart from their unmistakeable uniforms. Angels of mercy.

CHAPTER TWENTY-ONE

Eddie had tried to help Alex through his emotional crisis. He'd lots of brilliant advice to pass on – all well-meant but irrelevant, patronising or juvenile. Alex seemed reluctant to listen. Not so much deaf to Eddie's less than sound advice, more to do with his innate ability to handle the crisis without interference,

'Why do you have to be so fucking independent, Brownlow?' asked Eddie. He always used Alex's surname when he was annoyed or upset.

Alex shrugged noncommittally, which added coals to the fire. To be fair, Eddie was trying to be helpful, but Eddie didn't realise that him being helpful was likely to end badly.

Alex did spend some time thinking about his independence, and where it might have originated. Eddie, in his effort to give the situation perspective, had introduced him to a Phillip Larkin poem which he was convinced summed everything up, including the reasons why Alex's mum and dad ended up in such a state! Eddie liked the swear words and felt it was relevant. Alex recalled the first few lines.

They fuck you up, your mum and dad. They may not mean to, but they do.

They fill you with the faults they had and add some extra just for you...

He didn't feel he'd been a victim, though Eddie thought he must have been, given his propensity to stick out as such a lonely bastard.

That said, as a baby and child, Alex couldn't remember ever being held by his father and not that often by his mother. Yet he hadn't felt deprived – perhaps some people in his situation would have done. Maybe Florence and George Brownlow had simply inherited that disposition, like in Larkin's poem. Perhaps they'd never been held either. Touching might not have come easy to the Brownlows.

'Look, Eddie,' he said. 'You're a good mate, at our age we haven't had a great deal of life experience. We can't understand how grownups can make such a hash of things. They should be getting more intelligent not less. But I can handle it. I'm not going to get depressed or anything. I've felt things coming for a long time. Okay, it was still a shock when it happened, but I was more or less ready for it.'

'Even for your ma being queer?'

'Not quite ready for that, but it doesn't seem as bad as her going for another man.'

'It's not normal,' replied Eddie, looking down his nose as if wearing a pair of bifocal glasses.

'Nothing much is, in our family, Eddie. Your mum and dad seem nice people though, they talk to each other. Seems like a proper...a normal family...apart from you,' said Alex, laughing affectionately at his pal.

'What do you think your ma and Harris get up to, Alex? Do you think they use...things... so they can act like a man and a woman?'

'If they're both trying to escape men, because of...*things*, what would be the use of that? Let's not go there. No point.'

'Do they meet up often?' asked Eddie.

'Don't know. Not sure when Ma's working a shift or visiting Dad or seeing Miss Harris. Not important anymore. Everything is focussed on the house now. Some bossy woman has bought it. They're going to knock hell out of it; virtually rebuild the place by the sounds of it.'

'Where will you live? Will you still be at our school?' asked Eddie, anxiously tying a knot in a piece of string he always carried in his pocket. A sort of comfort blanket for mature boys.

'Not sure about where we'll live but I'll still be at the same school. Ma has given her word on that.'

Eddie undid the knot and slipped the string back into his pocket.

Florence must have got the date wrong; she was sure this was the day they'd arranged. She tried Vera's phone several times before deciding to leave her car at home and take the bus. From memory, finding space in the mews looked like a nightmare, and her parking technique left something to be desired.

The bus dropped her a couple of hundred yards from the narrow entry. There was a public call box in a small cul-de-sac right there, so Florence rang once more. Vera didn't pick up.

It seemed strange walking alone toward her lover's pad. She liked the feel of cobbles under the soles of her feet, the buildings closing in on the snug narrow alley, and the air seemed different too, ancient, if that was possible. She could have driven after all, there were no cars in the mews today.

The front door was ajar, but she rang the bell anyway. No reply. Perhaps Vera forgot to shut it, maybe took her car somewhere, if she had one. It certainly wasn't in the street.

'Vera, it's me, Flo,' she shouted from the hallway. No response. After three attempts she decided to climb the narrow stairs, calling as she went, worried that Vera might be unwell or, God forbid, lying dead somewhere in the flat.

She reached the landing. There was a smell of burning

candlewax and the sound of classical music. It was daylight outside but there were dozens of candles blazing away. Every exposed surface had one or two, flickering their haloes against the pale walls. She could see into every room as she walked through. No one in the hall, lounge, or kitchen. She was trembling now. The flickering lights gave off an eerie glow to the bedroom, the music muted the sound of her footsteps. Florence could see shapes in the king-sized bed, two bodies completely covered with silky sheets and a quilted duvet. One started to move. Vera poked her head over the edge of the bedclothes and met Florence's horrified gaze. Vera's hand, resting lightly on the body hidden under the covers, increased pressure in an attempt to pass on a subtle instruction; *a don't move or I'll kill you,* kind of message.

The music was from a Chopin nocturne. Florence wouldn't have known that. She'd never listened to classical music unless it was part of a film soundtrack or featured on *Desert Island Discs*. But she couldn't escape the fact that it was a romantic piece. Romance! The thing that was missing from her association with Vera. The emotion she'd hoped for most but was denied.

'F…Florence!' cried Vera. She was no longer Flo.

Vera pulled the duvet up to cover her breasts. Not really the time for modesty but…

Florence, full of fury – everything hitting her at the same time; flashbacks of her facial injury, her dying husband, her house being sold, her distant son and now her cheating lover – exploded across the room, grabbed the duvet and gave it a mighty yank. Despite all attempts from those hanging on, it came away and flew across the room as if it had been tossed by an athlete or like a net being cast from a small boat by a tribal fisherman. Underneath it, two naked bodies cowered, one familiar the other a very well-built woman with a crew cut and a skull tattooed on her muscular shoulder. Not a fellow academic then? Someone who lifted weights and loaded ships by the looks of her. But not dumb enough to miss the gravity of the situation.

Vera and the tattooed woman rose as one, grabbing the nearest crumpled sheet to cover themselves. They looked like a pair of cocooned creatures from another planet. It was as if a predator had entered their territory, one who was about to unleash the most terrible fate on them. Florence had never felt so powerful. Her love for Vera was dashed in that moment of fury, flung across the room with the duvet, and remained so as it slid into a heap on the bedroom floor.

Why had Vera been so critical about her 4711? It must have been a thousand times better than the stale sweaty aroma that swirled around the overheated room. It reeked to the point of gagging her. Harris had obviously misjudged the temperature that a few dozen candles would generate.

Florence's scars burned a vivid red before paling quickly as her face took on the hue. Quite obviously, she'd got the date of their meeting wrong. Or Vera Harris had…

Vera made no attempt to speak, realising fairly quickly that there was nothing she could say or do to salvage the moment. Why was she in bed with a naked woman listening to romantic music with a houseful of blazing candles?

Florence left the stunned couple, the smoking candles, the Chopin finale, and the overpowering smell of stale sweat. She walked down the stairs in a dream, her determination and fury intact. The adrenaline had kicked in, and she was oddly alert but numbed to the core. Anaesthetised.

CHAPTER TWENTY-TWO

Vera Harris's English Literature lecture was cancelled for that week without explanation. Pupils turned up, but she didn't. It was a first time in the history of her association with the school that she'd failed to take a lesson. The class were unprepared, her absence had not been announced in advance.

Alex was disappointed, as he was looking forward to some light relief. His ma had looked tired that morning, picking at her toast, disinclined to conversation.

He'd asked her what was up. 'Life,' she'd said, taking a sudden aggressive bite at the crusty black edge of the burnt offering.

Not quite in the mood to share her conundrum, Florence was at a loss to understand why lesbians – which to her meant women preferring their own sex as partners – should choose someone more male than the men she knew. It was a mystery. And why would anyone, anyone at all, choose the aroma of sweat over 4711 cologne? Or hard muscle over soft flesh?

Sitting in the class now, which started to get noisy as no one came to take over the lecture, Alex tried to reason things out. Ma in a bad mood and Miss Harris not around – had they fallen out or something? Or were they putting two fingers up to the school and meeting for a date? Surely Ma would have mentioned it. Not a secret since they'd had their 'chat'.

In the playground Eddie suggested that maybe the two women had run off together, a speculation which had already travelled round the class. 'I don't think so,' said Alex. 'I think Ma would have told me. It's all out in the open now, we've talked about it.'

Eddie was on the edge of pressing for more detail but decided to hold back for the moment. He wanted to protect Alex from what was going on in the class, and the school. He'd already removed a drawing pinned to Alex's desk. The artist, Greg Smart presumably, had drawn two stick figures, one seated upstairs on a number 27 bus (huge for emphasis) the other waving from the pavement. The name Romeo had been written then crossed out and replaced with Alex. An effigy of Juliet had been changed to Mary, a stream of roughly drawn hearts and kisses flowing between them. It was stupid rather than offensive, but Eddie still felt the need to act as censor.

Alex had experienced quite enough of the day, but by the time he got home, his ma seemed in a better mood and she'd baked a pie. A rare event. Not that she couldn't cook but she did so sparingly. Exotic fare like pies and cakes usually appeared when she was feeling her best.

'How was your day, Alex?' She was upbeat and smiling. 'They've paid the deposit on the house. They want to complete before the end of next month so we'd better get looking for somewhere else,' she said, annoyed that she hadn't considered things would move so quickly.

'That's great, Ma. One less thing to worry about,' he said cheerily.

His optimism hadn't registered. 'Miss Harris didn't turn up today. Is she ill or something?' he asked, determined to normalise his attitude toward their affair.

'How would I know?' said Florence picking up a tea towel and drying a few bits of crockery while she stared out of the window.

The starlings were back on the clothesline, making a hell of a racket.

'Any news on Dad?' he asked, changing tack, surprised his ma didn't have an update on Vera Harris and her missed lecture.

Florence hadn't really thought much about George since her last visit to the mews. She needed to make an effort now. 'The hospital hasn't been in touch, but I was going to ring at some point,' she lied. 'It's good you're home, Alex. Let's call them now. We can get the latest news together.'

'No plans to visit then?'

'Not unless he's conscious. Too distressing and not helpful for anyone.'

'Is it possible that Dad would know we were there, even if he wasn't conscious?' he asked, genuinely believing it was still a reasonable consideration.

'Maybe, but we've been through all that, Alex, I told you what the consultant said. I'm not sure your father would be that pleased to see us anyway. Who knows?'

Florence took the hospital number from the card on a rack and dialled. A direct line through to the ward. 'Staff nurse here. Who am I speaking to?'

'Florence Brownlow, George's wife. I wonder if you can tell me how he is, please,' she said, tilting the phone so that Alex could listen in on the conversation.

'Hang on, Mrs Brownlow, I'll get the nurse looking after your husband and check the consultant's notes. Give me a few secs,' she said. The sound of trolleys footsteps and chatter amplified, as the staff nurse put the phone on her desk. Florence could almost smell the antiseptic aura of the ward. And visualise George, corpse-like, innocent and out of it all.

The nurse was gone for some time. Florence's intuition told her the news wasn't going to be good. She could hear two voices now but didn't know who they belonged to. There was a noisy clatter as the staff nurse picked up the phone. 'Sorry to keep you, Mrs Brownlow, but the nurse looking after George couldn't speak for long, she was on her way to an emergency. It's very busy here. But the good news is there are positive signs. I don't want to give you false hope as I don't have enough detail, but nurse suggested you ring back later or call in at the hospital over the next day or so. Better if you can speak to someone directly. It'll give you a chance to visit your husband at the same time. Is that okay with you?'

'Yes, thank you,' she said, a sinking feeling overcoming her. She felt faint. Alex gripped her arm and encouraged her to sit down. The possibility that George might be recovering filled Florence with dread rather than hope.

Alex had heard the conversation too. The nurse sounded positive, his father was improving. They sat quietly for a moment, not quite in the mood for opening a celebratory bottle of something – or eating a pie for that matter.

'I'll come with you, Ma, share the load a bit,' he said, looking at his mother's unhappy face. The early optimism of tucking into the pie, baked in honour of the house sale, had mellowed somewhat.

CHAPTER TWENTY-THREE

George felt changes. He heard things, not all the time, but voices, tea trolleys, gurneys moving, sometimes even footsteps. He felt activity when a nurse made his bed or connected and disconnected apparatus.

Florence and Alex walked through the ward as if they were approaching a crèche at night. Not that they were afraid of waking George, it was something to do with the atmosphere and occasion. A nurse at the desk was smiling. 'Good afternoon, Mrs Brownlow,' she said. 'We've been expecting you. Follow me,' she said.

George looked no different to either of them, but was there a slight turn of the Head as they approached his bed? Alex touched the blanket covering his father's leg, and Florence, because the nurse hovered expectantly, made a show of it, holding George's hand, and giving him a peck on the cheek. She didn't linger with the hand. He felt warm.

Nurse checked her notes. 'Well, there's some news. The neurologist reported that George has opened and closed his eyes a couple of times. Sometimes his head turns toward a sound, he has pupillary activity, which means his eyes respond to light.'

Alex and Florence looked at each other. George still seemed quite dead.

'Obviously there's not a lot to show physically but they're signs that your husband might be recovering. His scores on the Glasgow Coma Scale have improved. My notes tell me that George's consultant explained what GCS means: it's an accurate guide to a coma patient's progress. Too early to say how much, or at what pace he'll continue to make headway, but we suggest you visit frequently. Patients are more likely to react positively to those they love,' said the nurse, a little tongue-in-cheek, aware of the marital situation from her case file and fully informed on how George managed to put himself in a coma.

Florence could feel a black cloud hovering.

'Let's grab a coffee, Alex, we could both do with one,' she said with a grim smile. She gripped his elbow and steered him at a pace toward the café.

It couldn't have been better timed for Alex, he'd no idea what to do or say in response to the visit. The plain facts seemed obvious; Father would be getting through this and coming home... What home? The house was sold, and Ma hadn't looked for another place to live.

They walked into the hospital café. 'Find a seat, Alex. Coffee or what?'

'Coffee's fine, Ma...and a sausage roll,' he said, smiling.

The place wasn't crowded so he took a seat by the window and looked out across the gardens. Pigeons pecked at invisible sources of food on a well-kept lawn and medical staff crisscrossed paths to various departments. He was full of admiration for what they did here. How difficult it must be, treating sick patients and watching people die.

He beckoned his ma toward the table as she walked across the space carrying a small tray. Two cups of coffee and a sausage roll. She looked smaller, older. He wasn't used to seeing her away from the home environment. Not quite a stranger but more of one than she should be.

Florence sat heavily on the spindly plastic seat. The sentence she'd been rehearsing had built up. She had to tell the boy now, while they were both in the mood for unsettling news. 'I've split up with Vera Harris.'

The words so shocked Alex that he coughed and spluttered, having just taken a bite out of the sausage roll. He wiped the wet crumbs off his school jumper. 'What happened, Ma?'

'I caught her with another woman. I happened to turn up on the wrong day.' *More like a man, to be fair!*

Alex didn't expect details and had no words to fit the occasion right now, so he took another bite of his sausage roll and washed it down quickly with coffee.

'Dad's going to be a problem too. It'll be chaos,' said Florence, steering away from further conversation about Vera Harris.

Ma was making statements which needed an answer, but they weren't actual questions. To Alex, she seemed in just as much chaos when Dad wasn't around.

'Was it hard, breaking up your…your friendship, Ma?' he asked politely.

'I was in such a temper, she made it easy,' said Florence, recalling the fury and the power she felt when confronting the secret lovers.

Alex couldn't quite picture the scene, but he'd seen his ma hit his dad, so he knew she was capable of violence.

'She must have been embarrassed knowing you'd be at her next lecture. That's probably why she didn't turn up,' Florence concluded, searching her handbag – for nothing, it seemed.

His ma had never been so open about her private life. Her confessions seemed more like those of a teenager than a mother. He wondered if Father John had heard about her more recent shenanigans.

There was a question he was burning to ask but wanted to make sure she wasn't holding her cup of hot coffee before he aired it.

'Will you still be a lesbian, Ma?' he enquired, the words

spilling out louder than intended. A couple on the nearest table craned their necks toward Florence, not quite believing that a mother and son were having such a risqué conversation in a hospital café.

Florence turned the colour of a ripe plum, somewhere between purple and red, with what appeared to be a sizeable storm cloud hovering above her.

Alex wasn't sure if the sudden change in Ma's demeanour was attributed to the question he'd asked or the reaction to it from the couple on the next table.

CHAPTER TWENTY-FOUR

Dansbury Street was wide, tree-lined, and led to some very nice houses, each with their own set of stone steps rising from a well-kept frontage. The perfectly glossed front door of number 12 had a polished brass plate bearing the name, *Dr Gordon Singer, Clinical Psychologist.*

Original Victorian tiled flooring led into a spacious hallway. Leaflets placed on the table next to a vase of fresh flowers displayed the summary of conditions Dr Singer and his team dealt with: *Working with people of all ages on a wide range of difficulties relating to mental and physical health. Including anxiety, depression, psychosis, 'personality disorder', eating disorders, addictions, learning disabilities and family or relationship issues.*

Mary was helping her father and mother, preparing for the day's clinic before she left for school. It was an odd but important part of the family day. A time when they were already fired up for study and work. They'd had their breakfast, and the conversation was usually an intelligent Q&A session related to things concerning school and clinic. If her father had a late start, the occasional personal concern was touched on: reactions to a particularly difficult patient, work overload, Mum not keeping up with the ever-increasing amount of paperwork and Dad's latest critiques regarding compulsory Association meetings. Bureaucracy gone mad!

Accountability and litigation were always hovering in the background.

The roomy clinic needed little tidying; the cleaner had been. Filing cabinets were kept locked, desks, tables and chairs dusted and polished with special attention paid to the upholstered chair and immediate area around where patients sat. Singer felt that the best possible start – and it made a surprising difference to how quickly people felt safe and comfortable – was to match the environment to the man they were about to trust with their problems.

Dr Singer was a clean-shaven six-foot academic with the authority, posture and serious features of a man who made patients feel he was capable of changing lives.

'Any news of the boy Alex?' he asked, placing the first case history on his desk, squaring it in line with the desk blotter. He placed a fountain pen parallel to one edge as he turned to Mary, waiting for an answer.

'He can't be as brave as he looks,' said Mary with obvious admiration. 'Despite the problems in his life, he never takes time off school, even though absence wouldn't affect his track record. You can't get lower than the bottom of the class, can you?' she said, letting out a nervous giggle.

'I thought you said he was bright.'

'He is, but not in a school sense. He's so different from the others, Dad. Interested in people stuff and doesn't see the point in learning things that don't help you cope with life.'

Singer looked at his watch and sat for a moment. 'And you like him?'

'He's nice.'

'Bring him to tea,' he said, looking to his wife Imogen for a nod of approval.

Imogen smiled with an *are you sure about this?* expression. They read each other's body language and facial nuances with an accuracy that could only come from years of familiarity and intensely psychotherapeutic interactions.

Imogen, in her early fifties, was also a qualified psychotherapist but decided she'd rather be Gordon's back-up than his competition. She knew everything that went on without having to solve patients' problems directly. Nevertheless, she was a powerful force when they discussed the day's list, and her acute powers of observation often stunned her husband. Imogen, a tad more glamorous than homely, wore her straight brown hair tied in a bun and fine around-the-eye wrinkles indicated she had a history of smiling a lot. Rimless glasses made the best of those features.

Mary walked to the bay window and looked out at the empty street, to avoid Father analysing her reaction to the invitation. 'He may not come,' she said, breaking her gaze, turning to check his response.

'You won't know till you ask, will you?' he smiled.

'Is the invitation for a cup of tea, or proper tea with cake?' she enquired.

'You choose. We'll talk about it later,' he said. The phone rang. Imogen picked up and waved at them both to keep quiet.

Mary was surprised at her parents' generous invitation, not quite sure how ready she'd be for this unexpected gathering. Alex sitting opposite her for a long period while parents quietly observed, analysed, and drew conclusions made her, excitedly nervous. She could already feel the colour rising in her face, even before the arrangements had been finalised.

She didn't get a chance to talk to Alex that day but did spot him crossing the tarmacked playground toward the gym. She didn't like to think of passing another letter through the school secretary. That sharp woman would put two and two together and might even make four. *Mary Singer must have more than a passing interest in Alex Brownlow.*

Mary and her parents sat down for their evening meal. All started off with a babble of routine questions about how their day had gone, highlights, if there were any, followed by a relative silence while they tucked into the remains of yesterday's shepherd's pie. They all agreed that it tasted better on the second day.

'What about this tea with Alex?' prompted Imogen. 'I'll bake a cake. Saturday would be ideal, he could come on the bus, or you could bring him back one day after school, make it a Thursday when Dad has a half-day off.'

'We'll drop him back home,' added Gordon. 'Is he shy?'

'Not shy. Just quieter than the rest,' replied Mary, having no idea whether he'd clam up in new company. Knowing Dad and Mum, they wouldn't expect too much; Alex had had a tough time, so they'd be aware of his situation before he arrived. They've seen every sort in the world pass through their clinic.

Mary thought about getting a message to Alex without making it obvious to the whole bloody school. But why be so secretive? Greg Smart would have made sure that all the boys knew about the waving scene on the bus... And then the girls would have caught wind of it, so – why not just walk up to Alex and invite him outright?

'Do we need a bit more background before we meet him?' asked Gordon.

'Well, you're aware he's bright,' she started, 'more likely to blossom when he leaves school than while he's in it.'

She had to get the worst bits over with now, it was only fair on Alex and all concerned. 'His parents fell out big time. His mum's having an affair with Vera Harris, one of the lecturers – the whole school knows. His dad is in a coma after falling off a stool in a pub. He was drunk. They're selling up and moving, somewhere local, I think. That's a rough outline,' she said, unable to stare them in the eye while she rattled off the facts.

Father John had nearly finished his course of therapy. He'd done well. Suicidal tendencies put in perspective, anxiety and depression helped by his weekly visits and sage advice from Dr Gordon. He'd explained that a priest couldn't listen to all those disturbing confessions without being deeply affected. Even more difficult, because Father John was forced to listen and absorb all this stuff without having any way of letting off steam.

'I understand that you have your faith, prayer, and meditation, Father John, but as you've discovered, a bit of earthlier help can be very beneficial...'

In a sense, they did a similar job, Dr Gordon took confessions too. Patient confidentiality promised. The difference being that clinical psychotherapists were able to use their skills and experience to work out a restorative programme. Face to face was imperative, both for patient and therapist. Being in a closed confessional with supposed anonymity, couldn't possibly lead to a solution. Offloading without accountability.

Dr Singer had stressed the point. *Body language, a major part of the way humans and animals communicate, is denied by the confessional. Non-verbal communication provides significant clues, essential to formulating a therapeutic process, one leading to improved mental and physical health.*

Maybe that's why the priest found his consultation and early visits to Dr Singer so difficult. Father John was used to hearing secrets, without ever having to disclose his own. Never exposed to the rigours of revealing his inner self through subtle facial expression and body language – without being in the dark, divided from any interrogator.

He wasn't the only priest Gordon had seen with these problems. In fact, no career or time of life was safe from the instability caused by anxiety, depression, overthinking, and suicidal thoughts. 'Help is always at hand' was his maxim...but you do have to seek it.

CHAPTER TWENTY-FIVE

Something moved her to visit the hospital. She tried to attribute the act to conscience or some latent desire to make peace with her husband. But it was neither, more like being on automatic pilot; an unpleasant duty against her will but necessary for any deity who might be watching, Catholic or otherwise.

'Hello, Florence,' came a voice from behind the screen surrounding George's bed. Must be the medics' round or the friendly male nurse assigned to her husband, she thought.

'Is that you, doctor?' she asked.

No reply. She moved the curtain a little. There was no one behind the screen apart from George. He was awake and, apparently, able to speak. A cold shiver took her, as if he'd risen from the dead, which was close to what seemed to have happened.

'Is the boy with you?' he asked, unable to remember his son's name, but it was early days. At least he'd opened his eyes and remembered his wife's name.

To her, it was creepy rather than reassuring. Florence didn't know what to do and looked around for a nurse or medic in case George suddenly decided to leave his bed and give her a hug – or throttle her. Either way, she'd die!

A nurse, seeing Florence backing away from George's bed, stepped away from her workstation, put an arm round Florence's shoulder and asked if she was feeling alright.

'It's a bit of a shock,' said Florence, with a sharp intake of breath, placing a hand over her chest to calm herself. 'Someone should have warned me!'

'I'm sorry, Mrs Brownlow, but your husband's attempt to speak has only just happened. Twelve hours ago, he'd not said a thing. Please sit down,' said the nurse, moving a chair close to where Florence was standing. 'Can I get you a glass of water? You look a bit pale.'

Florence sat and stared at the curtains surrounding George's bed, expecting them to move at any moment. 'What's going on?' she asked.

'Well, as you can see, your husband is improving. Since this morning he's been mentioning the odd name and a few isolated words which don't seem to make sense, probably fragments of something he remembers.'

'Like what?'

'Is Vera your daughter? George mentions her name a lot.'

'She's not my daughter. Just someone we know,' she replied, her head spinning with uncomfortable memories.

The nurse nodded. 'Perhaps Vera could visit. I believe you've already been informed how beneficial loved ones are for patients' recovery.'

Florence bristled and sagged at the same time. 'Did he say anything about…Vera?' she asked.

'Only mentioned her name. Lots of times. Vera must be very dear to you both,' said the nurse, waiting for Florence to look pleased about the way things were going.

Florence had nearly destroyed the strap of her handbag by constantly twisting it throughout the conversation. Unable to nod or shake her head at the nurse's comment, Florence needed to know how much better George was going to get and what a likely plan might be for his rehabilitation.

'What happens now?' asked Florence.

'Your husband will be moved to a general ward. If he maintains progress, specialist staff will get involved, occupational therapists, physios, that sort of thing. Depends on what he might need. Every patient is different. Progress varies, but starting to speak is a huge step forward. At this stage he'll be confused, say things we don't understand or make inappropriate comments but it's all part of the brain learning to function properly again.'

Florence felt a tightening in her stomach, wondering if George's inappropriate comments might involve monologues on Vera Harris and Florence Brownlow. Nothing she could do but hope, that if George started to spill beans, staff would attribute the spillage to a less than reliable, brain-damaged patient.

When Florence arrived home, Alex was back from school. She told him about George's unexpected progress and that he was able to call out her name. She avoided mentioning Vera Harris.

Alex smiled. 'I'm pleased, Ma. Does that mean he'll be out of hospital soon?' he asked, with some trepidation, at a complete loss as to how on earth they were going to manage the house move while upholding Ma's decision to part from Father.

'I think that's a little way off. He'll need to get some sort of mobility and be able to eat without tubes. But it certainly looks as if it's on the cards,' she replied. 'Put the kettle on, there's a love, I'll be back in a minute,' she said, making a dash for the stairs just in time to throw up into the toilet bowl.

She cleaned her teeth, gargled away the salty residue in her throat and touched up the colour of her face by rubbing a bit of lipstick into it. *Difficult to hide the haggard look of a beaten woman.*

'You've got a bit of lipstick on your nose,' said Alex on her return, aware of what had just happened. 'I'll make some tea.' The kettle boiled. Florence sat in a kitchen chair, leaning on her elbows, her head in her hands. 'I don't know what to do, Alex. We're in such a bloody mess.'

We? Alex couldn't quite work out what part he might have played in this continuing drama. None, as far as he could tell, it all happened around him; grownups telling lies for most of their lives and acting irresponsibly.

He put his arm around his mother's shoulder. 'Why don't we start with things we can do, Ma? Practical stuff. We could sort the house out ready for the new owners. Collect all the things we don't need and chuck them in the dustcart. Then we should look for somewhere to move into.'

'We'll never manage to buy a house before the sale is completed. We'll have nowhere to live.' She started to cry.

'Why don't we rent somewhere for a few months until we see where we are and know what's happening to Dad?' he said, knowing there really was no other option. But he didn't want his ma thinking she had no choice. 'What do you think?'

She wiped her eyes with her cardigan sleeve and stared up at her son. 'You're a good boy, Alex.'

He took the rare compliment as agreement and checked the kitchen clock. 'We could pop down to the estate agents now and see what the rental situation is. I'll get your coat,' he said, reaching for it on the hook at the back of the door before she had a chance to change her mind.

Thirty minutes later they were in town deciding on which of the three estate agents they'd approach first. They settled on Peacocks, who seemed to be well established and displayed the largest range of properties for sale and rent. The entrance door was glazed with bevelled glass panels which, for some odd reason, Florence felt was a sign of good taste and reliability,

The company was old but the young guy who approached them looked as if he'd just left school. Maybe he had. He stuck his hand out toward Florence, giving hers an enthusiastic shake as if they'd already agreed a deal. Alex held his hand out, ready for the same welcome, but was disappointed.

'Good afternoon. I'm Mathew Lowry, sales advisor. Are you looking to buy or rent?' he asked, smiling at Florence but yet to acknowledge her young son. Alex held back while his ma asked about rentals. He'd no idea what these transactions cost, or what the family's financial situation might be.

He was surprised at how quickly and confidently his ma stepped forward to explain the situation. Alex had noted this quirky talent before. Ma could be upset as hell but once exposed to practical things that needed attention, her 'other personality' took over. No other 'inner self' came forward when the situation involved an emotional perspective. Ma was absolute rubbish when it came to that stuff!

'Good morning, Mathew. I'm Florence Brownlow and this is my son Alex,' she said, placing a hand on her son's shoulder, noting the agent's reluctance to treat him as an adult. 'Here's our situation. I'll be brief. Our house is being sold but we might need to rent until we find somewhere suitable to buy,' she said, glancing at the prolific display of properties.

Mathew would have made the connection and factored in that a rental and sale were on the cards. And his bonus would reflect on the amount of effort he was about to put in. 'We think of minimum rental as being around six months,' he said, 'but most landlords prefer longer because of all the vetting and paperwork involved. Any idea when your contracts will be exchanged? Timing might make big difference.'

'We're not quite sure yet,' said Florence, 'just making enquiries at the moment. I've never done this before,' she admitted. 'Usually my husband…' She hesitated, wanting to leave him out of it but realised that much of the contract might depend on George's ability to sign documents.

'Well, I'm sure we'll be able to sort something out,' said Mathew, gripping his chin in a thoughtful pose. 'If you allow us to handle the house purchase as well, we'd give you a bit of discount,' he said, straightening his tie and tugging his shirtsleeves.

From a glass-walled side office Alex saw a large bald man in shirtsleeves give a nod of encouragement toward Mathew.

'In the meantime, I can give you some leaflets, details of houses to rent. And if you have some idea of the property price range you'll be looking at, I'll give you some info on them too.'

The man in the office stood and smiled toward them as Mathew handed Florence some leaflets. He'd tapped them in perfect line on the nearest desk and popped them into a glossy folder with Peacocks emblazoned across the front. Pictures of houses filled the front and back cover, all bearing sold signs accompanying each image.

'Here's my card. Call me anytime,' he said, shaking Florence's hand once more and affording Alex a cursory smile.

'You did ever so well, Ma,' said Alex, surprised at how together she was. He guessed she was beginning to realise that whatever the situation, they had to start somewhere, do something.

'He was very young, wasn't he? But he seemed okay, genuine enough – for an estate agent,' said Florence, tapping the side of her nose.

They were home by six. Oddly, although nothing much had happened, Florence felt a little better. Optimistic would be pushing it, but she'd taken steps and actually done something.

Florence spread the leaflets out on the kitchen table while Alex made a pot of tea. She squinted closely at the house prices she thought might be within their range, considering the house would be smaller, cheaper than the one they were living in. Properties varied from between twenty-six and thirty thousand pounds. They'd have less of a mortgage, which really would help. The big problem would be George's earnings being taken into account. *What earnings?* Maybe the accident insurance and the bit of respite pay from the termination of his employment would be enough. Either that, or she'd have to get a better paid job. She wished Alex was a bit older, old enough to get work and contribute. His continuing education was way down her list of priorities.

CHAPTER TWENTY-SIX

Father John hadn't heard from Florence Brownlow or Vera Harris for some considerable time and could only guess that they'd either burnt themselves out with the intensity of their devilment or they'd been exposed, named and shamed in some way. He couldn't imagine their current confessions would be any more sensational than those he'd already heard. But he'd been surprised before, and no doubt at least one of them would turn up asking for absolution.

Vera Harris was suffering from depression. Following her doctor's advice, she was prescribed a course of antidepressants and took a month's sabbatical. Her intention? To disappear for a while, recalibrate her life and face up to the fact that she was bordering alcoholic. *Bordering*, a subtle term used to lessen the blow of having to admit to needing AA and the Twelve Steps to sobriety. She'd seen programmes and read all the information, deciding it was a scheme for dropouts and losers. But she changed her mind on discovering that some of the brightest, richest, talented, and most respected members of the community had taken that route. Plus, her drinking had got way out of control and her career was suffering. She'd become so unreliable and unpredictable that she was missing appointments, dodging commitments, and falling asleep before she even got into bed with her latest lover.

When her depression dipped, she managed to get through part of the day by opening another bottle. Her brain was as sharp as ever but her capacity to carry out the things which were in it, did not come to fruition.

Her bust-up with Flo wasn't much of a problem. It had started well, the 'courting stage' showed real promise; the excitement of house-training a novice appealed. But Flo was hard work, a bit of a damp squib if she was to be totally honest.

Vera would like to have continued her lectures at the school but couldn't face *the boy*, and the residual echo of her misconduct. Not in her present state. In fact, there were so many things she couldn't face, she was compelled to address some terrible facts and seek the guidance of a professional. She thought of approaching the school's educational psychologist, Lance Grayling. They'd known each other for years and occasionally ventured from school life to have coffee. They'd discussed things academic, the school system, the poor levels of English grammar and the appalling standards of writing in particular.

The lack of discipline was a favourite theme for Grayling, who'd bring back the cane if he could. But despite being a disciplinarian at heart he was bound by the ethics of the school, answerable to governors and teaching staff. Developing practical strategies that could be implemented by teachers and parents was his brief. Fine, accountable, as it should be, but Grayling was convinced that over the last few years, school rules and discipline had gone soft, a namby-pamby affair that allowed governors, teachers and parents to collaborate in the obvious lack of discipline.

Vera tried to think kindly of Flo, recalling their courtship and anticipation of a bit more of a life together. Not to be. But she couldn't help wondering how Flo was dealing with the terrible shock she must have had at the mews; coming face to face with the woman whom everyone in Vera's circle called Mamazon, an earth mother type who looked as if she'd just stepped out of the jungle. Her appeal? She had the manners and rough sexuality of a gorilla.

Flo was probably on medication and seeking psychiatric help, decided Vera.

Florence and Alex did what they could to organise the next stages of their move and make a plan as to how they'd deal with George. But more pressing was finding somewhere to live. They'd picked out one or two places to rent, affordable and local. They'd decided not to look too hard at properties to buy because by the time their sale was completed, those houses would be long gone. It gave them an idea on price, but any purchase, or rental for that matter, relied on George being able to sign things.

'I've not asked anything about you, son. How's school going?' she asked, with a lack of interest obvious to Alex who'd expected nothing.

'The usual. But I've been invited to tea,' he said coyly.

'Eddie?'

'No. Mary,' he said, on the edge of blushing.

'Secret Mary… from school?' said Florence, smiling and feeling a lightness in the room.

Alex recalled that morning when Mary passed him in the hall and dropped a note into his gaping schoolbag. The buckle had broken ages ago, but he didn't want his mother facing such a petty problem as a satchel repair.

'Read it at home,' she'd said.

No way. Alex headed straight for the toilet block, locked himself in a cubicle, and read Mary's note.

Dear Alex,

Were your ears burning? We've been talking about you. Mum and Dad know we get on and they'd like to meet you. Could you to come to

tea? They've suggested a weekend or come back with me on the bus after
school, a Thursday ideally, when Dad has a half day off.
  Love,
  Mary

He was in shock. Rooted to the spot and losing confidence by
the second, his mind trying to unscramble the mess of conflicting
thoughts rushing through his head. He would be sitting opposite
Mary and parents who ran a psychotherapy practice. He might
not stand up to their scrutiny! It might be the biggest test yet for
his love affair with Mary. If they disapproved of him – *he imagined
Caesar giving the thumbs down to a beaten gladiator* – she'd be
banned from meeting him, forever. Game over. They'd hardly got
started…

Bang, bang, bang, a thumping on the toilet door followed by a
couple of kicks echoed around the heavily tiled toilet block.

'How much longer you gonna be in there Brownlow. Not
tossing yourself off, are you?'

Greg Smart and his pal were sniggering outside and threw a
toilet roll over the top of the cubicle letting it unravel as it went.

Alex stuffed Mary's note into his pocket, flushed the loo and
opened the door to face his nemesis. He smiled at the two lads,
and tried to look unruffled as he walked over to the basin, taking
time to wash his hands while they looked on.

One lad held him from behind while Smart checked his
satchel, pulled books out and stuffed them back roughly without
looking at the content. 'All rubbish,' declared Smart as if he'd
speed read the contents. 'No wonder your bottom of the class,' he
said.

They were about to search Alex's pockets, when Eddie came
in. He was livid.

'What are you two queers up to? Trying to force my mate to
join in? Leave him alone now or I'll report you to the Head. I'll
say that Smart and his dumb friend were soliciting in the school

loos. You know what that means Greg?' he said using Smarts first name for friendly impact. 'It means you're like prostitutes.'

Eddie had read, in some detail, about such activities.

Smart and his pal backed away quickly, dropping their hold on Alex as if he'd suddenly been declared highly contagious.

'We're witnesses aren't we Alex?' he said, winking but not expecting his pal to join in with his threats.

Alex was so relieved that Smart hadn't got hold of Mary's note, he almost passed out on the spot.

CHAPTER TWENTY-SEVEN

They chose Thursday on the bus. Well Alex did, for a couple of reasons. He was nervous and didn't want to turn up at Mary's front door alone, imagining parents and daughter faced with a *rabbit in the headlights*. He wasn't even sure if he could find where the Singers lived, not without a bit more guidance.

Preparing for this day had all the elements of attending a royal visit; shoes were polished to perfection, a fresh white shirt, ironed trousers, and school jacket hung on a wooden hanger on the back of his bedroom door. Hair flattened with a wipe of a wet flannel and teeth scrubbed to a car showroom finish. He checked for zits but decided not to squeeze the couple of small ones he discovered on the side of his neck.

Sitting on the 2B with Mary felt totally okay, as if it were a daily occurrence. They chatted about school and Mary tried to put him at ease regarding the meeting with her parents. 'It'll be fine,' she said. 'They're looking forward to meeting you. Genuinely, Alex. Mum's flapping about whether you'll like the cakes she's made. And Dad aims to dress casually so's he won't scare you off,' she laughed. 'He can look quite formidable when he dresses formally,' she added, trying not to show her own nervousness. She wanted the meeting to go well, just as much as Alex did.

He wasn't sure if he felt better or worse for Mary's reassurance. He knew that whatever the situation, two psychoanalysts would be hanging on his every word, interpreting every nuance of body language and facial expression. Or maybe they'd insist on a polygraph test, he thought jokingly, having read up on the subject as one of great interest.

Once off the bus, Mary took his arm, for reassurance, but dropped her grip as they neared the house. He was pleased she didn't hold his damp hand, his attempt to dry it discreetly on his flannel trousers had failed.

Mary took a key from her pocket and opened the front door. The shiny black door and brass plate at the entrance did nothing to calm Alex. In fact, it felt like he'd turned up for an appointment.

'I'm home,' she shouted, along the hallway. 'I have a guest with me,' she said, giving Alex a playful look.

The parents appeared together, looking younger and more glamorous than he'd expected – relaxed, used to seeing strangers turn up at the door.

Imogen Singer stepped forward and embraced him warmly, like he was a long-lost son. She smelled of flowers and felt soft. He'd never been hugged quite like it before, not even by his ma, or anyone else for that matter.

'Thank you for inviting me,' said Alex, taking a small box of Bourneville chocolates out of his school bag. Ma had told him that professional and sophisticated people tended to prefer dark chocolate, without explaining why.

'That's so kind of you, Alex. We'll enjoy those later,' she said, placing them on the hall table.

Dr Gordon Singer looked formidable even in his casual outfit. He gave a manly handshake, one lasting longer than the occasion warranted. Alex returned the grip and kept a smile on his face feeling that to drop it would be impolite.

'Very pleased to meet you sir,' he said.

'Come in, come in. Make yourself at home,' said Imogen. 'Take Alex's coat and satchel Mary. I'll put the kettle on.'

Dr Singer led him into a room with a floor to ceiling bookcase on one wall, which Alex immediately wanted to browse through. He noted some of the titles as he walked past, a whole section on criminology, court procedures, and law as well as the obvious psychology, philosophy and psychiatry tomes.

A table was set with a white tablecloth, place mats, fine China, serviettes, and cakes covered with glass domes.

Alex felt a stab of lowness. He realised that Mary and her folk were from another planet or might just as well have been. Sophisticated, intelligent – on a different level. Civilised.

Mary Singer was top of her class at school, Alex Brownlow was at the bottom. And his wrecked parents completed the mental image of a hopeless case. There was no way these lovely decent folk would want Alex Brownlow and his broken family contaminating their lives. He wanted to escape, but his smile refused to leave. He wondered if Imogen's smile was born of the same awkward realisation.

'Take a seat Alex,' said Gordon, guiding him toward a fine dining chair. 'It can't be easy meeting us all for the first time but we're sure that a cup of tea and some fantastic cake will help,' he said, as his wife nodded agreement before leaving the room to make things happen.

Alex sat facing a bay window, his face lit by the bright afternoon sky. Singer walked over and touched his shoulder. 'We're sorry to hear about your mother and father Alex. Mary told us what's been happening and how brave you've been,' he said, noting his daughter's encouraging expression. 'Please don't feel you have to talk about those difficult times while you're with us… but it might make you feel more at ease knowing we're aware of things,' he finished, walking over to Mary, and kissing the top of her head.

Alex was relieved and embarrassed at the same time. But this was a family who talked to each other, aired their problems, learned to be straightforward and open. A proper family.

Imogen entered with a fine porcelain teapot, matching milk jug and a bowl containing cubes of white and brown sugar and a pair of mini tongs to grip with.

Alex looked apprehensively at the delicate cups and saucers which he felt would have a better chance of survival in a glass case rather than allowing a clumsy teenager to drink from them. He was used to hefty cups and mugs which stood up to misuse on a Brownlow scale.

Imogen poured. 'Help yourself to sugar and milk Alex, then we can talk about cake.' She was comforting, friendly, genuine.

He waited until they were all seated with a cup of tea in front of them before helping himself to milk and sugar. Neither of Mary's parents took any. Fortunately, Mary took one lump of brown, allowing him to follow suit. Short rations were the decent thing on this occasion. He might have to hold back when the cakes were uncovered.

Imogen stood with a large knife using it as a guide, pointing toward the three glass domes in turn. 'That's my special recipe fruit cake, there's my special chocolate layered cake and those are individual fairy cakes.'

'Mary Berry's,' shouted Mary.

Imogen looked at Alex who had no idea who or what they were referring to. 'Tumbled,' she said, waving the knife playfully at Mary. 'You've learnt my big secret Alex. They're not my recipe's they belong to a famous TV chef. But you won't be disappointed. Let me guess – you're a choc man, same as my husband,' she said, cutting a bigger slice than Alex would have had the courage to ask for. And another, of equal size, for Dr Singer.

Mary and Imogen went for the fruit cake.

Alex, ready to pick up the slice as it was, watched how Gordon used his strange little fork to eat the cake. He was learning something new every day…

'Tell us about school Alex. Is that tough at the moment, what with all the upset you have to deal with at home?' asked Gordon.

'I find school tough anyway,' he replied. 'I don't think problems at home affect my schoolwork too much. I expect Mary's told you I'm bottom of my class,' he said, taking a forkful of cake, managing to get it to his mouth before it fell off.

Gordon looked at Mary, then his wife. 'No, we didn't know that, did we, Imogen?'

Imogen had a mouthful of cake too, but she shook her head. Mary said nothing. Alex wasn't sure if they were just being polite or whether they really hadn't heard. Alex and Mary swapped looks, unspoken words which connected them on a different level.

'Don't you like school, Alex?' ventured Imogen.

'School's fine, and I like people but I'm not sure that what we're being taught prepares us for real life. Doesn't get us ready to face the big wide world.'

Singer shifted in his seat, all ears, he'd never heard a child give that reason before. Disliking school was usually because students were bored, or the lessons were dull, or they were too dim to learn at modern class level.

'What do you think should be taught?' asked Singer.

'Difficult to be specific but it doesn't seem helpful spending loads of hours learning a lot of stuff we'll never use.'

'But the point of school is to give you a broad spectrum so that you can make choices when you leave. The path you choose then will be based on what you found to be the most interesting of subjects at school,' Gordon pointed out.

'My mind wanders, during most classes.'

'That's what young minds do. They absorb things which have nothing to do with what's in front of them. Unconsciously. Attention span is usually short because of that. Any particular subject at school that interests you?'

'I like English; writing, creating essays, reading and working out how to put things on paper so you can keep records.'

'That's an excellent subject. It will stand you in good stead whatever you plan to do. Anything else?'

'I was interested when our new biology lecturer gave a talk on the brain and how parts of it governed different things. I liked the idea that she used a model of a human brain to show us what she was talking about. The whole class perked up at her easy style of teaching. She made it interesting.'

'Does that give you some clues about what you should be pursuing?'

'Yes, sir, it does,' he said, without elaboration.

Imogen and Mary gave each other that look – *Father's back in his clinic.* He can't help it. But they could tell Alex wasn't fazed. In fact, he seemed at ease with Gordon's approach to high tea questioning at the Singers.

Alex and Gordon picked up on Mary and Imogen hovering over their tea and cake, watching and waiting for any uncomfortable moments that might need intervention.

Imogen tapped the side of her cup with a teaspoon, ringing it like a tiny bell. 'I'd like to raise a toast, to Alex – for being brave enough to come to tea with the Singers. Cheers,' she said, they raised cups and took a swig of their cooling tea.

'You must try the fruitcake,' said Imogen, lifting the glass dome and cutting a decent slice for Alex. 'Mary?'

'No thanks Mum, I'll just have a fairy cake,' she said, patting her flat tummy while blowing her cheeks out.

'How are your parents, Alex? Any progress with your dad, is he responding to treatment?' asked Imogen.

'He's showing signs of improvement but there's no telling how he's going to be long term,' said Alex, unsure of just how much they already knew about the Brownlows.

Three heads nodded, faces full of sympathy.

'And Mum's doing okay. We're getting ready to move…' he forked a piece of cake and moved it across the plate '… because my parents plan to separate.'

'So sorry, Alex. Accept our apologies,' said Dr Singer. 'We

didn't want this to be an awkward time for you. I guess you were already anticipating walking into a lion's den when Mary invited you to tea,' he grinned. 'We would have understood if you'd turned the invite down. Tea with two psychotherapists would be my worst nightmare.'

Everyone laughed.

Alex felt confident enough to ask his own question. 'What do you plan to do Mary – when you've finished school? Will you go to university?' he asked, her answer determining in which direction his future might need adjusting.

Both parents seemed to freeze in anticipation of their daughter's answer. Alex guessed that this was a subject yet to be fully discussed.

'I'm only thirteen. Well nearly fourteen,' she added. 'Far too young to make such an important decision as picking a lifetime career. I'm undecided.'

'University though?'

'Probably.'

The rest of the afternoon took a more casual turn. They ate cake, drank tea, and talked about other things. But running through the teatime conversation was a theme: Mary was thinking about how much she liked Alex. Imogen and Gordon were taken with him too. And Alex wanted, very much, to be included in their lives.

Sitting opposite Mary had made his heart ache. He'd discounted indigestion from tension or too much cake, it was most definitely his heart. But the girl he intended to marry, knew enough about his family and their shenanigans to want to keep her head down.

CHAPTER TWENTY-EIGHT

Alex burst through the door like an excited puppy. Florence was dressed, ready to go out. 'The hospital rang, there's been some developments with your father,' she exclaimed, hurriedly putting on her gloves.

'What developments?' he asked, disappointed that Ma hadn't mentioned his tea with the Singers.

'They didn't say,' she replied, hoping George's rehabilitation wasn't progressing too quickly. But she needed him to be making some headway, because in the not-too-distant future, he'd have papers to sign. 'Do you want to come with me?' Florence asked, noting her son's forlorn look which she attributed to the proposed hospital visit.

'Sure Ma, if you need the company,' he offered. 'Then I can tell you all about my tea with the Singers.'

'I was going to ask about that,' she lied. 'Was it with the secret girlfriend?'

'It was,' he said, rushing up to the loo, dropping the satchel on his bed as he went. He pulled off his tie, flicked his hair with an ever-ready pocket comb and brushed his teeth with a squeeze of toothpaste on a fingertip.

Florence smiled. How on earth did he manage to be that ready in seconds?

The bus was late, but they didn't have a schedule – though they were both anxious to know just how much progress George was making. Or did *new development* mean something terrible?

'So, what do these Singer people do Alex – are they posh?'

'Posher than us Ma, but nice. Proper China cups and saucers, cakes made from recipes by a famous TV chef and sugar cubes with tittle tweezers to pick them up with.'

'And what about your girlfriend, not too snobby is she?'

'No Ma. They don't act snobby at all, they're just different from us.' *Happily married, educated, refined and comfortably off*, he wanted to add, but decided against it.

'You must bring her to tea Alex. I'm sure she'd like to meet me. Perhaps before we move. I'll bake a cake – you like my cakes,' she declared, with a, *don't you?* look that dared him to challenge the statement.

He did like his Ma's homemade cakes, but they were rare things.

Florence waited for a response, but Alex gave a weak reluctant nod which should have sent a message to his Ma, but it hadn't.

She folded her arms and looked out of the bus window. That's settled then!

Alex couldn't sink any lower in his seat despite powerful forces trying to make him. This is how depressed people feel, he thought, trying to find a chink of light in what was becoming a gloomy afternoon.

It was dusk by the time they arrived at the hospital. Medical staff and patients were seen smoking around the nearby bus terminals. Ambulances, taxis, and cars dropped patients off and picked others up.

Florence, tense as could be, grabbed her son's arm and marched him through the entrance. She let go once they'd taken the stairs to the ward. A receptionist smiled as they approached the nurse's workstation. A member of the staff they'd seen before, approached and welcomed them in.

'We've come to see George Brownlow,' said Florence. 'I understand there's been developments,' she said, a bit too brusquely.

'There has indeed. Better see for yourself,' said the nurse, smiling broadly. 'I'll escort you.'

'I know where his bed is,' said Florence.

'He's not in bed, Mrs Brownlow, he's in the lounge watching telly.'

Alex held on to his Ma's arm, she'd suddenly gone wobbly. Nurse grabbed the other arm, cursing herself for not delivering the dramatic news when Florence was sitting down.

They peered through the glass panel separating the corridor from the patients lounge and watched George laughing at something on telly; The Benny Hill show, a programme George had never seen, and wouldn't have watched, even before the accident.

The nurse and Alex were still holding Florence up. She looked pale, unwell, and not able to believe what she was seeing. No doubt it was a miracle. *He'd be able to sign things,* was one of the more positive aspects considered by Florence, but it also seemed he was on his way to a more rapid recovery. What the hell were they going to do with him?

Alex watched his father with only mild interest. He'd bothered to read up on coma from one of the hospital leaflets. His ma obviously hadn't, and he couldn't understand why, because if she had, George's *developments* would have been less of a surprise. People get over coma, mostly anyway, and according to the literature, and progress so far, his dad was going to get a whole lot better than he was now.

George turned his head as they walked into the room. He waved a finger at the telly and went into another bout of laughter. 'Sit down, watch this, it's really funny,' he said, without addressing either of them directly. His eyes remained fixed on the television. Alex felt he was sitting in a psychiatric unit and that his dad was a heavily medicated patient, oblivious to everything apart from the mesmerising television screen.

For a moment or two, the Brownlows' watched Benny Hill together. Alex thought it was funny, but George's laughter wasn't. Like it was coming from some automated device hidden at the back of his chair. Florence didn't even smile because, to her the screen was just an annoying flickering light destined to be switched off.

She wanted to say, *how are you, dear?* but couldn't.

Alex ventured, 'How are you feeling, Dad?'

'I'm watching this,' said George, without moving his head.

Florence couldn't bear it. She touched his arm and said, 'We're going now, George, we'll come again. Soon.'

George didn't respond but went into shrieks of laughter as Benny Hill chased scantily clad girls around strategically placed props.

'Goodbye, George,' said Florence, without attempting physical contact.

'Goodbye, Dad,' said Alex, gently squeezing his father's hand.

Alex put a comforting arm around his ma's shoulder as they left. Apart from a turn of the head when they'd entered the room, George hadn't taken his eyes off the screen for the duration of their brief visit.

George thought the boy looked good, healthy even, the wife not so much.

Lying or sitting in hospital for days on end was not good for the mind, there was a tendency to overthink and that's exactly what his muddled brain decided to do. He couldn't look either of them in the eye when they walked in and wasn't sure if he'd ever have the courage to do so again. What on earth would he say?

Benny Hill was the hero of the day, even though George didn't find him that funny. Puerile, was his summing up. His jaw ached

from all that strained laughing. He'd never been much of a
laugher, so it was quite a trial, but it did get him out of an
awkward spot.

Two pals from work had popped in earlier and were amazed
to witness George's unexpected progress. They decided it would
be worth having a word with the boss. If George continued
improving at this rate, maybe he could do something at Oakland's
Joinery after all. Not his old job as foreman, obviously, because it
involved a bit of hands-on instruction with dangerous machinery,
but something.

George was looking forward to seeing his physio the next day.
He liked the ex-army guy who'd been putting him through his
paces. The therapist had already got him sitting and standing.
Tomorrow he'd be taking his first steps.

By the time they got back, Florence felt like a wet rag. No one
could have prepared her for the scene at the hospital. Separation
and divorce seemed a distant dream. She was already predicting
the outcome, forced to look after George, dusting and hoovering
round him while he sat in a chair watching mindless television
programmes.

The journey home had been mostly silent. Alex tried to think
of something positive to say but couldn't, not without lying.
Better to keep his mouth shut than lie, he reckoned. He felt a bit
gone over too, so shifted his thoughts toward Mary and cake and
Imogen's soft warm hug. Close contact with another human being
had not been a big part of his life. His ma usually hugged briefly,
from one side, as if she was about to leave for an urgent
appointment. And when she kissed him on the cheek, screwed her
lips to minimise contact, a parental duty rather than affection.

CHAPTER TWENTY-NINE

'God, grant me the serenity to accept the things I cannot change, the courage to change the things I can, and the wisdom to know the difference.'

Vera wasn't quite entering into the spirit of the mantra and criticised, not only the way it was written, but how bloody obvious the message was.

The Chair asked if there was anyone new to Alcoholics Anonymous attending the meeting, who'd like to introduce themselves. Everyone glanced discreetly at the silent Vera, who decided that her first visit would be for observational purposes only.

She reflected on the lead-up to her determined plunge toward sobriety. Recent drinking bouts had given her false courage, enough to take that emotional trip back to the confessional. She needed a full cleansing of body and soul – the whole works – like the best programme on her washing machine.

Father John wasn't totally surprised; he was used to less than regular visitors turning up without warning and could recall Vera's graphic accounts of her shameless life. This time, she didn't stick to her usual pattern of revelation. Of course, he realised that Vera was very drunk; talking rapidly, sometimes incoherently, about another woman or maybe a creature she'd had nightmares about, Mamazon, which conjured up memories of his time in the South American jungle as a young priest.

Florence Brownlow was mentioned too, but the context was lost on him.

He detected true remorse in Vera's voice, the wind had been taken out of her sails. If that required an alcoholic breeze to drive it, then the obvious aroma of a good scotch wafting through the grille toward Father John provided proof.

Vera sat with her arms and legs crossed listening to the various AA confessions and progress made by those who were more accustomed to the set-up.

She didn't believe all their stories. Several stood up and admitted to being recovering alcoholics, revealing they'd been dry for two weeks, or a year or whatever. One or two looked as if they'd come straight from the pub. But she was being harsh and unkind, and realised as the meeting went on that many of the stories and people involved in them were about much tougher problems and of longer duration than hers. Vera's drinking habit was purely hedonistic, but some of these poor souls were homeless, addicted for long periods with a history of abuse, of lost jobs, lost homes and lost loved ones.

But she still had reservations. There were those who'd obviously had a good education and articulated well, spoke like seasoned actors, their stories dramatic but less believable. As if this were their stage, and fellow sufferers were supporting players. It's harder to convince people you need help when you're self-assured and egotistical, because it looks as if you already have life nicely tied up, she reflected.

There was a social air in the room once the meeting was over. Some introduced themselves and offered help or wanted to share their experiences of getting sober. She was tempted to approach a woman who looked like she'd recently had a drink, closer to Vera's category and maybe an easier connection all round.

Her instincts were right; the woman, Betty, had tried to give up whatever she'd been on, without success. This wasn't her first failure, and she had no qualms about giving the facts in lurid detail. Vera lost interest once it occurred to her that Betty was experienced at failing and enjoyed regaling the group with how and why she couldn't give up. What was the point in attending? Because people still listened and encouraged, receiving attention which no one outside would give her. AA were family, and she was the errant child; always forgiven, always allowed another chance. Hardly a child, the woman was fifty if she was a day.

With a confession and an AA meeting under her belt, Vera felt virtuous. A state of mind which deserved a celebratory drink or two, but this early in her new programme, if so much as a drop touched her lips, a five-star rating couldn't be maintained.

She was already suffering withdrawal symptoms; nightmares, partly to do with her sudden desire to get her life together and partly to do with being rejected by Dr Grayling. He'd decided that his association with the school and lack of experience dealing with seriously disturbed people – *like Vera Harris* – meant that she was not something he felt capable of taking on. He was not the friend or the help she'd expected!

'I can refer you to someone else,' he'd suggested. 'Dr Gordon Singer's a good man – experienced in cases like yours.'

Her eyes bored deep into Grayling's. 'Does he even treat people as pathologically disturbed as me?' she replied, her voice heavy with sarcasm.

Her indignation struck home; he'd made an error of judgment, and Grayling's face turned from the milky paleness of a serious professional to the scarlet complexion of a competitive wrestler.

Florence suffered nightmares too, but the theme had changed from being attacked in the jungle by Mamazon and Vera Harris to George leaving his hospital bed to scare the living daylights out of her at home.

George, on the other hand, seemed to have dispensed with nightmares and swung toward pleasant dreams. Neither Florence nor Alex featured. They were about getting back to work, instructing his fellow joiners about how to use an electric planer, and emphasising the precision required for perfecting dovetail or mortise and tenon joints. His thoughts about what he'd be doing at home or after work had yet to be considered.

The arm-waving wife and the demolition-obsessed husband were trying to hurry things along. They wanted to make sure the completion date hadn't been changed. They'd workmen and architects standing by. Florence's solicitor was trying to ensure that George and Florence Brownlow were all set to do the right thing on the right day.

The tone of their request annoyed Florence. 'You'd think they were going to demolish the street and build a palace,' she said to Alex over breakfast, having picked up the morning mail and selected the envelope marked, *For your urgent attention.*

'They're probably excited, Ma,' he said, not believing the new owners got genuinely excited in the normal scheme of things.

'Well, if your father can sit and laugh at stupid television programmes, he must be able to scrawl his name on paperwork,' she said, without thinking about exactly how she was going to face the man and get him to sign. She was almost certain George chose to ignore her at the hospital rather than being incapable of communication or recognition.

'Have you asked Mary if she's coming to tea sometime soon, Alex? Might be best to do it before we actually start moving,' said Florence, her brain switching to a fresh topic.

'No, Ma, I haven't,' said Alex, taken completely by surprise.

'Why not?'

'I don't think you're in the right place at the moment, Ma,' he said. 'What with everything going on with Dad, the house being sold and all that other stuff.'

'What other stuff?' she responded, knowing damn well what stuff, but hoping it hadn't messed up the whole of her future.

'All the rumours about the lecturer at school and you... Ms Harris,' he said softly, hoping that Ma wouldn't press him on the detail.

'What has any of that to do with your girlfriend coming round for a cup of tea and piece of cake?' she said, collapsing inside but adopting the tone of an innocent victim.

'Nothing to do with cake and tea, Ma, but you must be finding life difficult right now...I know I am...and I don't want things to end up...' *a disaster,* he wanted to say.

'End up like what?'

'Can you let me ask Mary at the right moment? Please, Ma. It's not an easy thing to do, especially as her parents made such a big thing of it only last week. I don't want anyone to feel under pressure. Especially Mary,' he said, though the softness in the last two words might not have registered with his ma.

Florence didn't know how to react. She pressed the fingers of both hands hard into her forehead as if doing so might elicit a reasonable response – and give Alex an opportunity to change the subject.

'I've been thinking about Dad signing things. We could get the solicitor and Father's consultant to arrange a time with the hospital. Dad wouldn't be able to play up if they were there, they'd make sure he signed everything,' said Alex, recalling his last visit to the ward. The patient was not in the state he pretended to be. *Paying his wife back maybe?* Alex thought so.

CHAPTER THIRTY

Oakland's Joinery was abuzz. The two employees who'd visited George in hospital had reported back. The juicy rumours, garnered from many sources including wives and husbands of employees, were distributed amongst the workers while the boss was regaled with the story of George's steady progress.

On a suspended floor, the offices of the joinery were set halfway up a solid open-plan staircase built as a showpiece. George Brownlow had played a key part in its construction, so his reputation was clear for all to see. The faultless creation used several examples of exotic timbers and incorporated every joint imaginable in its construction. The whole building was open plan, designed for everything and everyone to be visible from Oliver Oakland's glass-walled office in its lofty position. Anyone looking toward it, client, visitor, or employee, would be reminded of the perfect craftsmanship expected of all who worked there. The imposing staircase and Oliver's office were impossible to miss.

Oliver, son of the man who'd started the business, dressed daily in a white shirt and pinstripe suit. He greased his hair, manicured his nails and shaved with a safety razor. Not a looker but tall and slim, gawky even. He listened intently to his employees' accounts. George Brownlow, as a worker, had been sorely missed.

'It really was remarkable, guv,' said one, 'quite on the ball. It seemed very early days to be doing so well, considering what we'd all expected. Thought he'd be a goner for sure. But he seems to be improving daily.'

'What are you two thinking?' asked Oliver, ready to hear from his trusted staff. They often managed to spot things he'd missed. A boss wasn't at ground level frequently enough to get the full picture, particularly regarding the latest gripes and gossip amongst his workforce.

'We think that George might eventually be able to come back to work,' said one, glancing at his fellow worker, who nodded support.

Oliver gripped his chin, removed his reading glasses, and looked out across the busy floor-space, thinking aloud. 'He's a good man, no doubt about that. But his expected recuperation may not be enough – not for his position as a working foreman. It won't be a full recovery, surely? He's been in a coma for God's sake!'

The two, unable to disagree, let the moment hang.

'He's actively hands-on in the joinery shop, unnecessarily so on occasion. George can't stop getting in there, interfering sometimes,' continued Oliver.

They couldn't argue with that comment either, but he was invaluable, a star worker with flaws and problems. Like all stars. And elevated to virtual sainthood by surviving his near-death experience. 'There's no one better, boss.'

'True. I'll have to think about it. Maybe he could be supervising a new chap… He'd have to take a drop in wages though, I can't be paying two men full pay for doing one job. 'But' he said, hoping not to sound mercenary, 'a lower wage is better than being out of work, isn't it, lads?'

The two employees smiled, reassured, certain that George

would be back. 'Everyone still thinks he built that fabulous staircase on his own…'

They all laughed.

'Would you consider paying him a visit in a week or two, boss, see how he's doing, maybe give him a bit of hope first hand?'

He was torn. Oliver knew about the Brownlows' intended house move, but Oakland's Joinery wasn't a charity. Employing a new foreman was a gamble. The chap might not turn out to be as good as George, but he might be safer. Safety was paramount. But then, so was keeping up with the busy workload.

Oliver also knew a hell of a lot more about the Brownlow family. It was a small town. Any business owner or professional was bound to keep up to date with local news and gossip. The web of information and people involved in discussion groups, business meetings, women's institutes, health clubs, golf clubs, pubs, restaurants and bars, all produced fragments of an ever-changing picture.

Oliver felt sorry for Florence, of course he did, but what would he have done if his wife had suddenly taken up with a lesbian and asked for a divorce? Killed her probably.

Florence was in reflective mood. It was Sunday, Alex was out with Eddie, and she was having a lie-in after a heavy night's sleep. The morning sun struck dust motes; the sudden draught swirled them around as she pulled the covers up to her chin. Disturbed particles floated onto the dresser and other bits of rarely polished furniture. The brightness filling the room was a sharp reminder that housework remained a less than important item on her to-do list.

She'd been thinking about George's unexpected recovery, optimistic it now seemed, outlined in detail when she asked the nursing staff how much progress he was truly making. Much more than he'd demonstrated on her last visit, that was clear.

The physio was amazed at George's progress and said he'd

rarely seen such enthusiasm; the man had progressed from a virtual cabbage to a highly motivated patient in a very short space of time.

She felt optimistic about Alex too, but in quite a different way. He seems to have taken it all so well, too well: Father's coma, her disfigurement, the move, her affair with Vera. All very grown up – and it looked like a romance was on the horizon for her little boy. Maybe that's how Alex was able to bear it all, he'd been too busy nurturing his developing relationship with Mary. But Florence had a sneaking suspicion that he'd have been okay anyway. Alex didn't do what others might. He was still a bit of a puzzle.

She wanted to meet Mary and connect with this mysterious girl.

Florence couldn't praise herself for being a good mother but then she had no idea how that would have helped, with such an independent son. At some point, she remembered hearing a strict utterance from her grandmother; *we must let our children go.* Florence didn't think she meant that to happen quite so soon...

But she realised, with some optimism, that George's recovery meant he'd be able to work – he could move out and they'd get divorced. Her heart lifted, and she threw back the bedclothes and went down to make a celebratory cup of tea. It was back to her original plan, but things might take just a little longer.

For some unconnected reason, Florence also thought about her affair with Vera. It had started well; gentle, slow, soft, everything she'd expected in an intimate relationship with another woman. Tenderness was the attraction – kissing, cuddling, holding hands, comforting embraces...

But Florence had never experienced an orgasm before, so when Vera's gentleness turned to something more frenzied – a similar attitude to George in his...how could she describe it, *premature climax?* – she became frightened, the act so aggressive that Florence felt she'd been raped.

But Vera had given her the orgasm she'd often wondered about. On reflection, Florence could only compare the whole experience to an exhausted runner breaking the finishing tape only to be carted off to A&E with heart failure.

That said, she wouldn't rule out another liaison in the future, not with a man, it went without saying, but someone with a little less vigour. Maybe an older woman, closer to a mother than a lover. Then she realised what a ridiculous idea it was and how unrealistic and stupid she was being.

Florence jumped when she heard the key turn in the front door and a heavy clattering along the hall. Alex burst into the kitchen, holding a bloodstained handkerchief to a face wound.

She panicked. She wasn't good with blood. Coupled with the sudden interruption of her reverie, she became flustered, erring toward clumsy.

'What on earth?' asked Florence, suddenly pale, anxious, dumbfounded.

'Fighting,' he said, smiling and wincing at the same time. He knew his ma would be like this.

She dashed into the bathroom and came back with a tin of assorted Elastoplast, a bottle of TCP and some cotton wool swabs. 'Let's have a look,' she said bravely. 'What happened? You don't do fighting, Alex. Who did this to you?'

'Greg Smart. By accident.'

'No one fights by accident. What happened?' she said, pouring some TCP onto a cotton wool pad and dabbing at the blood oozing over his cheekbone.

'I was waiting for Eddie. We were going across the street to play table tennis in the park. They've set up some new outside tables for the summer. Greg Smart came by and started saying nasty things about our family.'

Florence had a pretty good idea what. 'That's not enough reason to start a fight. People gossip all the time,' she reasoned, especially about the Brownlows. 'Who started it?'

'Smart. He didn't see Eddie walking toward him, and he started ribbing me about Mary...the Virgin Mary, he called her. He was laughing right in my face. I went to push him away, but

Eddie stepped between us. It was a mess, the three of us, part wrestling, part punching. Then Smart swung at Eddie with all his might, Eddie ducked, and I was hit, smack in the face,' he said, pointing to the small gaping wound which Florence was drying up.

'Might need a stitch,' she said.

'It'll be fine, Ma, it's stopped bleeding.' Alex was more concerned with the class tomorrow, the English lecture which Mary was due to attend.

Florence took the biggest plaster from the tin, peeled off the backing, and stuck it quickly over the injury. The plaster was four times bigger than it need be – a belt and braces attitude to the smallest of injuries. *Panic treatment*, George used to call her nursing skills.

'How did it end?'

'Eddie really laid into him…' said Alex, hesitating before admitting to the full extent of the outcome. 'They had to call an ambulance.'

Alex felt the increased stinging pain in his cheekbone, which he guessed had more to do with mother's rough treatment than the injury.

Florence, hand on chest to calm her heart from the stressful activities of a reflective morning, finally put the kettle on. She needed to talk to Alex about her more positive take on their future but decided that might have to wait.

The kettle whistled away. Alex reached for the biscuit tin while his ma made a strong cup of tea.

CHAPTER THIRTY-ONE

A loudspeaker in the playground emitted a tinny message. *'Alex Brownlow, please report to the headmaster's office immediately.'*

He couldn't imagine what this was about, or maybe he could if he tried hard enough. He ran through the corridors as fast as he could and approached the secretary's desk breathless and sweating.

'Morning, Alex. Take a seat, the Head will be with you in a moment,' she said, peering over the top of her black-rimmed glasses, and smiling while shifting papers distractedly on her desk.

Miss Peel, the Head's new young secretary, seemed a tad nervous. He looked out of the office window and spotted the back of a police car. An officer stood outside; the other was probably in with the Head. *They always come in pairs;* he'd seen it on telly in crime programmes. This sudden call to the Head's office must be about Greg Smart and Eddie. Maybe they wanted to question him as a witness?

Alex sat upright on a hard bench. His partner in crime walked out of the Head's office, grinning but not daring to look Alex in the eye. Eddie showed no signs of serious injury, just grazed knuckles, which he flashed briefly at his friend.

'Plod's in there,' Eddie whispered, drawing the edge of his hand swiftly across his throat in mock execution.

'Brownlow!' shouted the Head.

'Your turn,' said the smiling secretary, pushing her glasses into position as she nodded toward the partly open door.

Alex, to make sure the dressing on his wound was intact, checked its current adhesive state. It was destined for permanence. That plaster would take some shifting!

A serious looking constable stood at the side of the Head's desk.

Not one of the big guns, thought Alex, *just a bobby*. He smiled at the officer, who didn't respond in kind.

Mr Hawkins, the Head, looked very stern indeed. 'I expected more of you, Brownlow, thought you'd be the last one to cause trouble.'

Alex wasn't quite ready for the accusation. 'What trouble, sir?' he said, looking wronged, touching the sizeable plaster again, and wincing – confirmation that he'd been wounded.

'This is Constable Picket. They've had a serious complaint down at the station,' he said, looking for signs of guilt on the boy's face. 'You may or may not know that Greg Smart is in hospital. He'll be there for a while. He's made a complaint against you and Eddie Burns. Said you'd attacked him and beat him up… Two boys against one will not be tolerated,' he said, waving a stubby finger at the accused. 'We'll have no bullying in my school. There will be consequences, Brownlow.'

Picket coughed and took out his notebook, licked the end of a pencil and wrote something down before flipping back to his notes on a previous page. Alex thought they only did that on the telly.

'The station had a call from Mrs Smart, the boy's mother, saying two school thugs had beaten her son within an inch of his life.' Picket didn't really need to check his notes but did so for dramatic effect. 'She knew who they were and named the pair as

Eddie Burns and Alex Brownlow. We've already questioned Burns...'

Alex felt a weakness in his legs. His face felt hot and his hands clammy.

'That's not true. He attacked us, sir,' he said, realising that Smart being hospitalised wouldn't help his case.

'Are you saying that Greg Smart took on two of you?' said Picket, in a. sarcastic tone. 'The lad's in hospital. He was knocked out cold.'

'Greg Smart bullied me first. He said terrible things about my family. Personal things. He was so close I could feel his breath and spittle on my face. I tried to push him away, but he was too strong. Then Eddie came along right at that moment and tried to help.'

'So did Smart give you that injury?' asked Picket, pointing at the obvious.

Alex felt for the plaster once more.

'Yes,' he said. 'But the blow was meant for Eddie.'

Picket looked confused. 'Smart's mother said you were the ringleader, is that true? Did you provoke the lad?'

'No, sir. Smart's lying...' He thought hard before adding, '... and must have got his mum to lie too,' he said, uneasy about calling anyone's mother a liar.

Alex thought how stupid it all was. How could anyone be a ringleader of two people? You needed a sizeable gang to carry that title. Smart was a known bully, Hawkins would know that. Eddie was a clown, ask anyone in the school, and Alex Brownlow was the quiet one. The Head should come to his defence pronto on this.

Hawkins looked to Picket for a response. Picket obliged. 'Obviously we'll be interviewing Greg Smart again, take a proper statement. He wasn't quite ready to give us the full details on our first visit,' said the officer, unable to divulge that Smart was in no fit state to give a reasonable explanation as to what happened. Medication for his pain had left the boy confused and...crying like a baby. Smart's mother however, had not been confused. She'd been so explicit, you'd have thought she'd been at the scene with a camera and notebook. In Picket's experience, mothers were never able to give an accurate account of their offspring's antics.

'What happens now?' asked Alex, unable to comprehend the situation.

'It depends on what happens to Greg Smart. How well he recovers, see if he still wants to pursue his claim against...' Picket took another look at his notes but didn't speak the words as he'd written them – *Smart claiming he'd been beaten nearly to death by school bullies* – the aforementioned lads, Burns and Brownlow.

'We might have to get you all to see Dr Grayling,' said Hawkins. 'He's the school's educational psychologist,' he explained to Picket. 'He keeps the pupils on track when they get out of hand.'

'Given all the available information so far, I think these lads might need a bit more than the school psychologist,' said Picket. 'No offence, sir,' he added, politely taking the initiative.

'None taken. Who do you have in mind?'

'There's a very good man, he acts as liaison for us in all sorts of situations but particularly good with...' *kids* he wanted to say. 'Growing lads,' sounded better in front of the Head.

The headmaster nodded, inclined to agree. Dealing with thuggery was not really Grayling's area of expertise.

'My experience,' continued Picket, writing an additional note in his little book, 'is, that when asked about such affairs, criminally accused individuals tend to say they didn't do it.' He glanced at Alex for effect. 'Denial is the constant cry of every prison inmate, it seems.'

A disturbing image, a rusty iron cage housing two desperate criminals, crossed Alex's mind.

'Who's the expert?' asked Hawkins.

'Dr Gordon Singer's the man. One of these three lads is the culprit, the author of this unfortunate episode, and Singer will find out exactly which one it is.'

Alex felt his world crumbling. Dr Singer would ask him what caused the fight. His daughter being called the Virgin Mary might not play in Alex's favour, unless he was seen as a heroic knight defending a maiden's honour. Because that's how it was.

'That's enough for now,' barked Hawkins. 'Constable Picket is on the case, and he'll keep us up to date. Until then Brownlow, I want you to stay out of trouble and keep away from Burns. We want no more of this antisocial behaviour.'

Picket made a few more notes, slammed his pocketbook shut and secured it with a strong elastic band. He shook hands with Hawkins and walked past Miss Peel, who seemed to be putting the finishing touches to her makeup. She rather liked the boys in blue and hoped that Constable Picket would be visiting again.

'Now, Brownlow. I'm not going to do anything yet because I'm not sure the true picture of what happened has been revealed. Although your academic record leaves a lot to be desired, you've never been reported for bad behaviour or any breach of school etiquette, unless you can include staring out of the window for extended periods in that category. But your pal Burns is a different kettle of fish,' he said, without divulging the numerous reports he'd had of Eddie's mischievous history. Hawkins checked his watch. 'You may leave now but go straight to your class.'

Alex was stopped by Miss Peel. 'How did it go?' she whispered.

'Someone's lying,' he said, without mentioning Smart's name. 'And that's made trouble for Eddie and me.'

'Did someone hit you?' she asked, assuming the giant plaster indicated a sizeable injury. Alex was about to answer when the Head appeared at the door. 'Please come in, Miss Peel, I need you to take some notes,' he said.

Alex had made up his mind. He was going to visit Greg Smart in hospital.

CHAPTER THIRTY-TWO

Mathew Lowry, Peacocks' sales advisor, had come up with what Florence and Alex thought was a bargain. Not a house but a very nice two-bedroom flat not far off the bus route. Florence could manage the deposit, a few weeks' rental up front. Bank percentage rates shifting downward helped. And Peacocks' contract stating six months as the shortest length of stay was not a problem. They'd planned to live there for some time.

George Brownlow was still on a full wage, but even with the proposed period of half pay, coupled with Florence's part time wage, they'd be able to afford it. Their house sale was about to complete, so there'd be capital due as well. All they needed to do was get George to sign some paperwork.

Lowry shook Alex's hand this time, though he did overdo the *grownup greeting a child* bit by smiling too much and stooping too far.

They decided to take a bus to the hospital. Alex ran his finger down the timetable displayed on a cast iron stop sign. It was a fifteen-minute wait. Florence kept checking her watch and fiddling with her gloves while Alex watched kids across the street doing wheelies on their bikes.

A grey car pulled up. A man got out and walked toward them.

'Flo…how are you,' he said, giving Florence an almighty hug. Florence resisted, trying to think who the hell it was. Men didn't hug her without some indication of consent. Even then…

'It's me, Simon, Vera's brother,' he declared, throwing out his arms and smiling like a Cheshire cat as if that might make recognition easier. 'Where are you off to? I'll give you a lift,' he said, moving swiftly to open the front passenger door. 'And this is your boy, Alex. Hi, Alex,' he said, stepping back onto the pavement to embrace the boy warmly.

Alex tried not to be rude by pulling away, but being hugged by strangers was a new experience. Not unpleasant, just a bit sudden.

'We're only going to the hospital, Simon,' she said, checking her watch. The bus would be another ten minutes.

'That's on my route, going right past the place,' said Simon. 'Visiting your husband, are you?'

'Yes,' she said, reluctant to update him, she hardly knew the bloke.

'Sit in the back, Alex, you'll have the whole bench to yourself,' he said.

There really was no escape. Florence slid in next to Simon and Alex enjoyed the luxury of a comfortable seat and a lot of room.

'Seatbelts please, everyone,' said Simon, clicking his into place with a practised flourish.

For the first part of the journey, Alex felt invisible. The conversation needn't have included him, obviously, but he could see his ma was in a difficult position and unable to stop it happening. A sitting duck, Dad would have labelled her.

'Really sorry about you and Sis,' Simon started. 'I thought it was true love at first, but I should have known better, my sister doesn't do true anything for very long. You were as close as it got, Flo,' he said, intending a compliment, glancing sideways quickly to catch her response.

Her face was expressionless, an icy sculpture. Shutting out the memory; she'd thought it was love too.

Alex settled down for what promised to be an uncomfortable journey.

'She's on the wagon now, you know. Had to get help in the end. Alcoholics Anonymous took her on; that was brave of them, not sure I'd want to do it,' he laughed.

'Sorry about this, Alex. Grownups, eh? What are we to do?' he said, feeling around the dashboard for a packet of cigarettes, the ashtray already full of butts.

'Please don't smoke, Simon. I've got asthma,' Florence lied. Helping Alex avoid lung cancer was the only thing she could protect him from right now.

Mother! Anything but the truth, thought Alex.

Simon stuck the cigarette in his mouth but didn't light up. It was as close as he could get without smoking the bloody thing.

'Do you miss Vera, Flo?' he asked innocently. Evidently oblivious to the Mamazon affair. Or was he just fishing? He certainly seemed aware that his sister was a loose cannon.

'Not after she betrayed me,' said Florence, reaching back to touch Alex's hand, so lightly he hardly felt it. A poor substitute for comfort, if that's what it was supposed to be.

'I didn't know about that, Flo. Do you want to talk about it?'

'No, I want to forget about it. Ask your sister if you want the details,' she said, wishing the journey would end. Now.

Despite the difficult atmosphere Alex found Simon's straightforwardness refreshing. The man didn't hold back from telling the truth, and even better, Alex hadn't been excluded from adult revelations. Ma must be squirming inside, he thought; her buttoned lip wouldn't help her now. She'd been more or less struck dumb anyway, by the looks of her.

For some unknown reason, Simon didn't enquire about George. Alex guessed it was because of Ma's petrification. A conversation stopper if ever there was one, a tactic she and Father used when buttoned lips moved on to the physically obvious stage. A total shutdown.

They approached the hospital in silence.

Alex and Florence entered the ward with some trepidation. They glanced at each other with that, *I wonder if he's going to play up again* look.

George was reading, or trying to read, the newspaper. It looked hard work, but was still amazing to witness.

'Have you read this?' he asked, as Florence and Alex appeared at his bedside. 'Tommy Cooper's had a heart attack,' he said, before flicking to another page. 'And Gandhi's been assassinated.' He looked at Florence and Alex for a response but received none. He turned another page. 'And the coal miners are still on strike,' he finished, folding the paper in half, and dropping it to the floor.

'What can I do for you two?' he asked, without any obvious signs he'd recognised them.

'We thought we'd pay you a visit George. See how you're doing…' she said, keeping her distance.

George wished he hadn't dropped the newspaper. He felt vulnerable now and wondered if he could pull the *I'm not feeling well card* and call a nurse.

Alex was still musing over the fact that Tommy Cooper's heart attack received more attention than Gandhi's death. He didn't know much about Mr Cooper, but he'd read and heard about Gandhi. A legend, a hero.

'Is that all?' said George. 'You could have rung, saved yourselves a journey.'

Alex and Florence were still unsure whether George recognised them. He hadn't addressed either of them by name.

'We wanted to tell you about the house sale too, Dad,' said Alex, believing that due to the not very conducive atmosphere, someone other than his ma ought to make the point.

'What about it?' said George. 'Have we got somewhere to live?'

Alex and Florence needed a seat. He knew what was going on! More or less at least.

'We will have,' said Florence, 'but we need you to sign some papers so we can go ahead and sort things out.'

'I'll need to read before I sign,' he said before sliding down and pulling a blanket over his head.

They walked back to the hospital entrance. Alex was feeling positive, but his ma didn't encourage an overly optimistic conversation. He thought the fact that his father had even considered looking at paperwork with the obvious intention of signing it was a miracle in itself. His ma had, it seemed, been put off by Father's infantile attempt to shut them out by hiding under blankets. But she wasn't seeing it for what it was, the petty snub had taken precedence over the bigger picture; Dad was lucid enough to listen, reason and respond to the transaction they were so dependent on. No doubt there would be a solicitor and maybe an agent present to make sure everything was signed and completed legally without coercion. That wouldn't be a problem. The stumbling block might come if Dad were to have a change of mind or a coma-related relapse on that particular day.

Through the glass doors of the entrance, they could see Simon's car in the visitor's car park. He was leaning, half sitting on the bonnet, looking toward the entrance puffing away on a cigarette which glowed like a warning beacon in the fading light. He was waiting for them.

He couldn't possibly see through the entry door. The plate glass merely reflected the scene outside the hospital, including Simon's distant image.

Florence put a steadying hand on Alex's shoulder. 'I don't think I can face another journey with Simon. I wonder if there's another way out.'

'You could just tell him it's over with his sister and too painful to talk about. He'd have to leave you alone then, Ma…'

She shook her head at his every word, unable to be so direct. The buttoned lip was pathological.

Alex would have liked to spend a little more time listening to Simon's account of his sister's love life. But Ma must come first.

There was another exit, through A&E where ambulances and emergencies pulled in. But Simon had crushed his cigarette with a vigorous heel spin and was already halfway toward the main entrance, close enough to see the two indecisive figures staring straight at him.

'I have an idea. You can hang on, Ma. Tell Simon you need to stay a while because I want to visit Greg Smart while I'm here. I was going to leave it for another time – but it's something I have to do. No time like the present, is there?' he said, already feeling nervous and on the edge of reconsidering his courageous plan. 'My visiting Smart will help you, Ma. You can wait for me in the coffee shop, then you won't need to ride back with Simon,' he smiled.

CHAPTER THIRTY-THREE

Alex had trouble locating the ward. There were lots of them and he had no idea what state Smart would be in, whether he'd be assigned to an ordinary ward or in some critical care unit. Or having an operation! He asked the busy receptionist, and she checked her list. 'Greg Smart is in Burrows Ward, first floor, left at the top of the stairs,' she said, already turning to the next visitor.

Alex entered Burrows ward with some trepidation. No one looked particularly ill. Only ten beds. Greg Smart was sitting in a chair wearing what appeared to be his father's dressing gown, and pyjamas inches too long in the leg. He hadn't noticed Alex because he was deep into reading the *Beano*, and had a small pile of similar publications next to his bed. There was no evidence of serious injury, no bandages or splints showing, or drips or anything remotely related to someone claiming to have been nearly beaten to death.

Alex coughed as he approached the bed. Smart looked up, his colour drained, and Alex felt this was more the look he'd expected.

'B – Brownlow,' he said, stuffing the *Beano* quickly under a ruffled sheet, realising that the stack next to him confirmed a juvenile taste in literature.

'How are you, Greg? Looks like you're doing okay,' said Alex, trying to keep the hint of sarcasm out of his voice. Seeing Smart looking so pathetic and vulnerable was a satisfying experience. With none of his support group hanging around he looked much smaller and a less formidable version of the guy he'd been bullied by. Apprehension left Alex, as if they'd swapped roles or his opponent had undergone a sort of emotional *fear transplant*. He looked terrified.

Once anxiety had left Alex, bravery moved in. 'Your ma said you were nearly beaten to death by Eddie and me,' he said, unable to make eye contact, because the patient had closed his eyes, attempting to shut out the nightmare scenario. Alex recalled that only Smart and he had battle scars.

Eddie hadn't a mark on him.

'Mum exaggerates,' he offered, 'But I was knocked out. That's why I'm still here, they're making sure I haven't got brain damage.'

Too late for that, thought Alex. 'What about the rest of you?'

Smart pulled up his pyjama leg to reveal an ankle in a flimsy crepe bandage. Then showed off some grazes on his elbow and a light bruising either side of his face. So indistinct, that Alex had to lean closer to see them. But near enough for Smart to get a good look at the gash on Alex's face. He couldn't possibly have missed seeing the vivid scarlet streak. It was more obvious than any of Smart's injuries.

'I should be out soon…' he said, rolling down the leg of his pyjamas.

This moment was an opportunity for Alex, who thought back to his ma being unable to escape Simon's questioning. Greg Smart was the second sitting duck of the day and Alex was about to make the most of it.

'Because of you and your mother's accusations, we were summoned before the Head and questioned by the police as if we were hardened criminals. They want to send us for psychotherapy…'

Greg tried to stifle a grin. They both smiled. *A first breakthrough connection,* thought Alex.

'Why have you got it in for me, Greg? You seem to take every opportunity to give me grief. Yet you don't seem like a bad person, not when you're sitting here on your own...' *in your dad's pyjamas,* he was tempted to add for effect.

Smart would have some difficulty admitting it because maintaining the reputation of bravado and bullying relied on an audience, an all-boys thing. A gang culture aimed to bring down anyone who appeared different to the rest of the class or school. It was especially tempting to perpetuate the image if those they picked on didn't or couldn't fight back. But now that Alex had caught him by surprise, and alone, and with a stack of kid's comics, his macho image was dented somewhat. He knew, deep down, that he should have moved on to more mature publications by now, like the *Eagle* comic with Dan Dare, about space travel and stuff.

'If you want to call a truce, tell your ma to drop all those wrongful accusations. It's not fair that you can ruin Eddie's future, and mine, because you and your mother are telling lies. I don't think you're a bully, Greg, not really, but I do think you're... easily led,' he blurted. *There, it's out.*

Smart stiffened, touched by the fact that Alex thought he might be a normal guy, doubting his bullying credentials, but annoyed that he could see below the surface of what Smart felt was an indestructible force. 'Ma might not back down,' he said, unprepared to throw the towel in yet.

'Your ma wasn't there, Greg! If you carry on with your claim against Eddie and me, just be careful. Don't forget you have a reputation, you're the known bully in the school, and we're not. I've never hit anyone, and Eddie just makes people laugh, unless he's severely provoked. And past witnesses will testify against you. Remember when you bullied me in front of Mary and a whole load of us on the school bus?' Alex was on a roll. Out of character? Maybe, but there'd never be a better time to say it like it was. Your enemy trapped by his pyjamas in a hospital with a pathetic catalogue of minor injuries and a stack of *Beanos* next to his bed said it all.

Smart sagged with the realisation that it really wasn't looking good for him and his ma. She was due in that afternoon and he had to work out the best way of telling her about Brownlow's visit. She wouldn't be happy.

Things couldn't have gone worse for him, but then they did. Alex was about to leave when a doctor came to assess his recovering patient.

'How do you feel, Greg? You're looking much better. Nice to see you have a pal visiting. Is he in your class?' asked the doctor.

He's not my pal and he's not in my class, Smart wanted to say, but nodded weakly.

'There's good news. You'll be out of here tomorrow,' he announced, flipping open his notes. 'There are no signs of a problem following your concussion, just some superficial abrasions from the little tussle you had,' he smiled. 'If you hadn't had that knock on the head, you'd have been sent home without hospitalisation. But we had to be sure. Well done, lad,' he said as he turned to check the rest of the ward.

Alex couldn't stop smiling. *Superficial? Smart going home with barely a mark on him?* He'd be back at school before the end of the week and his case would fall apart. He'd probably be fined for wasting police time and look ridiculous when the kids at school saw the notorious bully unmarked and looking healthier than he'd been for some time. Hospital food wasn't designed to keep weight on, and the holiday from bullying would feel like a few days on a spiritual retreat.

Brownlow wouldn't let him live this down, tales of his visit would be round the school in a flash, his reputation in tatters.

Smart wanted the loo, urgently.

Mother, a small woman, all bones and a pinched face, turned up with a bar of Cadbury's chocolate and a stern look. She didn't want him looking good this soon! And when he told her about Brownlow's visit, she visibly boiled with rage.

CHAPTER THIRTY-FOUR

The Singers were having the usual morning chat before work and school. Except it was far from their normal discussion. The whole conversation revolved around Alex Brownlow and his confrontation with Greg Smart.

Constable Picket, always quick to get the experts in, had already been onto Dr Gordon Singer, preparing him for a proposed interview with the boys. Picket didn't usually have to bother with school scraps. Bullying was often ignored, hard to prove, usually from lack of evidence. But when someone ended up unconscious and in hospital, it was always taken seriously.

Added to his determination to seek justice was Picket's own experience of being bullied as a young man. Due to a rather feminine sounding lisp, his sexuality had been called into question but never proven one way or the other. Once he got married, his case rested. But he would target bullies with enthusiasm for the rest of his life.

Alex Brownlow being bottom of the class and not the favourite kid in the school had come to his notice. Someone with a grudge maybe? A loser, like most bullies, Picket had decided.

With Alex being known by the Singers and on a first-time consultation list, Gordon's hands were tied about how much he could reveal regarding the upcoming case. Or anything that manifested during the process. Imogen would, of course, be working alongside, but sworn to confidentiality like her husband.

'So, what's the plan, Dad?' asked Mary, looking toward her father for encouraging signs.

It was a first for him; a case that would impinge so directly on family life and cause anxiety for his only child. He sipped his coffee slowly before answering. 'You know the score, Mary. I'll have to treat Alex like anyone else who comes into my clinic. Our personal feelings can't be helped but they mustn't influence my professional analysis, the fairness of the case. Impartiality is paramount.' He took another sip of his coffee, while he struggled to find some reassuring sense in his clinical tone. Of course, they'd all be influenced. With the best will in the world, if you'd taken a liking to someone bias became automatic.

Mary's shoulders drooped. 'I'll be discreet, Dad. Just give me a sign, a word or two... Keep me in the loop.' She smiled at herself for using 'in the loop'; her father employed it so often when talking amongst professionals.

Of course, Mary would be pressing for news and updates, it would be unkind to leave her out in the cold, but his reputation and the confidentiality clauses in his contract must be respected and upheld. It was the law. But wouldn't it be counterproductive to create an inter-family tension for what would be in the public domain soon enough?

'Alex can't possibly have done what Smart and his mother have accused him of,' said Imogen. 'We're good at spotting wrong 'uns and Alex Brownlow is most definitely not in that category,' she finished, as all three nodded in unison. But they knew that Constable Picket was a man who wouldn't let go of a bone once he'd got his teeth into it. The troubling thing was that whatever the outcome, Alex would have some sort of background slur on his reputation which would be hard to shake off. Documentation, however contentious, would be passed on and affect his chances in the world of education and career.

The old adage, *a lie can travel halfway round the world while truth is putting its shoes on*, was totally appropriate. Mary had already heard news of the incident which shot around the school faster than a bullet.

Greg Smart's gang were virtually in mourning. And there was an unsettled air, firstly of disbelief, that Eddie and Alex were even capable of putting the school bully in hospital. And secondly that Smart's mother, a known troublemaker like her son, would have the gall to try to frame such an innocent pair when the evidence and character references would show otherwise. She'd look a damn fool, but everything would be on Alex's and Eddie's record, maybe a criminal record.

Mary was sitting in the bedroom in front of a dressing table mirror brushing her hair without looking at her pretty image. Her heart was feeling sad for Alex, and the injustice being dealt him. It felt like she'd been hit too. How could her gentle friend be so wrongly accused? She hesitated at the word friend; he was more than that now. But how could that be, as she'd had little conversation with Alex and even less contact than she'd had with her most casual acquaintances?

Colour rose in her face, and she started brushing her hair with undue vigour. Her scalp started to feel sore. She smiled, remembering a scene from the film, South Pacific – Mitzi Gaynor singing, 'I'm Gonna Wash that Man right outta my Hair'. Her parents had taken her to the local cinema when it came round for the umpteenth time, and since then, musicals had dominated her film choices. Of course, she was brushing not washing, but there was no way she had any intention of brushing Alex Brownlow out of her life, despite having to deal with such sudden emotional turmoil. She stared at the mirror, trying to look serious, but it was impossible, her freckled prettiness and constant smile defied all attempts.

The continuing morning's brief pored over the feelings they already had for Alex, the Singers liked him, couldn't believe what was happening. If a character reference was needed from them, it would be difficult, Gordon would have to keep out of it completely. He'd be submitting a report but however good it was, it would appear in a file with Picket's harsh criticism of anyone labelled a 'young thug', and Greg Smart and his less than reasonable mother would give their accusation more weight than was justified. But there'd be physical evidence too; hospital report, medical opinions if necessary.

There were no physical scars on Eddie!

Gordon would like to see Alex soon. He'd get Picket, the Head and any solicitor involved to set Alex's assessment up ASAP. He'd do everything in his power to see justice done quickly and insist on Alex maintaining a clean record… He stopped himself mid thought. He wasn't being professional. The heart-over-head approach was not the attitude a clinical psychologist should be adopting. The truth might not be as cut and dried as he thought.

CHAPTER THIRTY-FIVE

George had never been what one might call an active person. Never a runner, a gym person or even a serious walker. On his feet for part of the day and walking around to the pub did not count as healthy exercise. A bit of a tummy had developed over the last few years – the inevitable middle-aged spread, he'd convinced himself – but that was about to change. His new physio was a striking brunette with sparkling eyes and a throbbing energy that hit you as she entered the room. Despite recovering from recent surgery or serious illness, men and women patients attempted to tuck their bellies in and pull back their shoulders. All that effort before Arlene had uttered a word about rehabilitation, posture or how she was going to get them ready for home. George reckoned she could have achieved that much by just standing there. Was the unexpected enthusiasm a sign of her powerful presence, their own ambition, or a shameful revelation of what they hadn't been doing?

George had got up to a passable walking pace on what he could only describe as a training machine for the seriously afflicted. He'd soon be out of the place; a couple of days had been indicated. But he needed a little more time with Arlene, who seemed to have taken him under her wing for some completely unaccountable reason. He was on the treadmill, doing his darnedest not to expose his dislike for team activity and competition. He'd imagined himself as more of a Tom Courtney in *The Loneliness of the Long Distance Runner:* exercise as an escape from harsh reality.

'You're doing well, George,' she said, her teeth glistening in the clever lighting, designed to make everyone look less ill than they were.

He tried to puff out his chest a bit more but failed due to breathlessness and muscle fatigue. He was sweating. Arlene spotted him struggling.

'Take it easy, George. When I said you were doing well, I didn't expect you to aim for a marathon,' she smiled, putting an arm on a shoulder to steady him.

George smiled back and felt encouraged to end his session.

He was mighty pleased to flop into the nearest chair and contemplate his situation. He knew he was well on the mend. The brain cells were coming back to life, and he was already revising a series of tricky dovetail joints on an imaginary suite of oak furniture.

But what about Florence and Alex? The boy would be alright, no doubt about that. Would the recovering patient be able to stay with his wife and son until he got on his feet a bit more? Surely Florence couldn't deny him that!

CHAPTER THIRTY-SIX

Two significant but unrelated events happened. The Brownlows' house sale had been confirmed, completion date was set for next Monday, and Vera Harris had embraced her Twelve-Step therapy to the point of...enthusiasm.

As self-appointed guest speaker for the session, she took to the floor like a seasoned professional. Well, more a well-oiled one, really. She'd been drinking heavily and made no attempt to disguise it.

Vera had been mentally running through her various relationships and rated them in order of enthusiasm and ultimate satisfaction. Florence Brownlow came an easy bottom of the class. Too timid, pathologically disinterested and a disappointment for all concerned. Mamazon was tops because she was the most straightforward and honest – *exactly what it says on the tin,* as they say. She looked and acted like a female gorilla who ate, drank, and did all the physical stuff – including sex and lifting weights – like anything wild might do; spontaneously, naturally, and sometimes very aggressively... Whether she drank or not didn't affect her performance, only its momentary urgency.

'I can't do anything without a drink,' declared Vera. 'I can't take a class, or write a lecture or face the public...' The group nodded. 'I can't even pick up the phone to contact someone I know, without having a drink first,' she smiled. 'I've tried, I really have but...' They'd all been there. 'I know you'll think I'm a failure, this is my third week and I've got nowhere.' Arms were ready to reach out, but no one actually moved. The group could easily have laughed at Vera's expectations. Three weeks was barely a minute in the programme of a recovering alcoholic.

Sympathetic mutterings were heard but no one attempted to speak. Not yet. This was a critical moment for Vera, a confession outside of Father John's tomb-like and overly protective confessional. And a moment each and everyone in the group must have gone through: the trying without any obvious signs of success; expecting too much too soon. But Vera thought that joining AA was as good as wrapping the whole thing up, that once she was in the system, sobriety was compelled to follow quickly. She didn't have the patience for journeys.

'They're important points, Vera,' said the team leader. 'The benefits of these seminal moments aren't fully realised until much later in most cases. You have to be patient as well as honest. Everyone here knows recovery is not a quick fix,' she said, sweeping her hand round the group, 'but with our concerted help and your determination it is possible.'

'Explain that?' said Vera in a sarcastic tone, unable to grasp the significance. She'd failed, for God's sake!

'Firstly, you've admitted trying to give up the booze and secondly, openly declared that you weren't able to make it happen. Acknowledging failure is a positive sign, not a negative one. Believe it or not, that's a big result, Vera.' All heads nodded reverentially. 'You're now saying it like it is and that starts a powerful series of unfolding steps.'

'So, all I have to do now is say it like it is without the booze, is that what you're saying?'

'Something like that,' she smiled. 'Anyway, you've got the idea.'

The Brownlows' house sale had not gone smoothly, but eventually the deal went through. The arm-waving buyer and her demolition husband made several attempts to rubbish the house further, called in a second survey, tried to provide evidence for defects that weren't there, offering to waive them for another reduction in price. At the end of the day the couple knew they had a bargain and could see that Florence and Alex were at the end of their patience. There was a choice; stop their mean-spirited practice or risk losing the house. They chose the house.

Florence had welcomed the removal men with a cup of tea and chocolate digestives. The packet disappeared along with a second cuppa. They'd travelled some way, and it was lunch time.

This must be teatime, she thought as, an hour later, they tucked into their lunchboxes and hinted that it was time for Florence to put the kettle on.

With their questionable strapline, WE WILL MOVE THE EARTH FOR YOU, writ large across the back and sides of the pristine black truck, they emptied the place in no time. That said, Alex, with the help of Florence, had boxed everything up apart from the furniture.

A little way down the street, builders with some serious equipment were ready to enter the vacated house. In the car behind them sat the arm-waving purchaser and her eager husband who'd come prepared with overalls, gloves, and a flat cap ready to converge, destroy then rebuild their new home. He had a clipboard with plans, instructions, and an envelope full of twenty-pound notes.

Builders liked cash, and customers expected a discount for helping the workers avoid the taxman. Especially these customers.

Florence took Alex on a goodbye tour of the house. They were dry-eyed, silent, and not quite in the mood for nostalgia.

CHAPTER THIRTY-SEVEN

While he was waiting for his session with Gordon Singer, Father John thought about Florence Brownlow and Vera Harris. He hadn't seen them for a while and wondered whether they'd drawn a line under their relationship or carried on to such an extent that even the confessional would give little respite from their rollercoaster existence.

'Please come in, Father,' said Gordon, from his clinic doorway. He shook the priest's hand and followed the greeting with a sustained guiding arm around the man's shoulders.

Gordon had learned early on in their relationship that the human touch, apart from shaking hands or embraces from the bereaved, was a less than frequent treat for Father John. The priest had never been married, never had a romantic relationship with a man or a woman – which might or might not be true – but yearned for the close contact that only such a relationship could ensure. Gordon knew that.

'Please take a seat,' he said, as he walked behind the desk to take his own.

Father John needed little bidding to sink into the enveloping warmth of the Singers' well-chosen patients' chair.

'How are you, Father? Has the week been kind to you?' asked

Gordon, knowing from experience that days could be kind as well as people. Especially in the caring professions.

Maybe it was time he signed this patient off? The priest said he'd benefitted greatly, absorbed all the strategies he could to cope with a life full of demanding people and their easily revealed secrets.

'I'm doing well, thanks to you, Gordon. I'm most grateful. I realise now that there is no *getting better*, as far as anyone in a priest's profession is concerned, it's more to do with *coping better*. You've taught me that, something I hadn't realised until depression brought me down a peg,' he said, gazing at his ecclesiastical ring which he started to turn distractedly.

Gordon nodded at the sense of it. 'Either way, the priesthood cannot be less than a lonely and sometimes painful existence. But the joy it brings to you, the priest, must be hard to measure because the result tends to manifest, ultimately, outside the confessional and away from the church.'

Father John had never quite thought of it that way.

'Often that's enough. People are grateful, and the priest is gratified,' continued Gordon, '...or should be. Not easy when you're depressed. Impossible, probably. At the end of the day, it's about perspective and contentment, and how much pleasure empathising with others gives us in our most testing moments. Things we try to impart through our sessions here at the clinic.'

'I didn't want this to turn into a weekly confessional, Gordon, but I can understand the advantage. Unburdening oneself when in the darkest of places, has more benefit than I ever imagined. Prayer is not enough.'

Thinking again, Gordon wasn't quite sure that this was the best moment to tell the priest that he should end therapy and see how things panned out. 'When perspective starts to slide, and anxiety and depression step in, the men and women involved in our profession are here and always eager to help,' said Gordon, implying that he was always on the end of a line for his patients. Just a phone call away.

But patients were known to lie. Saying they were doing well when they were too embarrassed to admit they weren't. Priests lied too. Everybody lied if they thought it was to their advantage or were scared to admit they'd failed – yet again. Lying was never a long-term solution because no one could sustain falsehoods for any length of time.

Father John leant forward in his chair as if about to reveal more than he'd done so far. The body language was that of a fellow conspirator. 'Listening to confessions over the years has made me less keen than ever to form a close relationship with another of my species... We're all so flawed, so unpredictable, so damaged by the vagaries of life. But I realise that true companionship can be the greatest comfort of all. Perhaps I ought to reconsider my thoughts on that.'

'The fact you're thinking that way proves that it might be where your heart wants to take you. But it's worth mentioning, this often happens after a course of therapy, the patient wants to change their life. That's a good thing, the whole idea of making the shift from struggling on one's own to seeking help. But taking the leap all in one go, especially when considering a long-term relationship, can be too much too soon and end in disaster.'

Father John sat back in his seat and steepled his hands against his lips in consideration. Or was it prayer?

Sometimes they slept in separate beds, occasionally in separate rooms. Nothing to do with a deterioration in their relationship, more to do with being free to choose where to be when the mood took, without offending a partner. Gordon and Imogen had agreed the unusual arrangement before they'd got married. No doubt it was a unique and unprecedented scheme.

The thing is, they were both loners at heart, yet the need for isolation and close human contact were a mix they decided needed a unique plan. Through their clinical practice they'd witnessed many a relationship fall apart, because neither partner could tell the other why they needed space, without causing offence. Breakups or even divorce would ensue! They could see why; moving to another bed or another room, without serious discussion, seemed a provocative and hostile act. Unless you'd both managed to agree terms before you bought the beds.

When their days had been long and testing, the same bed with arms entwined and silence, suited them. When they'd been enlivened by the day, energy and adrenaline up, they took to separate beds in the same room and discussed things that were troubling them without risking each other's warmth sending them off to sleep. But when they'd had too much of each other, separate rooms fitted the bill because the atmosphere of two emotionally saturated people in the same room did not facilitate a restful night.

Right now, they'd decided on space but not distance. The soft lights of wall lamps sent a glow onto the bedside tables and arced upward in a triangular beam. They were both on their backs.

'Lots going on,' said Gordon, staring at the ceiling.

'Sure is,' said Imogen, comfortable in the words they used to kick-start a meaningful discussion.

'Mary's birthday next week. Can you believe she'll be fourteen? Only yesterday she was holding our hand to cross the street. Look at her now,' said Gordon. He thought back to one of the toughest moments in parenthood, when a child no longer wants to hold your hand. Essential for the child, sad for the parent, but necessary for both.

'Will we invite Alex?' asked Imogen.

'I'd like to but it's tricky. I have to vet him and supply a report for the school and Picket. That hasn't been arranged yet. I don't want any upset at the party. But...'

'But what?'

'Mary won't be happy if he's not there. Do you think they've already discussed the issue? They must have, she's unlikely to let that go,' said Gordon.

'Let's talk to her tomorrow. See how the land lies,' she said, knowing darned well that Mary would not feel obliged to negotiate. It was her party and she could invite who she liked. 'How was Father John?'

'Doing well. Or so he says,' said Gordon, a hint of scepticism in his tone.

'Do you doubt him then? He looks a lot more relaxed.'

He turned to face her, pulling the duvet over his shoulders in the cooling room. 'We both know that feeling well, Imogen; what a person says doesn't always match up with the therapist's gut feeling. Something's not quite right, but maybe it's my interpretation. Do you remember, must be ten years ago, that disillusioned deacon had come up against a lot of opposition when he questioned the system too much. I asked him if he thought that priests told lies. His answer was funny but telling…'

'Is the pope Catholic?' That's what he said, she'd interrupted, before he could finish the sentence.

They both laughed. 'And when I asked if priests were prone to anxiety and depression, he gave exactly the same response.'

'We've been here before, Imogen. The more sophisticated and erudite the patient, the more easily fooled we are and the bigger and more well disguised the lies. They often manage to get the body language right too.'

'But we don't get many priests.'

'What's the difference? We shouldn't discriminate, we're all the same under the bonnet. Anyway, the thing is, Father John is considering a relationship. Companionship probably, but who knows, once you get close to a warm human body…anything can happen. He didn't exactly say the word celibate, but I got the impression he's been abstinent all his life.'

'A relationship? The shock will bloody kill him,' said Imogen, breaking into a fit of laughter.

Gordon loved her like this. Spontaneous – and from here, across the room propped up on his elbow in the facing bed, he could enjoy the spectacle.

'As I see it, the perfect solution would be a dog. What could possibly go wrong with that?'

'Might be the answer. At least it would be warm, cuddly, and faithful, but I'm not sure about any interesting dialogue. Father John's a theologian, he'll need an intellectual challenge in a partner.'

CHAPTER THIRTY-EIGHT

The issue was over for Greg Smart and his spiteful mother. They'd be compelled to take steps and withdraw their accusation against Eddie and Alex. The patient would be home for a few days recovering, not just from his hospitalisation but from Alex Brownlow's visit. An event that had a more traumatic effect than the one he was recovering from. And Mother needed to rehearse her address to the Head and Picket. Probably best done by letter. Something like:

Dear Sirs,

Thankfully my son Greg Smart has been released from hospital. He's been a brave boy and had excellent care and treatment. That and an inner strength has left him able to carry on with his life.

Under the circumstance it only seems fair that we withdraw our accusations against Eddie Burns and Alex Brownlow as it would have had a detrimental effect on their record.

Yours faithfully,

Mrs Ada Smart

No rush, she'd write it out again and get Greg to give it the once-over before she posted it. The last thing she needed was for him to play the invalid for much longer, she wanted him back at school facing whatever he had to face, not curling up in a corner reading comics, delaying the day.

When Alex relayed his hospital visit to Eddie, his pal buckled with laughter, punched the air, and attempted high fives as he jumped. Alex wasn't quite so taken with the moment.

'Well, we've won, mate. They can't touch us now, can they? We just need to be at the school gates when Smartypants walks in on his first day back.'

'Don't be unkind to him, Eddie. He'll have suffered enough. Telling his ma about my visit would have been an interesting scene. You know how spiteful she can be. Don't lower yourself to their level.'

'I won't. I'll just lean casually on the school gate and smile... What's that word we struggled with in English class... *Enigmatically*, that's the one. Yes, an enigmatic smile, that's what I'll give Smart.'

'That might be even worse, but it'd be hard not to show something of our victory. Just don't milk it,' said Alex, not convinced that he'd got the message through.

Eddie had the sense to realise that he needed to change the subject. 'How's the move going?' he asked.

'All okay, we'll be there tomorrow. The place is small, and Dad will be with us for a while, but he seems to have plans. Things have changed since he's had time to think about his problems in hospital. He wants to leave home ASAP. It looks like he'll be back at work shortly and able to rent a room somewhere.'

'Won't you miss him?'

He looked Eddie square on. 'I never really had him to miss, Eddie. Our family's different... We're not close like yours. It's what I've grown up with. Not a problem.'

'But your mum goes to church,' said Eddie, believing that Christians were all-round good people with lots of affection and close family ties. Eddie had no interest in religion but was quite intrigued, observing his parents attempt to find the right faith for them. They were interested in Quakers at the moment. They liked the idea of calm without effort, they could be silent and didn't have to sing hymns or go to confession. And no organ music. Which was a big plus for his dad.

The Brownlows' new home was neat but small. The flat, part of a terraced house in a busy little street without parking, suited them. None of the fittings were that old and the present décor would be okay for a while. They weren't that fussed about wallpaper and paint anyway. The spare room for Father was a nine-by-ten-foot box with a single narrow bed. Not great, but he wouldn't be staying long.

The coolness between his reunited parents was palpable. Ma provided meals but was silent most of the time. They ate what she cooked, which was not always the most nourishing diet, but she had a lot on her mind. Alex guessed he might help with the catering at some point.

CHAPTER THIRTY-NINE

The church was packed for Father John's funeral. People who'd never have met again had it not been for his death, turned up, oblivious of who would be there. But they'd all been under his wing, at some point, some just fleetingly. Regular congregation, confessionals, and a fair smattering of the homeless, combined to form a colourful tapestry. Nuns peppered the middle row with their stark black habits and pale faces.

George Brownlow decided to sit on his own at the rear of the nave and took a great interest in the building. The beautiful Norman church boasted the burial of a Wessex king. The flintstone chequered walls and shingled spire gave it a unique character. He admired the features of the cruciform building and would spend most of the funeral service surreptitiously admiring the woodwork, the clever joinery involved in the building of ancient pews and intricate roof timbers.

The stained glass was spectacular but didn't quite capture the same interest. He imagined himself as one of the craftsmen waving around on a vertiginous wooden scaffold directing his men toward the finishing detail. He puffed out his chest for a moment. He'd have been good at that.

Everyone sat quietly. Only one person outside remained once

the others filed in. Mamazon was almost lost, standing in the surrounding foliage of the church yard, like some primate about to step out of the jungle, except she didn't. People inside, particularly Vera and Florence, wondered why she'd turned up at all. The colossus was no shrinking violet, so why didn't she join the rest of the congregation? Neither were aware that she'd not been anywhere near a church for decades.

Mamazon, a lapsed Catholic for many years, was there on behalf of a bedridden mother who'd been a staunch supporter all her life, and one of Father John's greatest admirers. But once she'd spotted Vera and Florence, her courage failed.

She could at least report back to her mother that she'd been at the church, and just hope she didn't have to answer questions about the service.

Vera and Florence had already swapped unsettling looks whilst they waited to enter the church. Both had ignored the large figure of Mamazon looking lost amongst the sizeable privet hedges.

Vera used all available pillars and pews to steady herself as she headed toward a seat. Perhaps the liquid assistance she'd taken before leaving the house was a bit too much, considering the circumstance.

The usual pre-service bustle calmed as everyone settled, but only in the physical sense because most minds present were going through hell.

Vera and Florence sat on opposite sides of the aisle. Constable Picket, Mr Hawkins the Head, his secretary Miss Peel and deputy Ms Kinley sat in the same row midway down the church. Gordon, Imogen, and Mary sat together, slightly closer to the pews nearest the sanctuary, which were more or less empty. There appeared to be no family members or close friends intimate enough to claim their right to a front row seat.

Mary felt relaxed enough to wave across the aisle at Alex and Florence. They responded likewise. Gordon and Imogen smiled back, wondering why husband George, newly released from hospital – and having moved swiftly away from his wife as they entered the church – was sitting at the back studying the vaulted ceiling.

Florence attempted to hold Alex's hand, which he gently removed. Teenagers did not hold their mother's hand unless it was to comfort them in a grief-stricken moment. But he knew, this was not about grief, it was embarrassment and shame.

Gordon's instincts had been pointing in the right direction, but never fully alerted him to the fact that Father John had been lying about finally coming to terms with his suicide ideation. Psychotherapy had certainly given him perspective and hope, but Gordon was reluctant to admit that nothing could have saved the priest.

He opened the order of service as the organ struck up Bach's *Toccata and Fugue in D minor*. Not a favourite, and even less of one since the old instrument had obviously not been tuned recently. The opening chords were deafening and seemed to vibrate through every pew, and every member of the congregation.

The coffin was sprinkled with water before it was carried down the aisle.

Mr and Mrs Singer were not Catholics, so the ritual and the service was like something from a distant past. There would be no Mass but there was bowing and kneeling, prayers, hymns, readings from the Old Testament. One that struck Gordon in particular. He followed the words in the order of service as they were spoken.

Vera decided that the empty front pew deserved occupying. How sad that no one close to the minister was sitting there, she thought. She picked her moment to grope along the aisle as the governing cleric stood up to commence his reading.

The residing priest, Father Donovan, in a crystal-clear voice which reached every part of the church, would have been heard by Mamazon out in the grounds, if she was still there.

A reading from the book of Lamentations 3:17–26
It is good to wait in silence for the Lord to save. My soul is shut out from
peace; I have forgotten happiness. And now I say, 'My strength is gone,
that hope which came from the Lord…'

My goodness, thought Gordon, even a bible reading gave more
insight to Father John's state of mind. He must have chosen the
text in a dark moment – while he was in therapy! A brief wave of
depression swept over him, enough to inflict blame and doubt on
his ability. He reflected on his change of attitude as his practice
and experience matured, swinging from perpetual optimism to
perpetual realism. Which included painful periods of self-
analysis.

The much-loved Father had apparently overdosed on opioids
and consumed a large amount of alcohol. His housekeeper found
him, fully dressed, lying on his sofa with an open bible on his
chest. There was no note, just a highlighted biblical text, which
confused everyone who read it. *Ecclesiastes 3:1-8 – 'There is a time*
for everything, and a season for every activity under the heavens.'

Not so long ago, Father John would not have been able to have
this send-off. A ban on funerals for suicides had only recently
been lifted in the Catholic Church. Until the 1980s the taking of
anyone's life, including one's own, was considered murder.

The congregation tried to ignore the lone figure of Vera Harris
at the front of the church. They'd been successful for the most
part, until they knelt for prayer at which point her snoring could
have woken the dead. The church had an echo quality when a
congregation was silent which added extra weight to the snorting,
grumbling, rumbling, and whistling of Vera's emanations.

George stopped examining the architecture, Florence wanted
to die, while Mary and Alex had a fit of the giggles. Gordon and
Imogen stifled their laughter while Picket and the school heads
stiffened as if they'd been interrupted during court proceedings.
Prayers were short-lived and damage limitation included the

singing of a rousing version of 'Amazing Grace', which woke Vera
and calmed everything down.

Father Donovan delivered the brief tribute.

Congregations were often surprised when little gems of the
deceased's lives were revealed by someone close. Little insights
that were never revealed in the course of their friendships. Not
this time!

No one in the congregation had any idea of how well the two
priests had known each other but it sounded like a eulogy
delivered from a script written by a stranger. The voice
wonderful, the message, disappointing for all who knew him. It
could have been any man of the cloth.

'...He was a much-admired theologian, published some of his best
works, lectured extensively and was respected internationally. His work
in the community...' he paused for effect...'made a difference.
Something we all aspire to in our lives. He was loved by all, relentless in
his pursuit of the truth and lived a humble life serving others...

He finished, far too suddenly for most, by inviting everyone
back to the town hall for refreshment. Nothing much had been
revealed about the man who'd touched their lives, Father John,
except to learn that his father had been a pious man who'd never
pursued a career in the church.

On a bench outside the church, a lone guitarist played and
sang the Beatles number, 'Let It Be'. Rumour had it that Father
John loved this song, but it confirmed something else to Gordon
Singer; that even Father John's favourite song was steeped in
melancholia.

The reception, wake, bun fight was held in the event section of
the town's municipal building. The oak-panelled room smelling
of wax polish and food looked like a large classroom to Alex and
Mary. But they were delighted to discover they could just fill
their plates with food and wander off to a corner for a chat. They
were the only youngsters present. So long as they kept their

heads down, they'd be invisible to the congregation of grieving adults.

They chose a little bench seat close to the exit. Most people were standing, though chairs and small tables were scattered casually about the place making it an appealing option for the less gregarious. Several moved tables and chairs together, others went off to a corner carrying what they needed to enjoy their food and drink away from the masses.

Mary chose a cucumber sandwich and fruit cake while Alex, embarrassed once they'd sat down and checked each other's plates, piled his plate with two sandwiches, a fruit cake and a chocolate one.

'Are you vegetarian, Mary?'

'No, but I lose my appetite when I'm sad... I can see you're not affected,' she laughed. 'It's my birthday next week. You'll soon find out what a pig I can be.'

'Really?' he said, holding his breath in anticipation...

'You'll be invited of course.'

'Even though I'm going to be interrogated by your dad?'

'It's my party.'

'I don't want to make it awkward for your parents.'

'Don't worry, once everybody's arrived, they'll make a hasty exit. You won't see them for the rest of the party.'

'They trust you?' he asked, unable to grasp the concept; parents allowing teenagers the freedom to take over the house with their pals.

George had remained in the church studying, in depth, the construction of the hefty doors, the entrance arch and anything else that took his interest. He must have had a sign saying, *don't bother me I'm busy*, because no one approached him.

Mamazon had disappeared some while ago. They'd called a taxi and bundled Vera into it before she took advantage of the free alcohol now available in the town hall. Florence breathed a sigh of relief and gravitated to anyone standing alone twiddling an empty glass.

Gordon and Imogen got stuck with the school heads and Constable Picket who took on a different persona once food and a glass of wine entered the equation. The scene made Gordon optimistic about how the 'Alex Brownlow affair' would turn out. The atmosphere generally developed that of a low-key party. People lightened up and Father John's suicide became less a part of conversations.

Alex had managed to secure a can of beer which he shared with Mary. The sudden fizz tickled both their noses and made them cough. Mary had tasted good wine at home, but never beer. Alex had never tasted beer, only cheap red plonk left in his Ma's glass at the end of a testing day and an early night. For teenagers, their drinking history was laughable.

'Tell me the truth about the scrap with Greg,' inquired Mary. 'Did you really put him in hospital?'

Alex felt a little puffed up for a moment, chuffed that Mary thought he could beat such a bully. 'Course not. It's not in me. Eddie sorted it out, he took my side. But the reason Smart ended up unconscious wasn't due to a beating; he hit his head when he tripped backward over the kerb. It was an accident, not the vicious attack he claims.'

'So why the big fuss with Picket and the Heads – and my dad?' she asked.

'Smart and his mum got together and made things out to be worse than they were. Probably trying to get compensation or it might just be revenge. But I think I've scuppered their plan.'

'How?'

Alex hesitated, not wanting to be seen as a clever dick. 'I went to see Smart in hospital. There was nothing wrong with him. He'd look an absolute fool if he proceeds with his ridiculous claim. Once Picket and the Heads see how free of injury he is, they'll send him off – *with a flea in his ear*, as my mum would say. And to cap it all, he was reading the *Beano* in his dad's pyjamas, and blushed like hell when he saw me.' Alex had a pang of remorse for revealing Smart's secret indulgence.

Mary was laughing, more from relief than titillation.

'By the time the medical reports get into the hands of all concerned he'll look a complete idiot. I think he'll drop it. It's been all quiet on the Western Front since I visited him.'

'Do you know his mum?'

'No, but my guess is that she's a bully too. There's no dad on the scene, as far as we know, so I expect she's had to be tough...'

'Brownlow!' The Head walked over, stared sternly and fixedly at the beer can next to Alex and walked on.

Message received, loud and clear, thought Alex, his face flushed scarlet. Mary put a steadying hand on his arm.

CHAPTER FORTY

Everyone at Oakland's Joinery looked surprised to see George striding through the company gates to meet the boss. Apart from Oliver Oakland, of course, who wasn't, because he'd invited him and had kept all the results of George's healing progress close to his chest until he was certain the man was out of the woods and ready for work.

The smell of fresh timber was like a perfumery to George. He didn't work with the most aromatic, the cedars and cypresses, but he knew them all. The earthy, mossy aroma of oak was his favourite and it overpowered him now.

Employees nodded, and one or two shook his hand and welcomed him back. They'd all written him off, a goner ready to kick the bucket, but he was looking as officious as ever and maybe even a little healthier than when he was last at work.

They watched him climb the staircase, his staircase, to the open-plan office. His hand ran affectionately along the highly polished handrail. Oakland was at the office door, ready to welcome his old employee back.

'It's a miracle, George,' said the boss as he took the man into his office and ordered tea. 'You look fantastic. Take a seat, give me the latest, how do you feel?' he enquired in one breathless sentence.

'I'm ready for work,' said George. 'I've been signed off at the hospital, apart from a check-up in a few months' time. Just routine. I've been having regular sessions with my physio, Arlene, and feeling as fit as can be,' he laboured.

Oliver was a realist, and given what George had gone through and the rumours abounding his family life, he couldn't be quite as optimistic as the man in front of him.

'Well, George, here's the plan. I know you feel ready, but you've had a hell of a knock, and we want you to take it a step at a time...'

George went to interrupt. He was totally ready!

'... Hear me out. We want you to assist the present foreman for a month and see how it goes. He's not as experienced as you, or as good, if I'm honest, but until you can prove you're back to your old self, I'm not prepared to take risks. And when that time is up, we'll need you to undergo a full medical, both here and with the hospital or health centre, then we can decide how to go forward.'

George wanted to say more about how fit and reliable he would be but knew that the boss and the company would have to be one hundred percent reassured. The medicals would be stringent.

'So, what can I do?' he asked, unable to hide the disappointment in his voice.

'Be a second-in-command foreman. Use your experience and knowledge to help a younger man be as good as you. Follow him like a stalker. Don't be afraid to offer advice or take over when he's struggling. As long as you don't actually operate the machinery!' he said, unable to stop his finger wagging like a guiding parent.

George was certainly puffed up about the boss wanting the temporary foreman to be like him. He was sure that, following a month's trial, he'd come out top man with two glowing medical reports to confirm it.

'You'll get a drop in wages whilst you're on support duty, but once the probation month is over, that could change. Let's see how it goes. Good to have you back, George,' he said, slurping his tea noisily, hoping George wouldn't make a fuss about his reduced income. To be fair he had intimated that when he visited the hospital, so it shouldn't be a surprise. George would be able to pay some rent and who knew where his life will take him then?

'Let me introduce you to the guy you'll be working with,' he said, reaching for a button on the intercom system.

George could see the employee approaching the office through the surrounding glass. He was touched to see the guy run his fingers respectfully over 'George's handrail' as he ascended the unique staircase. This had a positive effect on George. *A man of taste*, he thought.

They were still sipping tea when the foreman tapped on the door before entering the office. 'Morning, Delroy, sorry to take you off the floor. It's busy down there,' said the boss looking out across the joinery shop and the bustle of a Monday morning. 'We won't keep you, but this is the legendary George Brownlow, the man you've taken over from,' he said.

George stood up and shook the hand of the young man in front of him. Delroy was a smiling six-foot-two Jamaican with the whitest teeth George had ever seen. He felt somewhat intimidated; Delroy's size and glamorous appearance had affected George's confidence. His hand felt small when the other man gripped it and shook it for longer than the occasion warranted.

'Pleased to meet you, George. Congratulations on that amazing staircase, it's a masterpiece. I'm looking forward to working with you.'

George rarely blushed but he came close.

Oliver sipped the last of his tea and suggested Delroy take George onto the shop floor and reintroduce him to his workmates. It would give the old hand a chance to pick up the atmosphere and see how well, or not, things had been going in his absence.

'Good idea,' declared Delroy putting an arm around George's shoulder as he guided him out onto the staircase.

George's immediate reaction was to shrug him off but decided not to. If he was going to work with this guy, they needed to get along. Boss would be watching, and no doubt Delroy would be reporting back at regular intervals.

George's eye swept the joiners shop as he descended the staircase. Things looked a bit more relaxed, too relaxed for his liking. People couldn't be like this and work hard at the same time. Not in his book at any rate. You had to get your head down, nose to the grindstone.

The workers obviously liked Delroy. The exchange of smiles as George was reintroduced to his workmates was not the usual Oakland's Joinery way. More like the Caribbean way as if they were on some sort of working holiday or a gap year.

The penny dropped. The workplace was happier, but production was down because Delroy was too laid back and the boss had been too polite to say so. Oaklands had employed a slightly less capable man but a more relaxed one. A combination which didn't always mean an increase in profits for the company.

George's heart lifted. He felt confident that his trial would end in success because the way things were going now, profits were probably being sacrificed for mateyness. Or maybe his colleagues had been introduced to marijuana, which he'd heard was popular in Delroy's part of the world.

As George was guided back to the factory gates, he turned and looked up toward Oliver in his high glass office. Oliver was staring right back and gave George a hearty wave.

George didn't do skipping, but inside he had all the light-hearted feelings that most probably preceded the act. He was smiling and couldn't wait to tell his family the good news. What family? He didn't belong to one now.

He let himself in through the front door of the new flat and met silence. No one at home. Alex was at school and Florence must be working hard on her morning shift at the bakery. He wouldn't know how to tell them anyway. Alex would be pleased. Florence would, in a sense, but only because it was a step closer to him being able to finance a rented room and be getting out of her life.

He put the kettle on and fumbled around looking in various kitchen units before finding the necessary mug, spoon, and tea. He switched the kettle on.

It was all very strange.

A key turned in the front door lock and he felt the draught of cold air funnel along the narrow hall into the kitchen. Florence was home from her shift. He stiffened involuntarily as she padded along the hallway.

There was a bitter wind outside. Her lack of makeup, worn off from the morning shift, and the cold against her skin, enlivened the old scars of her operation. They stood out vividly, like proud lifeless veins on the surface of her face.

'George!'

He was dumbstruck; this was the moment he'd been looking forward to telling her that he'd soon be back at work. But her appearance froze him to the spot and memories came flooding back.

Florence entered the kitchen, dropped her bag and took another cup for herself. 'Tea?' she asked, without turning to look at her husband.

'Please,' he replied. A tear formed as he watched her move along the worktop with her back to him. They'd been lovers, intimate, then companions for many years, and now they were as remote as strangers could possibly be. He started to cry, huge racking shoulder-trembling sobs. He buried his face in his hands. Florence placed a box of tissues on the table. The thought of placing an arm around his shoulders or uttering words of comfort did not see the light of day. She placed the mug of tea in front of him. He felt the heat of it but couldn't lower his hands. His face felt hot and clammy, his eyes sore from salty tears.

'Can you go back to Oaklands?' she asked. That was all she wanted to know.

Amidst an unrelenting gush of self-pity, he managed a few fragmented words. 'Oliver Oakland…wants me back,' he croaked, without filling in the detail, that he'd be on trial for a month and that follow-up medical reports would be needed to clinch his re-employment as foreman.

'Well, that's good news,' she said, a similar outpouring of memories passing through her mind, but without the tears or the emotional crisis. No need for all that, she was going to be free, and George would have to live with it and get on with his life. No going back. Forgiveness was not in her, not yet and might never be.

But to see him so broken did have some effect. On reflection, she need never have mentioned Vera Harris. The situation hadn't affected her sexual relationship with George, that finished years ago. And intimacy, touching, cuddling, even words of love and comfort had also been a thing of the past.

She hated to see men cry, it was embarrassing and unmanly. Watching George cry was even worse. 'Drink your tea.'

Two hours later Alex rattled the front door, he'd forgotten his key. 'Sorry Ma,' he said, as she welcomed him in with a peck on the cheek. 'You're freezing, Alex. Where's your scarf?' she asked.

'I'm alright, Ma, it's in my satchel,' he said, pulling it out as evidence. 'I was too hot 'till that wind blew up our street.'

He walked into the kitchen and saw two cups. 'Dad home?' he asked.

She flicked her eyes upward.

'How did he do?'

'He'll give you the details, but he'll be back at work sometime soon,' she said, mustering a wry smile.

'That's great,' he said, realising the impact it was going to have, but he didn't feel the time was right to discuss it. 'Wanna hear my news?' he asked, in an effort to rescue his ma from further discussion about Dad. She looked tired, the scars on her face were more prominent than he'd seen them for a while. No makeup, he guessed.

'Is it about Mary?'

'How did you know?'

'Because you've gone all pink,' she smiled.

'That's the cold weather,' he said. But it could have been Ma hitting the nail exactly on the head.

'She's asked me to her birthday party next week. She'll be fourteen.'

'What're you getting her for a present?' said Florence, feeling a sudden lift in spirit; her little boy was about to start his first romance.

His pocket money savings would stretch to a record, he'd have to find out her taste in music. Or maybe a box of chocs, or… He'd think about it.

He rushed upstairs to change out of his school uniform. The spare bedroom door was half open. Alex knocked gently before entering and saw his father's sorry figure lying fully clothed on the narrow bed.

George was wiping his eyes with a handkerchief. 'Come in, son, I'm awake. Just resting.'

Alex was surprised to see his father red-eyed with residual teardrops running down the side of his face.

'Why are you crying, Dad?'

'I'm not crying, son, it's the cold room, makes the eyes water. You could keep penguins in here,' he said, unable to control the sniffling.

Alex smiled grimly. This was what his father always did, never showed weakness or emotion. His parents' lives should be past that now, but Father still hasn't learned that this very trait was what finally killed the marriage.

He placed a hand on his father's cold arm.

'I'm pleased they're taking you back at Oaklands, Dad. That's really good news,' he said, unable to offer any other comfort. The marriage was still over, and Alex had no expectations that things would or should change.

'Where did it all go wrong, son?'

Alex had a pretty good idea but now was not the time. 'Not for me to say, Dad, but you've never been very straightforward with each other, you and Ma, perhaps that might have played a part.'

'What do you mean?' he asked defensively.

'When I walked in just now, instead of admitting to crying, you said it was the cold room. I know that you'd been crying, but you wouldn't admit it.'

'Well, that's a man's way, Alex. We can't admit to every bit of blubbing and embarrass other people.'

'Maybe that was a bad example, what I was trying to say was that you and Ma try to smooth life over all the time, you never admit to anything that might upset one another, never say it like it is.'

And that's when the dam burst, he thought, remembering that horrendous day when his father turned into an animal.

'We should talk, Dad. A proper conversation, before…before you leave.'

George started to cry again but got the emotion quickly under control. 'Let's do that, son. Not here though, too gloomy,' he said, running his eyes around the freshly decorated walls. 'Let's meet down the pub and grab a drink. Always easier to talk with a glass in your hand.'

'I'm thirteen, Dad, I won't be allowed in a pub or to sit and drink in one.'

George seemed to have some difficulty coming to terms with the fact that his son wasn't old enough to enjoy a drink in their local. 'We could sit outside; you could have a lemonade and I could have a beer.'

'Let's do that,' said Alex, patting his father's shoulder as he headed for the door.

CHAPTER FORTY-ONE

Greg Smart returned to school the very next morning. His pals welcomed him back like a conquering hero, oblivious of the outcome of his ridiculous claim against Alex Brownlow and Eddie Burns. They were surprised to see how normal he looked, without the swagger and the cocky air. No scars, but they assumed he'd been traumatised. Alex and Eddie gave him a wide berth, though he didn't seem the threat he once was. They could describe him as sheepish.

'Brownlow, Burns and Smart, my office, now!' came the Head's message over the speaker system.

Eddie and Alex made a dash for the corridor. If they got there first, they might have the edge. Hawkins favoured boys who snapped to attention.

Smart hung back and let the other two enter the headmaster's study first. Not from politeness, it was fear. He knew exactly what was coming; shame, disgrace, embarrassment, in front of two witnesses he'd rather not share those emotions with.

His mother's letter lay open on the Head's desk in front of them. Any sharp-eyed kid would be able to read it upside down. Alex and Eddie, self-trained in such talents, had read it by now. They tried not to grin at each other.

Constable Picket was sitting in the corner as passive as a policeman could be under the circumstances. Miss Penny the secretary sat on the other side of the room, legs crossed, tugging her skirt over exposed knees because schoolboys could not be trusted to divert their eyes.

'No doubt news has already spread,' said Hawkins, looking directly at Greg Smart, who now seemed to be the established villain of the piece. 'Mrs Smart, your mother,' he announced, eyes still fixed on the vanquished pupil, 'has been kind enough to write in and ask us to drop all previous charges levelled at Alex Brownlow and Eddie Burns.' He placed his long-distance glasses on his forehead and reread Mrs Smart's letter.

Picket coughed for attention. 'You've had a lucky escape, all of you,' he said, as if Mrs Smart's note had less of an influence in the scheme of things. 'Bullying is on the rise; street crime is on the rise, robberies, vandalism – thuggery. There are more youngsters breaking the law than at any other time in history...' It was obvious he wanted to rattle on about the vagaries of the teenage population, but Hawkins felt it wise to concentrate on the matter in hand, and touched Picket's arm.

Picket responded, diverted from a theme he was reluctant to leave; a lecture on the morals of the young. 'Thanks to Greg Smart's mother,' he said smugly, 'you're off the hook and still have a clean record in the eyes of the law. But let me say this,' he said, waving his finger at each boy in turn, 'you may not be so lucky next time. You're free to go,' he finished, without mentioning that Greg Smart and Eddie looked unscathed. It was only Alex who displayed evidence of the tussle, a small red scar.

Greg Smart's face turned from white to pink.

Miss Penny finished the interview notes by signing off with a theatrical flourish, an action which required her to adjust her skirt once more. None of the boys noticed, and only the eagle eye of Constable Picket, who dreamed of becoming a detective, took in the detail.

They filed out. Smart first as he needed the bathroom. Eddie and Alex smiled but decided to wait until they were outside before swapping notes on their meeting with the Head and Picket.

They leaned against a wall and watched Smart exit the building. Two of his pals rushed over to greet him but were put out when he told them he wanted to be alone. It didn't take them long to realise that things hadn't gone well, and they shrugged and walked away, leaving Greg Smart to come to terms with his defeat.

'I want to go over and say something,' said Alex.

'Like what?' asked Eddie, who'd no intention of talking to the guy who'd caused them so much trouble. As far as he was concerned, Greg Smart was an outcast and deserved it.

'Something a bit friendly. When I visited Smart in hospital, I saw a different side to him. I think he'd been bullied himself, at home maybe. I don't know his dad, but they say bullies have usually been bullied themselves. Being caught out by us probably made him look foolish.'

Eddie tried to work out Alex's bizarre reasoning. Why would someone who'd been bullied want to make friends with a bully? Smart was the enemy for God's sake, always had been and always would be.

'I don't want to be his friend, but I'd like to be able to pass him without confrontation,' continued Alex. 'It may be the only chance we have because once he gets back with his gang, he may start thinking he's the tough guy again.'

'But then you can remind him of that hospital visit; when you caught him reading the *Beano* in his dad's pyjamas,' said Eddie, chuffed that he'd managed to find the perfect solution.

'I could do that, but it would be using the same tactics as Smart. I want to be better than him, not so unkind.' *But not such a bad idea, if all else fails.*

Eddie struggled with the logic. War is war. You didn't start cosying up to the enemy just because he'd gone all soft and girly. 'I don't get it, Alex. What're you going to say anyway? Whatever it is, please leave me out of it. I've no intention of trying to pal up with that creep.'

'Not pal up, Eddie, just draw a line under things.'

Alex left Eddie to ponder the situation and walked over to Greg Smart who was leaning on a brick pier at the school entrance. It was some seconds before either made eye contact.

'Greg.'

'Alex.'

Greg stood silent, unable to comprehend the moment.

'Tough in there, wasn't it, Greg?' asked Alex. Drawing them both into the same awkward situation was a good start. No one could deny the truth of it.

'Yeah,' replied Greg, needing Brownlow to say more if he expected any sort of response.

'I've been thinking. When I saw you at the hospital it wasn't easy for either of us, but I knew things weren't as they seemed. You were different without your mates around. I guess we all are. But I think we should be able to rub along somehow. Not be friends exactly, but less than the enemies we've been so far. A bit kinder maybe.'

Greg made direct eye contact and held it for some moments. 'I'm in a gang, Brownlow, I can't afford to be girly, or I'll lose my mates, they'll laugh and give me a hard time.'

'If they laugh at you for being one of the good guys, you have to ask yourself, what sort of mates are they? But I understand, I think.' Alex was racking his brain. These guys must have had different lives, maybe they'd been brought up with bullying and violence, it was probably their norm.

'We've got a reputation.'

'Not a good one though.'

At that moment, Mary crossed the schoolyard with a couple of her pals and gave Alex an enthusiastic wave. He gave an even more energetic one back. No need to keep their relationship secret anymore. He'd met her parents, they liked him. Didn't matter who found out now, and all the rumours spread by the likes of

Greg Smart and his mates had no impact on current school tittle-tattle. It was old news and accepted that Alex Brownlow and Mary Singer were a couple.

Greg's eyes flickered, as he looked down at his shoes and avoided taking in the romantic scene playing out in front of him.

'Do you have a girlfriend, Greg?'

'Not steady. Why? What's that got to do with anything?' he said, aware he'd had a sudden attack of envy.

'You and your pals always give me and Eddie a hard time, and in front of Mary Singer too,' he said, noticing a sudden increase in Greg's blink reflex. 'Girls don't like bullies. I never see you or your mates with a girl, I'm curious.'

Greg didn't have an answer. He thought girls went for the tough macho type. But couldn't explain why neither he nor his mates had ever gone on a proper date.

'Is that what you came over to talk about, Brownlow?'

'No, I want us to shake hands and stop the unpleasantness between us. I think you're a good guy mixing with…guys who are not so good. I want us to pass each other in the playground or street or on the bus without the threat of you and your mates giving us a hard time. It's not nice. You wouldn't like it. And it only gets you hated and feared.'

Smart could see nothing wrong at all in being feared but he didn't want to be hated. 'I'll try,' he said, remembering Alex's hospital visit and him being less damaged than he'd made out. If he was to be totally honest, he was living in fear too, scared Alex Brownlow might spread that hospital scene around the school.

'What if I don't shake hands?'

'*Beano*, your dad's pyjamas and a lying mother doesn't do you any favours, Greg.'

'Is that a threat?'

'A reminder.'

Alex offered his hand and Greg Smart took it. Alex's was dry while Greg's was clammy. Both boys knew at that precise moment who'd won the day.

CHAPTER FORTY-TWO

Alex ran a hand over his face but remained undecided as to whether he would start shaving. The hairs were darker and a little thicker than when he last checked. He'd heard that once you started, it was destined to be a daily chore. And who was going to look that closely? No one. Not with such scrutiny anyway. But suppose Mary kissed him on the cheek when he arrived? He smiled at himself in the mirror. Live dangerously, put the shaving on hold for a while.

So, he ran himself a decent bath with lots of bubbles and wallowed for longer than intended. Excitement and nervousness, and not an insignificant amount of fear, washed like waves through his lengthy ritual.

Ma had left early for her shift at the bakery and Father was enjoying his last few days of relative freedom. He was asleep. Alex was grateful because he wanted this moment, this day, to be exclusively his.

Ma had left the ironing board up, so he pressed his party outfit which only trumped his day-to-day clothes by having a bit less wear to them. But by the time he'd finished, his shirt, jumper, jeans and shoes looked pretty good. He didn't spend too much time on his hair, it had just been cut and given a style that the barber said suited him and the occasion. Short and sweet, Eddie had described it, a statement which had more to do with time taken than a haircut, but the message was clear. Not a style at all, just a barber taking the easy way out with his clippers.

The party was set for teatime, to fit in with the Singers' other arrangements. Mary didn't care too much when it was, as long as it happened, and she could invite who she liked. The weather was good, so they'd eat it outside.

He'd bought her a record, *The Bee Gees Greatest*. He thought it was good music with a subtle romantic element. Everyone loved the Bee Gees.

It was barely lunchtime, but Alex was nervous and ready, three hours before he needed to leave.

He'd picked up a book at the school library and thought he might start it. The title captivated him; *Man's Search for Meaning*, by Viktor Frankl. He knew little about the content except that he found it in the psychology section – the Singers' section he called it – and someone had left a makeshift bookmark in the last page, a strip of lined paper with the words; *If you're interested in the human condition, read this book*. Alex wasn't quite sure what *human condition* meant but the short volume and the scribbled note intrigued him. And Gordon Singer, his girlfriend's father, might be impressed to hear that Alex was interested in such a serious subject.

Two hours had gone before he checked the kitchen clock and decided to review his appearance; haircut, clothes, the wrapped record, and the birthday card; not too smoochy, *Hope you have a great day, Mary. Happy Birthday, love Alex*. He stopped short of adding a kiss and a heart.

It might have been a mistake reading that book on surviving the Holocaust, just hours before a celebration. It was deeply disturbing. But the author had a surprisingly optimistic viewpoint despite suffering terribly and observing others enduring the same conditions, or worse.

He wasn't in the mood for a party now, but he looked in the

mirror and gave himself a stern lecture. He was going to spend the whole afternoon with Mary.

He counted today as one of the biggest moments in his life so far.

There were no good luck notes from his parents. He knew that the event was only a big thing for him and Mary. Better this way than the other, he thought, all that fussing and advising about the way he looked, how to behave and not to be home late. None of that.

Gordon Singer met him at the front door with a manly handshake, Imogen hugged and kissed him gently on the cheek. He could hear music through the French doors as they steered him down the hallway and out toward the walled garden. It wasn't the Bee Gees playing, or anything he recognised. It was jazz. Old jazz. Nothing he could do about his record now. Anyway, the jazz might be her parents' choice.

There were only a dozen people there, half boys, half girls. He'd seen most of them at school but there were a couple of new faces. No one was dancing but they all had glasses of what looked like lemonade.

They must have turned up early. He checked his watch; he wasn't late.

Mary bounded over, threw her arms around his neck, and kissed him on his flushed cheek. She gripped his hand and took him to meet the rest of the gathering.

He felt shy, and a few he knew from school, the ones who'd never taken to him, gave him the welcome reserved for those awkward moments. Like when you turn up at a party that no one had invited you to. But the people he didn't know made him feel at ease, presumably because Mary had put a good word in, and they'd have witnessed her affectionate greeting.

'I've bought you this, Mary. A Bee Gees album,' he said, handing her the record wrapped in tissue paper. 'Sorry if it's not what you like but I can change it. I still have the receipt.'

'Don't worry, I like most music,' she commented politely. 'Do you like Miles Davis?'

'Is this him now?' he asked innocently, having never heard the name, let alone listened to him play.

She nodded. 'Dance with me, Alex,' she asked, taking his hand, and leading him onto a section of lawn which had been boarded over to protect the grass. The closest he'd ever been to dancing was to tap his foot vigorously to a catchy tune on the radio.

Heads turned to watch them. They all knew the score, but this was the first demonstration of their affection acted out so publicly and intimately.

'I can't dance, Mary,' he said, catching her scent as she whisked him away. His head spun with their sudden proximity.

'Neither can I,' she laughed, 'just follow me and we'll learn together.' She twirled, caught Alex around the waist, and spun him gently before moving to a rhythm, pulling him closer, leading him back and around in a series of unfamiliar manoeuvres that left him breathless. Not the movements alone but the smell of Mary, like something out of a garden, the closeness, the intimacy of moving back and forth in a rhythm, he found difficult to interpret. Sensual yet oddly innocent. Others started to dance. Girls stayed together at first then, as time wore on, boys got braver and before long couples formed. No booze to be had, yet he could smell alcohol on Mary's breath, which was confirmed when she gave him a quick wet kiss on the lips.

Another boy asked Mary to dance. She accepted graciously but kept her eyes on Alex, who decided to chat to one of the other boys. The conversation was short because an attractive girl asked him to dance.

He smiled. 'You don't know what you're letting yourself in for,' he confessed, 'If you'd watched me dancing with Mary, you'll have spotted my two left feet.'

The girl laughed. 'It's only moving to music,' she said, pulling him onto the lawn. 'Follow me.'

She was talented. Alex didn't feel he had to take part, it was a solo display by a girl who loved her music and didn't really need a partner to get the best out of it. Alex reckoned she must practise in front of a mirror every day to get that good.

He was dancing with a pretty girl, but his eyes were on Mary and her eyes were on him. They wanted to get close again.

'Cake!' came a shout from the French doors. Imogen walked out with a huge chocolate cake displaying fourteen lit candles. The air was still but she sheltered the flames from any possible draught. Gordon followed her closely with a knife and stack of plates and napkins.

'It's okay, we're not staying,' he laughed, 'but we wanted to join in the important bit.'

Mary was looking a bit wobbly as she approached the table where her dad had placed the cake. The candles had burnt halfway down before she managed to direct her breath accurately enough to blow them out. With one almighty puff, cheeks bulged, face reddened, the candles went out a moment before she toppled face down onto the sticky chocolate surface of her mother's homemade cake.

Alex was close to Mary's exhalation. Almost pure alcohol, it seemed. Had the candles not gone out before she toppled Mary might have gone up in flames.

The dancing stopped. Gordon and Imogen rushed forward. Alex guessed that everyone at the party was making a split-second decision, whether to laugh or cry.

Mary was standing now. Well, almost, Gordon and Imogen were holding her up, face covered in chocolate, a big dollop remaining on the end of her nose and a half-burnt candle clinging to her hair.

Mary wasn't so much guided back through the French doors, more like frogmarched by two very embarrassed parents.

Alex wanted to follow but held back. Everyone read the situation. Mary had secretly got drunk, and the parents would have to deal with the fallout.

'Wanna dance?' asked the girl who'd already performed her solo routine in front of him.

'Shouldn't we be waiting for news of Mary?' he suggested. 'Her parents might want us to go.'

'She's done this before, she'll be fine. Dance.'

Imogen and Gordon were puzzled. There was no readily available drink in the house, it was kept in a locked cabinet and only they had a key. All Mary's guests had been welcomed in by them and there'd been no signs of anything alcoholic coming into the Singers' residence.

'What shall we tell her pals? We'll have to call a halt to everything, she's fast asleep and in no fit state to be woken up to continue celebrating. How bloody embarrassing. It'll be round the school in no time.'

'That's the least of our worries,' said Imogen. 'We have an underage secret drinker in the family. A fourteen-year-old secret drinker.'

CHAPTER FORTY-THREE

Many teenage boys, for a variety of reasons, carry a few yards of string and a penknife in their pockets or hidden in a schoolbag. Eddie was one of them, in fact he was a most skilled and innovative user of such items. Unfortunately, he lost a whole length of heavy-duty twine when he lowered a half bottle of vodka over the Singers' Garden wall. The plan had gone well to begin with. Mary had reassured him that she was quite able to deal with a drink or two, but that her parents weren't ready to indulge her.

How could she party without it?

'What about your guests?' he'd asked.

'Use your brain, Eddie, they won't be getting any, will they? My parents would go mad if they saw everyone staggering around the garden. But I'm the hostess, I need help...'

'They won't be best pleased to see you rolling around drunk either,' he laughed. Mary didn't respond, so the jolly moment faded quickly.

'So, what's the plan?' he asked.

'If you walk along the path behind our house, you'll see an old tree. Exactly beneath that, on the garden side of the wall, is a compost heap. I want you to tie string around the neck of one of those flat half bottles of Smirnoff – you'll need about twelve feet. Lower it over the wall and drop it straight onto the compost. It's a big pile of grass cuttings and leaves so no one will hear it or see it. The gardener comes once a fortnight but he's not due for another week.'

'What about the string hanging around when I let it go?'

'Duh! Make a slip knot, I'll show you if you don't know how. Then you can pull it back over the wall and no one will be any the wiser.'

'I do know about knots!' he said defensively.

She smiled. 'Sorry, Eddie, I didn't mean to doubt your skills, only I'm nervous about it all. I'm not a party person but they'll expect me to be the confident hostess.'

'Well, you will be now,' he said, pocketing the money she'd given him.

'I added a bit extra for doing me a favour… And keeping our little plan to yourself,' she said, tapping the side of her nose.

Mary had known Eddie for as long as she'd known Alex. Most of the school knew Eddie Burns, he had a reputation, he was brave, daring, and mischievous. Teaching staff were aware of his notoriety too, but he had a talent for getting out of difficult situations and there were plenty of friends willing to lie for him. If he were to enter the criminal world, he'd definitely be labelled The Fixer. In fact, he'd already been called that.

Eddie agreed to Mary's plan at once. 'No problem,' was his cheerful response. He had good reason to want Mary taking a sip or two. She was more likely to loosen up for Alex. Eddie was exasperated with the slow pace of their courtship.

'It's painful, mate, like watching paint dry,' he'd told Alex.

'True love isn't a race, Eddie. It's for life,' Alex had replied.

Eddie, unable to visualise anything lasting much longer than a week, responded with a fit of laughter. 'Fuck's sake, Alex, you're thirteen not thirty.'

Eddie didn't get it. The way they were carrying on, so slow, *soooo* painfully polite, they'd be dead and buried before they managed a snog.

As it turned out Eddie's slip knot failed to slip, but the vodka, stolen from his Grandad's secret stash, landed safely amongst grass cuttings and leaf mould. The string got tangled and six feet of it hung from a low branch of the old tree. Mary was unable to shift it in time for the party but managed to secrete the bottle. She'd deal with the string later. No one would see it unless they were searching the place.

Gordon and Imogen, addressing their young guests, didn't try to hide the fact that Mary had drunk herself into a virtual coma. 'You all saw what happened,' said Gordon, his pained expression having a powerful effect on his teenage audience. 'Please put your glasses on the table. We don't want anyone else leaving here drunk.'

Everyone did what they were told, the request felt more like part of a police investigation. And hearing the Singers being so upfront about their daughter's disturbing episode was unexpected to say the least.

Imogen took on the task of testing each drink. She was surprised and relieved that none of the glasses contained alcohol, but distressed to realise that her daughter was the devil of the piece. *At least Mary had the sense not to have included anyone else in her...spree,* thought Imogen. A small mercy indeed.

By the time they were ready to turn in, Mary was asleep in her room, or pretending to be. Gordon and Imogen decided to share a bed that night, a comforting physical contact now essential. Their day had been unsettling to say the least, and they felt a big part of their life was about to change. Credibility and social standing could take a dive when one's beloved, bright, educated daughter disgraced herself so publicly. The school would know all about it within twenty-four hours and the rest of the town not so far behind.

Gordon stared at the ceiling, as a rush of potential scenarios ran through his mind like a fast forward video; how to deal with Mary and the school and how to save the family and their successful clinical practice from adverse publicity. There would be some, of course, but he'd seen these things get out of hand before, when press and public joined forces. Clients/patients, depending on their perspective, could so easily change therapists based on negative media attention.

'I'm pleased the others weren't involved,' said Imogen. 'At least it didn't turn into a drunken orgy and end up with us having to face other horrified parents. We'd have been sued for sure. How did she get hold of the booze anyway?'

'No idea, but we'll find out. She'll have to face the consequences, as will we. Damn that girl, what the hell was she thinking?' he said.

'What will those consequences be…for Mary?'

'So much depends on how she faces up to it in the cold light of day, when we've all had a night's sleep,' said Gordon. 'Tomorrow, I hope to get some answers. No excuses, just some solid reasons that'll give us a sense of hope, that this was a one-off!'

'I'm disappointed,' said Imogen, on the edge of tears. 'She's thrown up a couple of times since we carried her in, taken plenty of water and does seem settled now, but I'll check on her before we get off to sleep.'

'At least Alex wasn't involved in her shenanigans. It would have been worrying, especially after all that trouble with the school bully, Greg Sharp,' said Gordon, clinging to the vestiges of his dying optimism.

'What happened about that, in the end?' asked Imogen, her hand still resting affectionately on Gordon's chest. 'With everything going on I forgot to ask.'

'The Head rang while you were out, cancelled all our arranged consultations with the three boys involved, and admitted that Sharp and his mother had collaborated in a false accusation. Picket will know what's happened by now and won't be that pleased. He was on a mission with those lads, they'd have all gone to prison if he'd had his way,' he said, smiling grimly, thinking of the copper's lack of judgement. 'Hawkins is going to put the detail in a letter so we can file it for future reference. Alex Brownlow would have been in serious trouble, a black mark against his reputation if the process had gone ahead.'

'I'm pleased. I just hope he's not been put off Mary because of today. She made quite a spectacle of herself,' said Imogen.

'I don't think it'll make that much difference,' he said, drawing his wife closer for comfort. 'We've seen the way he looks at her, he's fallen for Mary big time. Could be puppy love but I have a feeling it's more than that. Apart from the teenage love interest, or whatever it turns out to be, he seems like a good honest lad. I like him even more now we know he's not involved in our daughter's drunken escapade.'

They could have talked and speculated all night long but knew it would be a waste of time. They needed the freshness of a morning to enable them to see things clearly.

'I'll just check on Mary,' said Imogen. She moved out from the warm covers, shivering slightly before slipping into her dressing gown and walking toward Mary's bedroom. The girl was asleep. On her bed lay a single sheet of notepaper with one word written in thick felt-tip, 'SORRY'.

Despite herself, Imogen smiled. She took the note to show Gordon, who viewed it in a more serious light. They both knew this was not going to wash, the next morning's confrontation was going to be difficult.

They held each other more closely than they had for some time. Their sense of unity magnified, not because of a sudden burst of love; it was more to do with fear. Within minutes they were asleep. The word *sorry*, from their errant daughter, had given them momentary peace.

CHAPTER FORTY-FOUR

Mary's class had all the news by the end of the morning and most of the school got the message within a couple of days. The situation wasn't helped by her absence from school; such a rare event would have caused speculation anyway.

Vera Harris had heard the latest from Dr Grayling, the school's educational psychologist, who occasionally rang her up to see how she was. It wasn't a close relationship, but they'd developed respect for each other's position at the school and their professional status.

Grayling also felt a strong sense of duty to the pupils under his care. Gordon Singer would undoubtedly speak to his daughter Mary, but being family, the perspective needed to take an unbiased view would be lost. The Head had no option but to refer Mary Singer for sessions with the school's educational psychologist for guidance. Same profession as Singer, not that Grayling kept score, but he felt it was a school related matter. A pupil's unprecedented absence and the report of extremely bad behaviour was something he was quite capable of taking on.

Vera couldn't help smiling to herself. Mary Singer had started on the road to ruin even younger than she. There was something deliciously entertaining about an apparent innocent taking a fall from grace. Especially *little miss perfect knickers* who was top of her class, pretty, and from a privileged background. She remembered her from lectures, the perfect child it seemed. Well, look at her now. The disgrace would stay with Mary Singer for quite a while, but the outcome could go one way or the other. It was a wakeup call, warning the teenager, in plenty of time, where this could lead. Or as so often happens in these situations, she'd consider her reputation shot and decide she might as well enjoy the infamy. Much depended on how the parents handled it, but even then, there were no guarantees.

Vera was still taking the Twelve Steps to sobriety. Despite all attempts to block out the irritating mantra, she found herself reciting it several times a day. At each meeting, she admitted her inability to quit drinking but had, to everyone's surprise, managed a full twenty-four hours without a drop. She received smiles of encouragement from the group while omitting the fact that she'd been asleep for that period following a bad night at the club.

As part of her attempt at rehabilitation, she'd revisited the Catholic church to suss out the new priest. Spilling the beans to a devoted listener without others joining in and airing their twopenn'orth was quite appealing. The thing holding her back initially was her much talked about performance during Father John's funeral; the staggering drunkenness and the snoring, loud enough to... *wake the dead.*

But wasn't that what priests were there for, to forgive all this stuff?

Confession with Father Donovan, the cleric who'd given the eulogy at Father John's funeral, did not turn out to be such a therapeutic experience. Mainly because whenever he was moved to speak, his voice came across loud and abrasive. His words were kind but the manner in which he delivered them resembled admonishment and felt judgmental in tone. She'd spotted him on his way to the confessional, and he had the bearing and strutting walk of a man who was not averse to harshness. The last thing she needed in her delicate state.

She was suffering her first and last visit to this particular priest, unable to shake off the feeling that every word she said was being written in a little black book to be used against her later. She was being silly, but that's how it felt.

Vera had been in reflective mode over the last few days. Some years ago, she'd read an intriguing article written by a critic, an academic turned psychologist, summarising research and his thoughts about people who fell in and out of love. The title was something like, *When Love Fails*. Apparently, it was a three-stage process. She thought it was all a bit silly at the time, something concocted by a lifelong cynic who'd never been in love at all. But now she wasn't so sure. That memory had been preying on her mind for some time.

Once the height of a love affair had been reached, quoted the author, there was a tendency for time and familiarity to take its toll. The first casualty, he'd determined, was romance; a slow deterioration in the effort of pursuit, often unnoticed by one partner but strongly felt by the other – *no need to try so hard now we're in an established relationship*. The second was sex, often to the point where alcohol was needed to enable the act to take place at all, or with any amount of enthusiasm. The third was intimacy; less touching generally, shorter on kindness and words of affection, and only holding hands in a crisis or at a funeral.

So, what was left of those relationships that had exhausted the physical element? Best guess, companionship! A togetherness that made life worth living. *If you like that sort of thing*, she'd thought at the time, but now she longed for it. And it was no big deal providing, at the end of the day, that state turned out to be… mutually acceptable.

She'd been reassured by the following data from the same source. It was possible, in rare cases, to maintain all three qualities. But the good news, for most, was it was also possible to live a fulfilled happy life without them. Perhaps she could embrace companionship a bit more fully now that her interests in carnality had waned. Was her decline due the effects of excess alcohol and too much sex? Or was it age and vital bits of her body getting worn out and numbed from overuse?

Reflecting on her more recent affairs, Mamazon had failed on the first point, excelled on the second but nosedived again on the third. It really was just sex. Florence was great on the courting bit, the 'will she, won't she' anticipation. The heightened expectations of moving on to satisfying sex kept her interested. Like seducing a virgin. But Mrs Brownlow had failed miserably when it came to the deed, it turned out to be a big disappointment.

The third stage, continuing an affectionate intimacy, was missed completely; Vera's betrayal had killed everything. She'd burned her boats the minute Florence turned up at the mews to witness Mamazon in full flow. It was, of course, unforgivable, and certainly unforgettable. But as she lay awake at night, full of alcohol and remorse, she realised how important and enjoyable the courting stage was. The promised intimacy, the kind gestures, the pre-sexual gentleness and consideration. As close to companionship as she'd ever been, and it was…to use a word she tended to avoid…lovely.

Perhaps Florence had reflected too.

Florence had indeed. The most tumultuous affair she could have imagined had set her expectations of a loving relationship back somewhat.

Companionship was high on her list, her one and only priority, always had been, nothing to do with being numbed by overindulgence in alcohol or sex. The resulting sexual escapade with Vera Harris had only confirmed what she'd feared. Her attraction to Vera, though intriguing, turned out to be less than a sexual one.

A friendship with the odd cuddle wasn't a great deal to ask, was it?

Florence was finishing her shift at the bakery and drinking a cup of tea while she tidied up. It was a nice part of the day, especially more recently as George had moved into a decent bedsit not far from his work. She felt his absence as a relief, like a thorn being removed, or the sudden lifting of a dark cloud.

He'd acquired his new residence through a lucky introduction. One instigated by Delroy, the friendly Jamaican from work who'd kept the home fires burning at Oakland's Joinery, while George recovered from brain damage.

Florence, now living with easy-going Alex, found the atmosphere remained pleasant without the underlying tension which had been impossible to escape.

It was bucketing down. She looked across the street but was unable to see clearly as far as the bus stop. The shopfront window had started to mist up forming rivulets and baffling distortions. There was a closed sign on the bakery door, but someone was trying to get in. Florence shouted from behind the counter, 'We're closed. Read the sign.'

The door kept rattling; the boss went out to see who was blind to the obvious, fearing some sort of disturbance. It had happened before, louts busting in to empty his till at the end of a busy day. He cleared the condensation with his sleeve and squinted at the obscure image; a woman he'd never seen.

She shouted, her voice muffled by the double-glazed door. 'I want to see Flo,' said the woman. 'I'm an old friend.'

'It's someone for you. Florence. Tell them to come back when we're open,' he said, stepping aside. 'On second thoughts, you're

due to go anyway,' he said, checking his watch. 'The muffins
didn't go well today, so take some home for Alex, but don't miss
that bus. See you in the morning.'

Florence felt her blood rise. She knew exactly who it was but
was at a complete loss as to why the woman who'd treated her so
badly was attempting to face her now. And how did she know
where *Flo* worked?

'Only one person calls me Flo. I don't want to see her. I'll leave
out the back.'

'What shall I tell her?' he said, checking his watch again. 'It's
pissing down out there?'

'Tell her I left early,' she said, aware that Vera Harris might
have made her out through the misty shopfront.

The door kept rattling. Vera started banging on the glass. 'Just
give me a minute, Flo. That's all I need…'

The boss opened the door, 'Sorry, luv, you missed her. Want to
leave a message?' he said, picking up a scrap of paper and taking
a pencil from behind his ear.

Vera was soaked. No umbrella and no raincoat.

'Step inside, you'll drown out there,' he offered reluctantly. He
wanted to finish his day. He gave her the pencil and she scribbled
something, folded it, and pressed it into his hand. 'Please see that
Flo gets this as soon as possible. Please.'

'That'll be tomorrow,' he said.

'Of course… By the way, is she still living in the same place?'

'I'm sorry, but we don't give staff's details to strangers,' he
said, trying not to sound unfriendly, but with Florence escaping
out the back of the building, he realised this was not someone she
was keen to meet up with.

CHAPTER FORTY-FIVE

Saturday morning at the Singers' place was usually a relaxed affair; late breakfast, reading the papers and catching up on news, personal, local, and global. This weekend was different. Gordon and Imogen were waiting for Mary to make an appearance. Both felt the tension, the anticipation of a family gathering that neither were sure they could handle well.

Their ears, finely tuned, listened for any movement emanating from upstairs. There was a soft thump as Mary got out of bed. They looked up at the ceiling, mentally following her footsteps to the bathroom. The toilet flushed, then the weekend ritual started. Mary usually spent a long time in the shower.

'She won't be down anytime soon,' said Imogen. 'More coffee?'

'Please,' said Gordon. 'Put the grill on and I'll make some toast. Might as well have ours now,' he said, picking up a newspaper. Neither needed to discuss the situation further, they'd talked it through and decided the stage would be Mary's. She would have to steer the conversation. What she said, and the way she said it, would determine the way they'd handle things. Contrition or confrontation?

The puzzle remained as to who supplied the vodka and how

Mary smuggled it in without anyone else noticing. Someone must have seen something!

Only a short amount of time had passed but as Imogen poured coffee and Gordon scraped butter and marmalade onto toast, they checked the kitchen clock and made sure it was in sync with his watch.

Mary was dragging out her ritual. It was deliberate, ensuring her parents had thrashed their interrogation plans out over morning coffee, hopefully with a new day's perspective. To face them yesterday would have been a mistake. Whatever happened, she wouldn't be naming her vodka supplier, Eddie Burns.

There were advantages and disadvantages to having parents in the psychology field. Best part was that they were more acutely aware of the human condition and all its frailties, forgave easily and were hot on problem solving. The downside was, being their daughter, tolerance levels adjusted downward and problem solving with someone so intimately related became more difficult.

She ran several potential scenes through her mind, all dependent on the way her parents looked, their first line of greeting, body language and any atmospheric clues she picked up on entering the room. She'd try not to lie, but she had to protect Eddie, especially as he was such a close pal to Alex. Guilt by association would be conferred on him for sure. *Why would Alex's (emphasis on the name) best friend supply you with booze?*

Half an hour later they heard Mary's footsteps on the stairs. Gordon had eaten his toast, drunk his coffee and turned over every page in the morning paper with only a fuzzy recollection of the latest news. Imogen was wiping surfaces and tidying kitchen cupboards, reluctant to leave the kitchen at this critical time.

They were both sitting when Mary entered. She kissed them both on the cheek and took the initiative. Maybe attempting a little humour to start the proceedings would help, she decided.

'Please don't ask how I got the vodka. I could tell you but then I'd have to kill you,' she smiled. Despite themselves, Gordon and

Imogen smiled. It lifted the mood and paved the way for reasonable dialogue.

'I know I'm in trouble,' she said. 'I just wanted to be the outgoing and charming hostess. I couldn't do it without a little help...' she added, realising in the blink of an eye that it was a bad idea to reveal the need for a drink in order to oversee such a friendly gathering.

Gordon and Imogen frowned but held back on comment at this stage. They knew from clinical experience that if someone needed alcohol to enjoy a tea party with friends, it was the thin end of the wedge. Their home was not a seedy nightclub.

'I'm really sorry. I embarrassed you and all my friends. It was my fault, but my intentions were good. I'm learning about life, doing what I can to be a nice person. It takes time. I've heard you both say that, when you're discussing young patients. After all, I'm only thirteen,' she said, in her most reasonable, intelligent 'child of a psychotherapist' tone.

'Fourteen,' said Imogen, portraying her daughter closer to adulthood.

'Is this a first for you?' asked Gordon. "Have you been legless before?'

His choice of words stung; they were spot-on, true, but not the usual tone he used for his little girl.

'Not my first,' she said, without further explanation.

'Then we have a problem,' he said. 'I don't expect you to elaborate but thank you for being honest enough to admit some sort of frequency. Same supplier?'

She looked down at her feet. That was all the affirmation he needed.

'How are you going to deal with this at school? Everyone will know by now, and your absence for the last couple of days will add coals to the fire,' he added, rising to put the kettle on again.

She wanted to say it would up her street cred, the latest cool compliment for teenage notoriety, but now was not the time. 'I'll be as honest as I can, but they'll make up their own minds, there'll be different versions of the event, depending on who's on my side and who isn't.'

'What about Alex? Did he know about the vodka?' asked Imogen.

Mary blushed. 'No, he didn't. I think he would have tried to stop me. But I thought everything would be alright. I was only going to take a few mouthfuls to help get the party going,' she said, digging an even deeper hole with her naive reasoning.

'You realise this is going to reflect on the whole family and the practice, as well as your school status, don't you?

She nodded weakly. A front-page headline popped into her mind; *'Top girl collapses face down into chocolate cake after underage drinking spree.'*

'If you've done it before, and repeated the same mistake without learning your lesson, you have some serious thinking to do. We're here for you, of course, but as we've never talked about the issue…'

'We're talking about it now,' snapped Mary, realising how this was looking.

'But only because it happened right in front of us, and all your friends,' he said, indicating toward the garden, 'Otherwise we'd never have known. And if Alex was innocent of all this, he must be thinking twice about his relationship with you.'

That really hurt, but it was true. And when Alex found out who supplied her…

'Let's stop there,' said Imogen. 'We can't wind the clock back. If this discussion and your foolish episode hasn't moved you toward some serious thinking and a positive decision, I don't know what will,' she finished, mentally ringing her hands because she'd no idea what they'd do if Mary had already become addicted to alcohol.

'There were no signs of the bottle when we cleared up. Is there any vodka left? Where is it?' asked Gordon, making an effort to avoid sounding like a television detective.

'Can't remember, I wasn't in a fit state, was I?' she said, in what her father would call defensive teenager speak.

'The gardener's due soon, he'll find it.'

'Does it really matter, Dad, Mum?' she said. Tears of shame welled up, at the thought of her parents finding an empty bottle. And maybe the string caught on the old tree would provide another clue to the mystery. Then the forensic work would follow, which usually produced results. They love solving puzzles and problems. Psychologists seemed to be good detectives.

'At the end of the day it's a confidence issue,' she said, looking from one parent to the other. 'Not something obvious at school because I can bury my head in study, like everyone else, and I'm good at what I do, I'm top girl. Confident.'

'Then why need a drink for this?'

'Hormones probably, that's what everyone talks about at school. We're all changing into women...and confused.'

'It's called growing up and you can't do it in one mighty leap,' said Imogen, remembering her own teenage difficulties.

'Confusion is part of the package,' said Gordon, 'but you can't fix it with booze,' he added, remembering his own difficult association with the dreaded bottle.

'You sound like a couple of psychologists,' said Mary. They all smiled. Message received and understood. She wasn't too worried about what the class would think, they'd all done naughty things. She was used to the bitchy chit-chat which went on between teenage girls when anyone was in trouble, and the laddish, sometimes bullying aspects of how boys treated such spicy news. But she was worried about what Alex might think; that she was a stupid, silly, spoilt child, and someone he'd never want to see again.

CHAPTER FORTY-SIX

A few days later Mary turned up for school, her head held high as she walked through the gates to be heartily greeted by some of her friends who'd been at the party. There were hugs without words at first, all glad to see her back. They wanted to escort her into the school, but Mary shrugged their affectionate grip away and said, 'Thank you all, but I must do the next bit on my own.'

Alex passed on the other side of the forecourt as she made towards the entrance doors. He smiled and waved, she smiled and waved back, more enthusiastically than intended because his friendly greeting was unexpected, and her heart and emotions lifted on realising what that brief encounter meant. They were still friends.

Shuffling and whispering rose and fell as she entered the classroom. The odd snide comment was typically juvenile, but if ignored, things tended to die down quickly. She'd witnessed that sort of behaviour before and it only did harm when taken too much to heart, with the victim ending up feeling stupid and depressed. Dad taught her that at a very young age. *When people try to hurt with words and unkindness, they run out of steam if you ignore them or laugh it off. Because meanness loses its effect if you decide not to be a victim.* It always worked.

Her desk by the window had a view of Greg Smart on the forecourt. He was looking straight at her and once he recognised who it was, staggered about like a drunk, holding on to his pals and grinning maliciously. She'd expected nothing else. Good job Eddie or Alex hadn't seen it – he'd be back in A&E in no time. She smiled.

She opened the lid of her desk to find a small cake. It was covered in thick chocolate icing. The donor had not been brave enough to leave a note.

It seemed unkind, but humorous in a way. She decided to make a point. Not all the class had arrived, but those present watched in wonder as Mary took the cake and placed it on the teacher's desk. She scribbled a quick note.

'I believe this was meant for you but found it in my desk. Obviously, a mistake, but apologies if I got it wrong. Mary.'

As she turned to go back to her desk, her eyes scanned the room. She spotted a particular girl blushing furiously.

A new lecturer had replaced the absent Vera Harris. Mrs Brown walked in and viewed the cake with some delight. 'What's this?' she said, smiling while reading the note. 'Thank you, Mary. Was it a mistake?' she asked, addressing the class. 'Whose gift was it? I want to thank them. That's such a nice welcome on my first day. Everyone likes chocolate cake,' she said, looking at each pupil in turn.

The blushing girl could not control her remaining flush. Mrs Brown spotted it. 'Aah, I see. I won't ask anyone to stand. No need to be embarrassed it's quite a brave thing to do, buy your new teacher a cake. Not sure I deserve it but thank you.'

The class laughed and the girl didn't quite know what to do with herself. She stared briefly at Mary, who was concentrating on not returning the icy look.

Mary was pleased to see the back of that first day. She'd handled it well and couldn't help mentally thanking her parents for their good advice on how to tackle confrontation and bullying.

Tomorrow she'd be seeing the Head and the education

psychologist. Her dad was going to intervene in the ongoing
process at some point but felt it was best for Mary to turn up for
an initial meeting and briefed her on what might happen and how
she should respond.

CHAPTER FORTY-SEVEN

Florence was ready for work. She had time to spare so made an extra cup of tea and called Alex in to sit with her for a moment. '

'How are things at school, Alex? And how did Mary's party go? You haven't mentioned it,' she said, blowing across the surface of her hot tea.

'School is school. I was embarrassed to mention Mary's party, but you'll get to hear about it anyway. The news will have spread fast… She was drunk,' he said, hoping his ma wouldn't press for too many details.

'Where did she get the booze? I can't imagine her parents allowing it.'

'They didn't, but I can't tell you. I'm not a snitch. But she definitely didn't get it from me.'

'Were they all drinking?' asked Florence anxiously.

'Only Mary.'

'Was she ill, staggering about, or being sick?'

'She had to be helped indoors after she fell face down into her birthday cake,' he said, knowing the story would reach his ma through town gossip and the customers at the bakery. Better to get the story from him, then she'd be prepared.

Florence laughed. 'Do you still like her?'

'Course I do,' he snapped. *I'm going to marry her.*

She'd read Vera Harris's note left on the scrap of paper at the bakery but had no intention of rekindling their disastrous relationship.

As she stepped off the bus, Vera, looking serious and nervous, walked across the street toward her.

There was no way Florence could have avoided contact in the long term now that she had discovered the bakery. She decided to face the inevitable meeting head on, aware that Vera could turn up at all hours.

'I'm working, Vera,' she said, checking her watch. 'We'll be opening soon. If you want to say something, make it quick. It's over with us, I don't need to explain it all again, do I?'

'I'm a different person now, Flo. I've been going to Alcoholics Anonymous. I'm on a programme to kick the booze, the Twelve Steps. Everyone swears by it,' she said, without adding that so far she'd only managed twenty-four hours without alcohol. 'Haven't had sex since. Not that interested anymore, it was the drink, you know. Besides, we had something more, something deeper, I realise that now. Couldn't we meet up, just the once, and you'll see how I've changed? Hear me out. No strings. I know you liked me before...before that incident at the mews.'

'The total betrayal incident?' she said. 'A leopard doesn't change its spots, Vera. Please don't turn up at my workplace again, it's embarrassing, especially when you started banging on doors while my boss was there, and the bakery closed. He knows I don't want to see you, so he'll be on guard too. I have to go, or I'll be late.'

'Give me your phone number then,' she said in a commanding tone.

'No way. I have yours and that's the way it's going to stay. You've made your thoughts known, and I hope I've made mine clear too. Good luck with the Twelve Steps,' she finished, certain she detected a whiff of alcohol when Vera stepped closer, attempting to embrace her.

The boss guessed what was happening and moved hastily toward the door, allowing Florence to escape into the safe warmth of the bakery.

CHAPTER FORTY-EIGHT

George had mellowed. Since being back at work and accepting the status quo, everyone noticed he'd changed. Was it a delayed reaction to his accident or just a more recent take on life? Neither as it turns out, it was due to the care Delroy and his family took in making sure George settled in comfortably. The recommended digs were not far from where the Jamaican and his family lived, and close to others who'd emigrated from the Caribbean.

The day he moved in they invited him for a meal, curried goat and rice. A first for George but he enjoyed it, though he wasn't quite sure about the rum, which went straight to his head.

He'd never seen so many smiling faces. Delroy and Lorna had two kids, nine-year-old twins, who made George feel uncomfortable at first – were they smiling at his expense? He felt pale, old, and scruffy amongst such vibrant looking people.

Lorna, wise enough not to ask George about his home life, kept to the subject of work, Delroy's praise of George's expertise and his magnificent staircase.

After the feast Delroy and George sat out in the small garden while the family cleared away and washed up. George looked on with interest as the Jamaican made a ritual of hand-rolling a cigarette, inspecting it and twisting the tissue at its tip before lighting up. His first draw of the cigarette was slow and measured, his face relaxed as he sucked in slowly, holding the effect for a moment before exhaling.

'Do you smoke, George?'

'Now and again,' he said, unable to remember much about his history in that area, not even sure where or when he last lit up.

Delroy drew again on his scruffy hand-rolled cigarette. George picked up the aroma as the smoke drifted lazily toward him. He felt at ease. The friendly company, the generous meal, the rum and the residue of whatever Delroy was smoking, had turned him into a relaxed but sleepy guest.

The man who George feared would take his job no longer seemed such a threat. He couldn't quite explain why, because Delroy had obviously replaced him. He was unsure how it was going to work out. If Oakland gave George his job back at the end of this trial period, Delroy would be out of there and looking for work. Not fair, thought George. He only needed to look after himself, while Delroy had a family to support. Florence or Alex might as well be on another planet.

'I didn't mean to take your job, George. Must be hard recovering from such a serious accident. I guess you'll be back in position if all goes well,' he said, staring at the grass between his feet, while contemplating the situation.

'Perhaps we can work something out,' said George, unable to understand how he came to care so much about someone he hardly knew. Yet, in a way, he did know him. Delroy and his family were a likeable, happy, devoted couple surviving the best they could in a country they weren't born to. They'd drawn him in with their undemanding friendliness.

'Maybe,' said Delroy. 'We'll survive.'

Lorna came out with mugs of coffee and sat with them. The twins ran down to the end of the garden, taking turns to push each other on a homemade swing, a piece of wood with two holes drilled in it for the support rope and suspended from an old tree branch.

'Not his greatest piece of joinery,' said Lorna, laughing.

'Don't point it out in front of the boss, Lorna. You'll get me sacked.' They laughed.

George was touched by their generous spirit. And that Delroy referred to him as the boss.

'Do you smoke, Lorna?' he asked.

'Not as much as my husband,' she declared, patting Delroy lightly on the knee, as if he was a naughty boy. 'He loves his *ganja*.'

George couldn't remember the last time he felt so relaxed. Being with this lovely family was like...nothing that came to mind in his past. And the *Jamaican cigarette* which Delroy had rolled for him was something he might get used to.

CHAPTER FORTY-NINE

It was a busy clinic day when Imogen picked up the phone; the afternoon testing, as Gordon tried to catch up on his workload. Patients didn't always turn up on time and it only took one or two latecomers to shift the schedule from routine to an extra hard day. Trying not to let anyone down meant that rest periods took the brunt.

'Mum, it's Mary…'

'You're due home in an hour, why the phone call? Something happened?'

'I've got a chance to chat to Alex. I want to apologise for my behaviour at the party. I want him to still be my friend…'

Imogen smiled to herself.

'Hang on, Mary, the next patient's here,' she said, switching the phone to silent while she booked a young man in and guided him to the waiting room.

'Sounds like a good idea,' said Imogen, on getting back to the phone. 'He deserves an explanation – I hope you have a good excuse ready. Go ahead, meet up with Alex, send our regards but don't be late, dinner's still at six.'

'Thanks, Mum. I'll be there.'

Alex was outside. Mary had been waiting for him at the school gate, both managing to ignore or smile through the various comments and gestures made by the less mature members of their peers as they walked into town.

He felt very grown up ordering two takeaway coffees from Franco's – the newly opened coffee shop, run by an Italian family – but he was unsure what drink to choose, a coffee menu being a new experience.

The young guy, who had *barista* printed on his overall, recommended espresso; it would be his choice if he wanted to appear *raffinato*, a man of taste. He winked at Alex and nodded at the smiling Mary who stood out on the pavement peering through the shopfront window.

'And two chocolate muffins, please...' Then he remembered Mary's headfirst dive into her chocolate birthday cake. It might awaken painful memories.

'Oh, sorry...can I change that to flapjacks?'

'You sure?' he asked, with an *I prefer the muffins* look.

'Positive,' he said, looking out toward Mary who'd turned and raised her face toward the sun.

With the disappearance of a light blanket of cloud, the air warmed quickly. Mary removed her school blazer to display soft smooth arms, a part of her he'd never seen before. He tried to stop staring, but Mary noted his look of interest before he'd a chance to revert to the casual demeanour intended.

She liked what was happening. A stronger physical attraction was developing. Partly from the memory of that drunken kiss but also to do with the anticipation of their bonus afternoon.

'Shall we take this to the park?' he asked, proudly displaying the bag and two small coffees, eager to divert from his momentary embarrassment.

'How's school for you, Alex?' she asked, reluctant to get to the nitty-gritty of their meeting just yet.

'Okay,' he said. 'But I'll never be a scholar. Not at that school anyway, not enough interest for me. I miss Vera Harris's lectures, but she hasn't been around much for a while,' he declared with no intention of elaborating on her single aborted lesson at this point. 'But there's a plus side too, we've had more lessons with Jennifer Mayhew, the biology teacher. She's good, everyone likes her teaching style. We were so impressed with that lecture on the brain, she decided to divert from the syllabus to keep us interested. Does your class have her, Mary?'

'No, thank God, I get enough brain stuff at home,' she laughed.

They chose the first seat overlooking a duck pond. Timber slats composing the bulk of it warmed their backs as they sat. Ducks quacked, skimmed across the water, and waddled ashore, heading for the paper bag of goodies.

Alex was the first to sip his coffee which he nearly spat out; it was hot and very strong, not a bit like the Nescafé at home. Controlling his reaction, he watched in fascination as Mary sipped her espresso without a flicker.

'Do you like the coffee? It's espresso,' he said, with the air of a connoisseur.

'Just like it is in Italy. Excellent choice,' she said, without commenting further on Italy or Alex's reaction to his latest coffee experience.

'Oh, they look nice,' she said, as Alex took flapjacks out of the bag and handed her a serviette. Ducks squawked.

They sat for a moment, Alex in anticipation of Mary's account of her party and running through several scenarios about how he'd react. He was hoping for the truth, because anything else... He didn't want to think further than that.

Mary was eager to apologise without resorting to rubbish excuses. 'I'm sorry about the party, Alex,' she blurted, gauging his initial reaction before rattling on.

'Apology accepted,' he said, with a smile that might have appeared a little forced. Maybe because he was determined not to let that incident ruin their relationship. 'Did your mum and dad blow their tops? They must have been pretty angry.'

'They sure were, and worried about how you might take it too. It was quite a spectacle, I gather,' she said, as if giving an account of someone else's drunken escapade.

'How did the kids at school take it – the day you came back?'

'You know what they're like, some cruel, some kind.'

He did know, exactly. 'What were you drinking, that had such an effect?'

'Vodka. An absolute disaster: I'd never drunk it before. I usually go for wine. But I needed something clear which didn't smell of alcohol. A drink I could put in a glass of water or lemonade.'

Alex was trying to work out why anyone would take that risk in front of their mum and dad. And wondered what 'I usually go for wine' meant in the context of her day-to-day life.

'Have you been…'

'…Legless before? Yes, but not at home.' She looked down for a moment at the untouched flapjack before taking a huge bite, filling her cheeks, and coughing as a result. Ducks rushed for the projected crumbs.

'Why?'

'I like alcohol and I'm shy.'

'But you're only fourteen, Mary, and I'd never have you down as shy,' he said, unable to erase his impression of this pretty, top of the class girl, whom he thought was full of confidence.

'Well, I am.'

'So how did you get hold of the stuff in the first place? Obviously not from home, and you're too young to buy it from a shop.'

Alex tried but failed to erase the image of Eddie floating in and out of his consciousness.

'I couldn't possibly betray my source, Alex.'

'But drinking's not the way. Have you discussed it with your parents?'

'Of course not. Besides, they have their own problems.'

Really? Alex hadn't thought of two psychoanalysts being unable to work their own problems out.

'They sometimes sleep separately,' she admitted.

'Does that matter?' he asked, confused by the revelation, after all, his parents did.

'Sometimes separate beds, sometimes separate rooms, and sometimes together in the same bed. That's weird by anyone's standard.'

Alex had to admit, they didn't sound like a contented couple. Perhaps they needed to see a psychologist? He held back a smile.

'They're buttoned up in so many ways. The trouble is, Alex, when you're as bright and clever as they are, it's easier to pretend everything's okay when it isn't. But they don't realise how much it shows to someone as observant as me.'

'Could've fooled me, Mary, they look perfectly happy and well adjusted.'

'Of course they do. That's the whole bloody point, isn't it?' she said, leaving the comment hanging.

'Parents, eh? You know how mine ended up,' he said, flicking his eyes skyward. 'That was all due to keeping lips buttoned for too long, often over unnecessary things just to avoid confrontation or serious discussion.'

'Everyone does it. Haven't you twigged that yet?'

'But alcohol isn't going to solve anything, that's just another escape from life.'

'You sound like my father.'

'Talking of fathers,' he said, knowing it was time to change tack. 'How did he handle it with the school? I expect Grayling and the Head demanded some kind of punishment to be meted out...'

'He had a word with the Head and pulled rank on Grayling. Father wanted to deal with me, said it was a family issue and nothing to do with school.'

'How'd he manage that, without causing a problem for Grayling?'

'Dad put it in perspective, said that my misdemeanour – don't you hate that word? – happened at home, outside school time and away from anything related to education. He admitted I'd been a naughty girl and justice would be served. He finished by stating the obvious – they were psychologists and used to dealing with such problems in the general population, on a regular basis.'

'What did the Head say to that?'

'Hawkins accepted the reasoning but said he'd like an update, without specifying exactly what that meant. Dad nodded and that was the end of it. Grayling was there at the time but had nothing to add. Outmanoeuvred, I guess.'

CHAPTER FIFTY

Vera Harris failed in all attempts to reconnect with Florence Brownlow. Visiting her at the bakers had been something of a disaster, and she couldn't even be sure that the boss man had given Flo the note she'd scribbled.

Desperate to get her life back on track, she requested the school give her another chance to deliver a few lectures, reassuring them that her association with AA had changed her life. Reluctantly the Head gave in, but was soon sorry he had when Vera turned up the worse for wear, insulted some of the pupils' intelligence, and had to be escorted from the building. Her exit elicited laughter and unkind words as she was rushed past the attending class and out through the doors. Her career was over, her disgrace complete. And as if that wasn't enough, Alex Brownlow was sitting in the front row. If he reported back to Flo about her...then all efforts in the reconnection department would have been in vain. But maybe he wouldn't tell her?

On turning up for her impromptu visit at Florence's old address, Vera was met by various tradesmen, builders' machinery, dust, and a woman waving her arms as if directing traffic.

'Sorry to bother you, but I'm looking for Flo Brownlow,' said

Vera, realising that whatever was happening here did not have Flo's stamp on it.

'If you mean Florence Brownlow, she's moved,' said the woman. 'And no, I don't know where she is now, in case you were going to ask.' The woman turned toward matters in hand, directing scaffolders and generally project-managing the alterations. 'Try the estate agents who sold us the place. Peacocks. They should know.'

'Thanks.'

Peacocks was easy to find, and Mathew Lowry, Sales Advisor, was ready with a handshake and every intention of doing business.

'I'm not buying or selling,' she stated, much to Lowry's disappointment, his shoulders visibly sagging. 'I've just been to a property you sold. My friend Flo Brownlow lived there but forgot to leave her new address. Any chance you could let me have it? I really need to get in touch.'

'Sorry, madam, we can't give you that information. Company policy. Haven't you got her phone number?' he asked, aware that no business was going on here and reasoning that if this woman didn't have a contact address or a telephone number then she couldn't be that close a friend.

Plan B. She'd wait for Flo to leave the bakery and confront her outside. Last chance.

It was cold, waiting across the street for the bakers to close. Condensation clouded the shopfront windows, but shapes moved across the fluorescently lit interior. She'd no idea whether Flo left at closing time or if there were extra duties to be dealt with before going home.

An hour after the place shut, Vera, shivering from the cooling temperature, went to cross the street as Flo walked toward the bus stop.

Florence froze when she saw her. Colour drained from her face. A reflex twitchiness took over. She felt sad and angry at the same time. Vera looked as if all life had been sucked out of her like a punctured blow-up doll. But anger dominated Florence as the distance between them closed.

'I don't want to do this, Vera. It's been a hard day, I'm tired, nothing's changed as far as I'm concerned. It's over. And you lied to me.'

Vera was trying to remember which particular lie. 'Did you get the note I left at the bakery?'

Florence ignored the question as a surge of emotion prompted some straightforward speaking. 'Alex told me what happened at the school. You were drunk and insulted the kids! They had to carry you out. Not exactly the best advert for a senior lecturer or a lady supposed to be on the wagon and full of remorse. You had no intention of giving up drink, so why did you lie?'

'I tried.'

'Really! There were no obvious signs.'

Vera took on the look of a grossly misjudged criminal.

The bus had just turned the corner and Florence made a dash for it before Vera could gather her senses. She didn't look out of the window as the bus pulled past a tearful Harris who'd decided to head straight for the nearest bar.

Florence, still shaking from the encounter, left the bus to walk up the street to her new home. George was waiting outside. He'd come to see 'his boy'.

The day couldn't have got any worse. Alex appeared at the door, in answer to his father ringing the bell. The three walked inside like three strangers approaching a doctor's waiting room. Alex and Florence noted a particular odour as George moved quickly along the narrow hallway. Neither were used to smelling marijuana at home.

Florence went straight to the kitchen and put the kettle on. George sat at the table without invitation and started telling Alex about his Jamaican family. And Alex filled in the news of school and added a little humour by mentioning Vera Harris's aborted lecture. Not in an unkind way, but it must have seemed like it to his mum.

The tea came quickly, and a plate of assorted biscuits was placed in front of them. Florence felt compelled to sit down, though it was the last thing she needed – to sit down with George after her hard day at work... Then Vera.

But she was pleased George was back in work, had some nice people around him, and seemed more settled than she'd seen him in years. He was off her back.

George placed an envelope of money on the table. 'Something to help with expenses,' he said, unable to look her directly in the eye, because each time he attempted it a wave of terrible guilt swept over him. So being here today was a brave act, helped along by a little pre-visit session with Delroy.

Alex decided to let the grownups talk and excused himself after hurrying his tea and biscuits. 'I'll be down shortly...before you go, Dad.'

Alex lay on his bed recalling his confrontation with Eddie. His pal had admitted to supplying Mary with vodka.

'I guessed it was you, Eddie. What on earth were you thinking of?'

'I was thinking of you, that's what,' he said.

'Me? That's crazy, Mary got into a lot of trouble.'

'She wanted to be at her best. Mary doesn't like parties much and wanted to impress you with her skills as a hostess.'

Put like that, Alex felt a rush of affection both for Mary and Eddie. Despite the stupid risks, their intentions were good. But if the Singers found out he'd really be for it.

Alex waited a bit longer, to give his parents enough time to have some sort of dialogue while being aware that it might not go smoothly. It was nearly an hour before there were signs of Father getting ready to leave.

CHAPTER FIFTY-ONE

The doorbell rang. Alex dashed down the stairs. Constable Picket stood at the door, accompanied by a woman officer.

'Good afternoon, Alex. Is your mother in?'

Florence was there in a flash, with George following swiftly behind.

'Can we come in?' asked Picket, about to step into the hallway.

'What's up? Is this to do with Alex?'

'Let's talk about this inside,' said Picket. 'Your son better leave, he's not involved,' he said, without looking directly at Alex.

Florence and George stood aside to let the two coppers in.

Alex was curious but went back to his room and looked at his notes from Jennifer Mayhew's lesson, then at one of the books she'd recommended, which was psychology rather than anatomy. She made a big thing of the prefrontal cortex, the part of the brain which regulates thoughts actions and emotions. Just his cup of tea.

Before he settled to read, he opened his door a little and heard the steady hum of reasonable conversation. Neither parent raised their voice. Picket had taken the floor, questioning and listening.

'There's been an accident, Mrs Brownlow. Vera Harris. We've

tried to contact her brother Simon, but he's not answering his phone.'

'But why contact me?' she said defensively, aware that George might be building up a head of steam at the mention of Vera's name. But he wasn't. When she turned toward him his face was calm, expressionless almost, certainly not angry.

'We're contacting you because we found this note, *Dear Flo,* written on a scrap of paper,' said Picket. 'That's short for Florence, isn't it?' he asked. Florence didn't answer but stared at the words.

'Dear Flo, I've tried to apologise, tried to get it right, but you've made it clear. It's all over, you no longer want to be my friend. I feel my life is over too. It could have been good, love Vera xx'

Florence flushed and steadied herself against the nearest wall. 'What sort of accident?'

'A fatal one,' said Picket, the fact confirmed by his companion officer. At this juncture he couldn't express the bloody obvious until medically proven, that love-struck Vera Harris had committed suicide.

'Was she driving?' asked Florence, unable to think of anything else to say.

'Drowning,' he answered. 'In the canal. They couldn't save her, I'm afraid.'

Florence stood rigid, overcome by a lightning sense of relief followed by a creeping pity and horror. She bit the back of her hand before looking at George who'd not changed his expression throughout.

He'd wanted Vera gone, but not like this.

There was a reason why Picket had never been promoted. More than one probably but his communication skills left something to be desired. He spoke in clipped sentences that gave the impression his heart wasn't in it, even though it was. Only Picket could have delivered such bad news in so few words, like an old-fashioned telegram system.

'We need to ask you a few questions,' said Picket, 'It might be worth putting the kettle on. Just routine.'

Florence was pleased to have the distraction. Her movement toward the kitchen was hasty. Then a terrible guilt crept in. Her rejection might have tipped Vera over the edge after being so desperate to rekindle their relationship. And she was probably drunk too.

While Florence was making tea, Picket turned his attention to George, who'd maintained the effects of his smoke with Delroy.

'Did you know the woman, Mr Brownlow? Ever met her?' he asked.

'Knew about her, never actually met her. Saw her once from a distance when I was in a pub.'

'As I understand it, Ms Harris's relationship with Florence played a part in ending your marriage.' Picket pronounced Ms with an emphasis on the S as a drawn-out Z. *Mizzz*. Making it clear to all present that he found the title...annoying. *Whatever happened to the perfectly acceptable Miss?*

'Yes, it did but what has that got to do with her falling in the canal?'

'Maybe nothing, but we must look at other possibilities. She may have been pushed, for example.'

George smiled. There was a time when he'd have liked to have done that very thing.

'You're smiling, Mr Brownlow. This is not amusing,' said Picket, scribbling across the page of his notebook.

'Only because I feel that you're implying I might have pushed Harris into the canal.'

'Did you?'

'No,' he said calmly, 'But I can see why you'd think that.'

Florence came in with tea and biscuits. Picket and his partner went straight for the shortbread. They were due a break.

'Back to business,' said Picket, after taking a quick slurp of his tea.

'We've been round to the bakery and your boss said he saw a lady fitting Mz Harris's description across the street as you were getting ready to close. Said he'd seen her before and that you wanted to avoid her for some reason.'

'I did want to avoid her, she was being a nuisance.'

'In what way?'

'It's not a secret here,' she said, looking carefully at George before returning her attention to the police officers. 'We had a relationship which has been over for some time. But she kept trying to contact me.'

'Seems like you might be the last person to see her alive, Mrs Brownlow.'

George had witnessed scenes like this played out on several TV programmes. Quite often the last one to see the dead person was usually the killer.

'Tell us what happened,' he said, flipping his notebook, pencil poised to record every last word.

'Quite simple. As I left the bakery, she walked toward me from the other side of the street, but I didn't want to get into a difficult conversation, for obvious reasons. We didn't get to speak much, just a few hurried words, told her I didn't want to meet up. The bus was turning the corner of the street, so I hurried toward the stop before Vera could get close to me, and jumped on it.'

Picket licked the end of his pencil, preparing for more. 'What happened after that?'

'That was it. The last time I saw her.'

'Time?'

'5.30 pm. You can check with the boss.'

'We've already done that.' He smiled at George and Florence in turn, ensuring that all were impressed with his efficiency – confirmed by the enthusiastic nodding of his companion officer.

CHAPTER FIFTY-TWO

Simon arranged the funeral. Florence had to be there, she owed Vera that.

Could Vera's death possibly have been an unfortunate accident? Of course not, she'd left a note, so it must be suicide. Facing facts, it was Flo's rejection that must have encouraged the distraught woman to kill herself. The only one to think it suspicious, possibly a murder, was Constable Picket, who seemed to want every death to be filed in that category so's he could play detective.

The woven casket containing Vera Harris's body seemed to sum up the wretched state of her life. It looked as if it could fall apart at any moment. The coffin was covered in lilies, Florence's least favourite flower, because they always reminded her of death and the pollen left yellow stains on anything it touched.

It was a surprising congregation, a real mix of adults and youngsters of all ages. Gordon Singer, the school Head, Hawkins, and a couple of teaching staff were present. Picket was there, no one was sure quite why, probably to suss out, in Agatha Christie style, who could have been the murderer.

Mamazon, all alone, took a back seat looking a little less like an all-in wrestler than Florence remembered; maybe because she was dressed. There was no eye contact, just an awkward moment of recognition.

Gordon Singer looked sombre. One could only guess the secrets such a therapist might be mulling over when forced to sit still and contemplate his association with the deceased. Grayling was there too and felt side-lined, disappointed he hadn't had a better chance to help Vera Harris through her life crisis. He might have made a difference...

The biggest surprise, to those who'd only experienced Vera as a very lonely loose cannon with no stability or people who cared for her, were the number of youngsters. How did they fit into her life? Her brother would know, he must have invited them.

The service was brief. Simon gave the eulogy. It was warm, heartfelt, and eloquent. He spoke of his rebellious sister in a way that pulled the heartstrings, because her life struggles had origins. He didn't labour the point but described her as a lost child who loved young people. Vera was stuck in a time warp, an innocent trying to fit in with a world which moved too fast, searching for love but never quite finding it.

It was this moment when he looked directly at Florence, who blushed on cue.

His single quote was short but fitting: *'Lives are like rivers: Eventually they go where they must. Not where we want them to.'* Richard Russo.

Heads nodded.

Everyone walked to the pub across the road where a room had been set aside for guests to take refreshments and interact.

Florence felt a strong arm around her shoulder, and the grip tightened, an affectionate moment rather than a threatening one, though she decided on an open mind as she turned to see who the embracer was. Mamazon! Looking tearful, and on the edge of high emotion, she was trembling as she squeezed Florence tighter and attempted some sort of apology. It was said in a mumble, but

Flo got the gist of it. Mamazon wished that Florence never had to witness Vera's betrayal. The penny dropped; all Vera Harris's relationships must have been transient, all part of her desperate search for love. Mamazon, it now seemed, was as shocked and disappointed as Florence. Candles and music had, apparently, given the mews tryst additional but inappropriate significance.

Without further comment, Mamazon released Florence and lumbered out of the building in a hurry, without speaking to anyone else. It dawned on the stunned Florence, who now felt a pang of pity for Mamazon, that the giant's main mission when entering the wake was to deliver her apology to Florence. She felt her legs give way, took to the nearest seat, picked up a half-glass of abandoned champagne and downed it in one. She felt dizzy and shaky, reliving the scene at the mews when she first saw the flickering candles, heard the music and smelt the sweat. She could smell it now.

Constable Picket and Gordon Singer witnessed the scene but neither rushed to console the distressed Florence, both thinking their presence at that moment might be more of an embarrassment than helpful.

Simon had witnessed it too and rushed over to her, asking if she was alright. Was she hurt? Did Mamazon upset her?

'You know that woman, Simon?' she asked, without giving a clue as to how she knew Mamazon.

'Don't know her but I know of her. Vera talked about her a bit. She did that occasionally, boasted about her lovers...' He stopped there, he'd already said more than intended. Poor Florence.

Alex completely understood why his mother didn't want company at the funeral. Not that her affair with Vera Harris was a secret, but it was obvious she wanted to get through that difficult moment alone.

Mary and Imogen decided from the very beginning against

accompanying Gordon to any of his patients' funerals. They always offered their support, but never attended, simply because – particularly on this occasion – apart from Imogen booking Ms Harris in and Mary being present at some of her lectures, their associations were light and brief; she hadn't touched their hearts.

George knew about the funeral through the grapevine. He was glad Harris was dead, but her passing did nothing to relieve the impact of his wife's affair. A memory which visited him all too frequently...

But there was some light at the end of his present life's tunnel. He recalled yesterday vividly.

Oliver Oakland had summoned Delroy and George to his office. They were both nervous. Surely one of them was about to get the push.

They climbed the showpiece staircase, *George's staircase,* and stood on the landing waiting for the boss to greet them. He opened the office door, and shook their hands with a tight meaningful grip.

'Come in, take a seat, there's coffee on the way,' he said, pleased to see his top men turning up in white shirts and conservative ties. Standards!

'Right, lads,' started Oliver, who was smiling. Delroy and George glanced nervously at each other, uncertain whether coffee was a good sign or a bad one. They knew it had been used to sack or praise people in the past. Oliver's way of treating the privileged and stricken with equal respect.

'Profits are up even though it's our least busy time of the year,' he said, staring at the two men as if searching for confirmation. 'We've had the best month ever and, as you're aware, we've had to implement overtime. Despite the workload, staff seem more relaxed and the two of you seem to have found a way of getting along without fighting for the top job. That was my biggest concern...' He paused again, shuffling papers absently. 'I want to think of keeping you both on... but only if the next couple of months proves the sudden surge in business is a genuine upward trend.'

Oliver picked up the loose paperwork, tidied it into a neat stack and tapped the edges square on his desk. A signal that the meeting was over and all was well at Oakland's Joinery. Coffee arrived. George and Delroy beamed at each other.

CHAPTER FIFTY-THREE

The local park wasn't so popular this time of day. Three acres of grassland peppered with bushes, the odd flowerbed, clumps of trees and a tennis court. People? There were a few dog walkers, and that about summed it up. But the near empty terrain in front of Alex freed his mind from distraction. He felt brave enough to ask the question now that they were alone. Ice creams and the sunny day helped. 'How did your parents deal with things at the party?' He'd been thinking about it for some time, assuming that Mary and her parents would rather it were swept under the carpet from a publicity point of view. No doubt admonishment and therapy would be the theme at home for some time to come.

'I'll tell you. But first I want to know when your birthday is. I promise not to embarrass you if I get an invite. I'm on the wagon now,' she said. Neither could remember a time when they'd laughed so easily together.

'My birthday's gone, Mary – it was two weeks after yours,' he said, without any sign of regret or embarrassment.

'Why didn't you tell me?'

'I never broadcast it.'

'Didn't your parents do anything about it?'

'Mum forgot the last couple of years, and Dad? Well, he always forgets...'

He wasn't sad, not being that keen to celebrate his own birthday anyway; he was self-conscious about it, not really a party person.

'You could have dropped a hint.'

He shrugged off the suggestion.

Mary gripped his hand in sympathy – *what a pleasure* – but was unable to understand why anyone would want to miss celebrating their own birthday. It was the saddest thing. 'Surely someone remembered. Eddie must have known...'

'He forgot too. Eddie doesn't remember birthdays, apart from his own, and only then because his mum and dad make sure everyone knows way in advance.' He mimicked Eddie's mother's voice: 'We're looking forward to our favourite son's big day. What would you like to do this year?'

Mary smiled at his squeaky interpretation of a voice she'd yet to compare it to. 'Really sorry to hear about your missed birthday.'

'Enough about me, how did things go afterwards...after your party?' he asked, feeling a little hot under the collar. He wasn't expecting Mary to grill him about his birthday celebrations, or lack of them. There was no escaping reality, he'd set himself up as a straightforward honest person, preferring everything out in the open. But he had to admit parents missing their child's birthday seemed a very odd thing indeed. Yet, he was just as guilty, he'd joined in the charade and ignored them too.

She felt excluded. Alex not letting her know about his birthday seemed to put a subtle distance between them.

'The gardener came a week later,' she started, determined to move on from her disappointment. 'Unfortunately, he's sharp-eyed, spots a weed at a hundred paces. He saw a bit of string dangling from the wall above the compost heap and tried to retrieve it. He needed steps because it was snagged on a bit of rough brickwork above his head. He took note of the slip knot and measured the length of twine, before showing it to Mum and Dad. They put two and two together and made four. The mystery of how vodka got into the party was solved.'

There was a moment's silence. A frown appeared on Mary's face, a rare event. 'You must have been drunk at some point in your life, Alex Brownlow,' she said, with a penetrating gaze that made him feel he might possibly be guilty.

In a way he wanted to be *in her club,* but alcohol wasn't for him. He'd never been drunk but had thrown up after his first and only full glass of red wine – with Eddie of course. Perhaps that counted, but throwing up and taking two or three days to recover was no encouragement to try it again. He'd had the odd sip from the cheap red his parents drank but that was bravado, a desire to integrate himself into the norm, rather than enjoyment.

'Not really,' he finally admitted, his face showing a flush of embarrassment.

Mary looked disappointed. 'Never?'

He had to admit it. 'Had a glass of red with Eddie once.'

'And?'

'Threw up,' he blurted. 'Eddie's advice was not that sound,' he continued, eager to put the event in context. 'It turned out to be the same wisdom he calls on to help those about to start smoking. *You need to keep doing it!* was his advice. *It's part of growing up.'*

She laughed. 'So, you're Mr Squeaky Clean then?'

It sounded unkind but wasn't meant to be. 'I'm full of admiration – really,' she said, wishing she could have faced her party without the vodka.

A momentary distraction, maybe because greedy flies were heading their way, but they both licked their melting ice creams at the same time. They locked eyes for a second. Synchronicity, Alex liked to think. He'd seen an article in a library magazine, *Psychology Today,* and probably read more into it than was good for him; that acts performed simultaneously by two people make a subtle but meaningful connection.

'So apart from the fact you can't tolerate alcohol, do you feel left out when you see others enjoying themselves after a few drinks? People loosen up. Surely that's a good thing?'

'Not having had the experience, I wouldn't know, would I?' he smiled, feeling slightly awkward. He didn't want to come across holier than thou, but he really didn't see the point in drinking so much, followed by feeling bad, hangovers, taking time off school or work for days after the event. He'd seen it in others, not nice, and people did stupid things when they were drunk. Even grownups. Especially grownups.

'What do you think about others drinking socially, Alex?'

'It's up to them. Depends on how much. From what I've seen, the odd drink seems okay, but legless doesn't seem such a happy state,' he said, aware that Mary would feel stung by his comment.

'What do you think, Mary? Do your parents attempt to guide you at all? Do they like a drink?'

'Grownups shouldn't point the finger, should they? They've no right! Parents have history; things they'd rather keep from their kids...' She hesitated. 'My father used to have a drink problem, a big one. He got a lot of help and Mother used to suffer long periods of depression. She needed help too. They talked about it openly and viewed their experiences as good reasons to end up as psychotherapists. Dad always goes on about it being impossible to help others unless you've had problems yourself – and solved them.'

Alex, surprised at Mary's sudden disclosure regarding her mum and dad, did his best not to show it and wondered if a tendency to drink too much might be a genetic thing. He reflected on his own parents, and adults in general. Did they all have to struggle so hard to keep their love and lives on track? When did it all start to go pear-shaped? Did they button their lips until it was too late?

...*had problems and solved them,* resonated with Alex.

'Seems reasonable. But that doesn't explain...' He couldn't stop now.

'Doesn't explain what?' she asked, knowing damned well exactly what Alex needed to know.

'What happened at the party?'

'Sounds like you're about to judge me,' she said, a little colour pinking her cheeks, along with an emotional blinking of the eyes to stop tears forming.

'Not at all. We're young, Mary, only fourteen for God's sake. What our parents do or say doesn't influence our behaviour much, does it? We're free to experiment, that's how we learn and grow,' he said, pleased with his wise words that came from nowhere. But not totally true to his innermost perceptions; he hoped Mary didn't go too far down the road of experimentation. If the scene at her party was anything to go by, things might not turn out well.

'But I hated seeing you so ill, Mary, like you'd turned into someone you didn't want to be... Sorry, I've said too much.'

'Well, I did ask.'

She hugged him tightly. A green light for Alex, who returned the embrace with enthusiasm, the closest the most intimate parts of their young bodies had ever been. The thrill was mutual.

She needed a moment to think. Alcohol was on the agenda, and she was trying to work out how it might feature in their developing relationship. She had a strong desire to take the odd drink, but it looked as if Alex might be a teetotaller. What? At fourteen?

She'd already got wind of something amiss. When Eddie performed the *vodka drop,* he told her not to mention anything about booze to Alex. That from Eddie meant the two pals must have had a serious discussion about drinking, one that wouldn't favour Mary's idea of them taking the odd glass or two together.

CHAPTER FIFTY-FOUR

Since their lives had settled somewhat, Florence and George had little need for the confessional. But they both remembered times with Father John when it was the only lifeline they had, the only release of pressure from their uptight and dishonest existence.

But life is never without problems; no sooner than you deal with one, another pops up to test your mettle and your sanity.

Picket had got wind of cannabis being used by some of the employees at Oakland's Joinery, including George Brownlow. It was...illegal. One of his favourite words. Oliver Oakland was never a man he could get on with; wrong political party for a start, and a bit too touchy feely for a businessman. Leanings which could lead to all sorts of trouble. Surely Oakland must be aware of this banned drug being used by his employees. If not he was in for a big surprise. Worst case scenario – he'd be forced to close the factory down.

Picket had only ever addressed the station sergeant as *Sarge* which seemed perfectly natural and acceptable. Contacting Sarge would be his first step in addressing the corruption being practised at Oakland's Joinery. *We can't have employees off their heads at work as well as at home, being a danger to themselves and others.* He'd swotted up on the subject, read a bit about psychosis amongst marijuana addicts. A relatively small number, but in Picket's opinion, a great enough threat to warrant intervention. Any mental aberration amongst the working population was worth taking note of.

Sarge was busy. Picket approached his desk and asked if he could have a word. 'Make it snappy, Picket, I'm late for a meeting as it is.' He was used to his constable's overly zealous attitude toward petty crime; more trouble than it was worth when it came to assigning valuable police time to sort it out.

'Drugs, Sarge.'

'What sort of drugs and where? Dealing, using or are we about to crack a local cartel?' asked Sarge, trying to keep the sarcasm out of his voice but failing.

'Oakland's Joinery. It's rife. There's dangerous machinery...'

'Let's stop you there for a moment, Picket. Not time for this now but presumably you've taken notes and got some sort of proof, witnesses maybe. Write a draft report and we'll talk it through,' he said, rising from his desk and picking up a file before heading for the Chief's office. 'Pop in after your shift tomorrow,' he finished, walking past Picket with a smile only used for necessary pleasantries.

That evening Picket started to write out his rather sketchy report. At certain points he ran a sentence or two past his wife, Penelope. She'd located an article which her husband used as an introduction: *Smoking marijuana in the workplace is not allowed. In general, the use of marijuana will be treated the same as alcohol and considered a serious case for dismissal of an employee.*

Everyone shortened her name, as is generally the case with most people. 'Penny' seemed friendlier and rolled off the tongue easier. Not a problem when she was young and unmarried, but being called Penny Picket became an easy tag for petty criminals and the public alike to be creative with her married name. It was one of the milder reasons as to why being married to a copper turned out to be less romantic than she'd expected.

Added to that, *Pickpocket* was Constable Picket's nickname, both inside and outside the force.

Penny was inclined to sniff at her husband's latest account of his fight against crime, namely the 'drug cloud' drifting across his patch.

'I don't think Sarge will be impressed with what you have so far, dear,' she offered, looking up from his page of rough notes. 'Where's the hard proof? Where's the witness accounts? Is business suffering or workers' absence increasing? Who tipped you off anyway?' she asked, passing the paper back to her husband.

Picket tapped the side of his nose emphatically, like a character out of *Dixon of Dock Green.* He had a witness, someone who needed protecting. If things got tough, they might have to be moved to a safe house or change their identity for fear of reprisals. He'd read about Yardies and criminal gangs in Jamaica...

'Come in, Picket,' said Sarge. 'Sorry to keep you.'

Sarge's desk was laid out neatly with paperwork and some important looking files marked *CONFIDENTIAL.* Picket felt his story might be trivial in comparison. He stood with his hands behind his back, twiddling his fingers, awaiting further instruction hoping for a cup of coffee.

'Take a seat, constable,' said Sarge, checking his watch. 'I've only got ten minutes, I'm afraid.'

Picket held back on producing his draft report and decided that with such a short time available, he'd better get straight to the point.

'I've been contacted by a whistle-blower, Sarge.'

'I hope this is not just hearsay, Picket. Who's the source?'

'Can't say yet, but she's worth listening to. I've got all the details here,' he said, waving a couple of pages, fanning himself from a rising temperature.

'How did she find out?' asked Sarge with little interest as he absently opened and closed a drawer.

'Husband was on it, apparently.'

'On what?'

'Cannabis. Smoking it or mixing it with tobacco, she said.'

Sarge stifled a grin and slammed the drawer shut, making Picket jump.

'I think the Chief should know,' said Picket, still holding his draft report which was becoming damp with perspiration.

'Don't be shy, constable, show me your report,' said Sarge.

He placed it cautiously on Sarge's desk… He'd been holding it rather tightly and the pages looked a little crumpled.

Sarge gripped his chin as he read the leading paragraph, designed, or so Picket thought, to ensure collaboration.

'Smoking marijuana in the workplace is not allowed. In general, the use of marijuana will be treated the same as alcohol and considered a serious case for dismissal of an employee.'

'What rag did you get this quote from?' asked Sarge.

Was there a sniff in his voice? Picket pulled back slightly at the way Sarge was reacting, as if the drug outbreak was something he'd made up. The sudden pause allowed Sarge to continue. 'It's complicated, Picket. The law changes all the time. Can't rely on anything these days.'

'This was in last week's *Herald*, quoting from government legislation, Sarge,' said Picket defensively, palms still damp, his shirt collar tight.

Sarge got up from his desk, opened the door and shouted across the busy office. 'Can someone get me a couple of coffees?' He turned to Picket. 'Sugar?'

'Three please,' replied Picket.

'And some sugar,' Sarge added to the coffee order.

'I don't want this to be an issue, Picket. I don't want it blown out of all proportion. So, I'm going to tell you what the bigger picture is.'

Picket nodded enthusiastically, like a model dog on the back shelf of a car.

'You may not know this, but the Chief and Oakland are good friends.'

In Picket's mind this made things worse, not better. He was about to point it out but somehow the right words evaded him.

'I'm not making excuses but here's the picture. Since our Caribbean friends moved into the area, the staff at Oaklands have embraced them and their culture.'

'But…'

Sarge held his hand up. 'Let me finish.'

Coffee arrived and Picket helped himself to three spoonfuls of sugar. Sarge took none and managed to convey his disapproval by not stirring his coffee.

'Oakland told the Chief that staff at the joinery are more relaxed, profits are up, and the place is in a better shape than ever. I'm not advocating drugs for anyone, Picket, but given the situation, I don't think we can do much about it.'

'You mean ignore it, Sarge? Ignore drug taking?'

'In this particular case, yes. We have enough going on as it is, with proper drug problems; hard drugs, serious addicts. Crime. Why would we want to interfere in something so positive? None of the staff are rolling about or off their heads, they turn up on time, do their work. No absences, no accidents…'

Picket knew this wasn't going well. But drug taking at work was still a crime – and on his watch! His career was stagnating. Promotion was a dream. He knew his brand of policing was a bit forensic. He cared about little things, made too much effort bringing petty criminals to justice. *Isn't that how you prevent larger crimes?*

Perhaps he'd leave the force after all, become a private investigator. He could do that. The courses welcomed experienced men with a background in law enforcement. He'd checked it out, it was possible. He'd be his own boss, catch the criminals early in their development, stop bigger crimes happening.

Sarge didn't want to compromise himself, but he was a bit fed up with Picket trying to make small crimes big ones; expecting high praise for catching an OAP shoplifting for example. With that attitude, he'd never get promoted.

Sarge handed the report back without reading the rest of it. 'Go home, loosen up a bit, try not to make big crimes out of small ones. Oaklands is doing better than ever. The Chief will not be happy with this…this nit-Picketing attitude,' he finished, grinning at his clever play on words.

CHAPTER FIFTY-FIVE

Alex's life was about to make a sudden detour. His association with Mary had blossomed and with it her parents' desire to meet up with Florence and George Brownlow; two families bonding through their beloved children. Alex knew that Imogen and Gordon Singer were fully informed about his parents' separation; the breakup of the marriage, the reasons for it, the parting of the ways and his mother's affair with Vera Harris.

Dear Alex, George and Florence.
You are invited to Gordon Singer's birthday party on August 15th.
2pm @ 12 Dansbury Street, London.
Dress casual. No presents thank you.
We're really looking forward to meeting you all.
Best wishes, Imogen Singer.

They were psychologists so how could they possibly expect the Brownlows to be playing happy families at a birthday party? Mother would jump at the chance. She was itching to meet the Singers, better on their turf than hers.

George wouldn't be so easy to tempt. Not that Florence wanted him at the party, but having been invited, he'd every right to be there. His inevitable embarrassment and inability to fit in with such sophisticated company would prove arduous.

Alex wasn't sure if he was shocked or just surprised at the invitation. Or if there was much of a difference between the two, except that shocked seemed to indicate being upset as well as surprised. He settled on surprised.

He'd talk to Mary, though he was certain that only his mother would accept the invitation. She would be fawning and well behaved without the toxic aura of Father and his burden of guilt. *For nearly killing his wife and destroying family life for a start.* Hard for him not to show it, especially after a few drinks and a captive audience. Alex couldn't quite believe how negatively he was thinking.

He sat with Mary in the park after school. The term was ending, and summer holidays stretched out for weeks ahead like a comfort blanket. They just looked and listened at first; songbirds singing their unrecognisable melodies, the whack of a cricket ball across the way, the smell of freshly mown grass and blossoming flowers which neither of them could name. On greeting, they'd hugged more naturally than either could remember, both feeling that thrill, a prelude to adult intimacy closing in.

'Did your family get the invites, Alex?'

'Mum and I did. Not sure about Dad. Did you know his address?'

'Mother seemed to have magicked it up from somewhere,' she answered, a little nervously, unsure about how her parents managed to get hold of the details without asking Alex.

'What's got into your mum and dad? They're psychologists for God's sake.'

He didn't mean the words to come out so sharply. But he sensed tension rising and saw it in her face. No doubt she thought the invitations were a bad idea too. Inviting Mum would be okay, she'd been hankering to meet Mary's parents for some time. But

Dad? He'd be manageable on his own if they'd got the timing right. But together? He could see the family gathering turning into a display of unspoken hostility.

The sun gave way to cloud. A breeze stirred, cool enough to produce goose bumps on Mary's arms. She looked pale. He offered her his school blazer, which she declined. She was wearing a little perfume or maybe washed with scented soap. He took a heady breath and placed his arm around her shoulder. She leant into him, neither of them wanting the moment to end. They watched two squirrels chase each other up and down a nearby tree. The little creatures stopped momentarily to face each other; rock steady, tactical. Playing or fighting?

Mary knew what was to come and who was invited. She knew her father and she knew what this particular birthday was about, not discussed but decided without room for change. It wasn't about his age, his birthday or a celebration, it was about getting a group of people – who had various issues with each other – together in one place. A psychological experiment. He'd write a paper on it, or publish an article, about how stressed-out people conducted themselves civilly, or not, when their nemeses were within arm's reach.

On this occasion Gordon wasn't interested in eating or drinking, he wanted to observe while at the same time working out if he could bear his daughter being linked to such a disparate family as the Brownlows.

Two things troubled Alex as he headed toward Dansbury Street. The first was his mother insisting on linking arms as they walked. It was unprecedented, awkward, and unnecessary. But Alex realised this was a big moment, her meeting Mary's family at the posh end of town. Florence's dress was years old, but she'd made a decent attempt to look her best by adding a bit of makeup, a colourful scarf and a never-before-seen handbag.

The second distraction was the billowing blue smoke rising above a rooftop somewhere along the very street they were due to walk along. Could it be a fire at the Singers' house?

Everyone invited might have expected a sit-down tea with flowered china cups and neat triangular sandwiches, but the Singers had prepared a barbecue. August sunshine stage lit the scene set out with umbrellas, proper linen napkins, cane furniture and glass-topped tables supporting stacks of white plates. Gordon and Imogen wore striped aprons and straw hats as if they were hired staff.

As guests arrived, the Singers casually waved tongs and forks, a kind of admission entrance confirmation, like punching tickets. And there was a relief for Alex as he watched barbecue smoke rise, heading into the trees and over the rooftops at the end of the garden.

Mother let go of Alex's arm as Mary ran across and hugged her warmly. Florence wasn't used to such spontaneous expressions of affection and displayed her awkwardness by adjusting her scarf and checking her handbag as if searching for lost train tickets. Mary hugged Alex and kissed him on the cheek.

Florence was even more taken aback when Imogen left her post at the barbecue and repeated the warm affectionate hug already demonstrated by her daughter. 'So pleased to meet you at last, Florence. It's been too long,' she said.

It's been too long, was something an old friend might say, thought Florence.

'Come and meet Gordon.' Imogen took Florence's hand and led her toward the barbecue which was sizzling away nicely. Gordon placed his metal tongs on a table, wiping his hands down a pristine apron before giving Florence a vigorous handshake. 'Welcome, Florence. Hope you're hungry.' She was momentarily lost for words. 'Isn't Alex a fine lad?' he asked.

Mary whisked Alex away toward a small bench. 'Apart from you and me, it's all adults,' she said. 'Hope you're okay with that.'

'Absolutely fine,' he replied. *Sitting with Mary and a promise of food?* Perfect.

'I'll have to help Mum and Dad when guests arrive. You were the first,' she said, squeezing his hand to confirm her delight. 'So nice to have your ma here too. I didn't think she'd come. Will your dad turn up?' she finished, knowing darned well how tricky the whole scene was going to be.

'I don't even know if he got the invite, we haven't heard from him for a while.'

Alex and Mary happened to look skyward at the same time, some minor distraction or fleeting shadow. A large sausage-shaped balloon with a pair of round ones secured to the string at one end, drifted lazily across the scene at Dansbury Street. A few guests followed their gaze, but only Mary and Alex came close to guessing what it was about. The artistic creation came from the same direction as the compost heap and was, undoubtedly, Eddie Burn's artistic impression of a penis complete with testicles. Eddie's subtle hint that romance was in the air.

Alex promised Mary that he would kill Eddie next time he saw him.

The next guests to arrive were Picket and his Sarge, both looking completely out of place in coloured shirts and jeans. The invitation did say casual but nothing could have disguised the fact that they were officers of the law.

Following the two coppers was Dr Grayling escorting his very attractive wife, who wore a low-cut dress displaying more feminine charm than Alex had ever witnessed in public. Father Donovan smiled at everyone as he headed for the party hosts. Headmaster Hawkins was accompanied by Miss Peel, his new young secretary.

Why was Simon Harris, Vera's brother there? He headed straight for Florence, who flushed scarlet at his approach. Fortunately, an affectionate greeting and a few words about meeting her wonderful son Alex, and he was off to the barbecue. After all, what could they possibly have to talk about?

Then Oliver Oakland walked in, accompanied by Delroy.

Guests started to queue for food. A kind of help-yourself bar with white wine on ice and a tapped barrel of beer. The coppers were there first.

A few faces turned toward the garden gate which was being closely inspected by a man in a floppy sun hat. He removed his sunglasses to illicit gasps of surprise from half the gathering. George Brownlow. He headed straight for Oakland and Delroy, who smiled and greeted him like a long-lost friend, not because they hadn't seen him for a while but because he was brave enough to turn up in the knowledge that wife Florence would be there, and sparks might fly.

'It's one of ours,' George said to Oakland.

'What's one of ours?' asked his puzzled boss.

'The gate. I checked it out. Only one firm could have produced an oak gate like that. Definitely one of ours... An Oakland's creation!' he emphasised, the boss still looking vague. 'I probably oversaw the making of it,' he said, beaming from ear to ear as if the gathering was all about his own past contribution to joinery. But his approach was partly a distraction. He knew Florence would be there and was still working out what he might do or say to her, given the situation.

CHAPTER FIFTY-SIX

It started to look like a scene from an Agatha Christie film. The arrival of the felon, George Brownlow completed the final scene where Hercule Poirot or Miss Marple reveals the identity of the dastardly villain. His deed, as close to a killing as one could get, would put him in the dock of a criminal court. The obvious conclusion for a tough jury: *attempted murder*.

Part of the morning's preparation at 12 Dansbury Street needed particular attention. Imogen hid the key to the lounge drinks cupboard, where Gordon's favourite – but heavily rationed – whisky was preciously stored. And knowing how difficult this birthday party was going to be, she gave her antidepressant regimen a careful review.

They were both stressed about the situation, but psychologists never reveal their weaker side, especially not to patients. The gathering was full of them, unaware of others being so, as far as they knew. Now all Gordon and Imogen had to do was observe and record. It had been many years since Gordon conducted a similar 'trial'. He'd finished the tough project by writing an award-winning paper and gaining international plaudits from his profession. He hoped to repeat that success, before he was too old.

This time he'd be mature enough to avoid the nervous breakdown which threatened to wreck his life following his last effort.

Alex, smiling for everyone's benefit, ran over to his father, who was making straight for his mother.

Breaths were held as George rushed past his son and threw his arms around Florence in a crushing hug, one that was impossible to get out of. She could never have guessed what was happening and wasn't quick enough, agile enough or mentally prepared enough to do anything about it. She couldn't remember the last time George had hugged or touched her with any sign of affection. He smelt vaguely of something...*planty*. She felt faint. Alex, witnessing the situation, rushed to her side as his mother's legs started to buckle. Mary, quick as a flash, helped Florence into a padded garden seat and, as the colour drained from her face, poured the troubled woman a glass of water.

George, bemused by his own behaviour, spluttered an apology. Not apologetic, the hug was genuine, but could only have been delivered under the influence of something helpful, something planty maybe.

Mother was recovering. As Mary watched over her, Alex surveyed the scene around him. Gordon and Imogen gave a reassuring thumbs-up as they saw that Florence was in safe hands. George drifted back toward Oliver Oakland and Delroy, who'd a strong desire to move away to avoid hearing details about the embarrassing situation which had set heads turning.

Picket and Sarge tried to ignore the scene too, by turning back toward the barbecue and pouring themselves another drink. The last thing they wanted right now was a family crisis with aggro while they were in civvies.

Something close to depression descended on Alex. He wasn't quite sure what depression – that much discussed emotional state adults talked about – really was. Feeling down for a bit longer than usual, maybe? But this was a blanket effect as if something upsetting had washed over the celebration. He noted that Gordon and Imogen were super-caring hosts, over the top in some ways, like doting parents of a large family.

Things had settled nicely for Florence. She'd got over the unexpected hug from George. She could forgive him that and now assumed the demeanour of someone who'd managed to clear their mind of past emotion and pain. He was a non-person who deserved only the same courtesies one might bestow on a stranger.

The coppers were frequent visitors to the barbecue and the barrel. But hey! They were off duty and enjoying their leisure time to the full. Now and again subliminal mental interruptions entered their heads as they were compelled to mix with some of the guests who'd spent time at the station, or been interviewed, for one reason or another. But the almost constant reminder that they were off duty kept bringing them quickly back to the day at hand.

Everyone knew about George and Florence. Pointed looks and whisperings were ignored throughout the afternoon, but nothing was missed by the two hosts.

Grayling was the only one who didn't get the same amount of attention when he turned up for his plate of food; just a pleasant nod as they piled his plate up with whatever he'd picked.

Alex and Mary, satisfied with Florence's recovery, left her in a comfortable chair with a glass of lemonade and a chicken sandwich while they moved to a more private part of the garden. Trees and shrubs decorated an L-shaped area, a dogleg, which turned back abruptly from the broad open lawn.

They sat silently for a moment, turning their faces up toward the warm sun. Mary took Alex's hand and placed it firmly on her breast, holding it there in case he shrugged it off. He'd no intention of doing so. She kissed him passionately, flicking her tongue across his lips. It was obvious to Alex that she'd been drinking, but he'd no idea what. It certainly wasn't vodka because her source was busy playing silly buggers with balloons. White wine was the obvious choice, but how she'd managed to slip it past her parents' eagle eyes remained a mystery.

Alex was taken aback by the sudden display of passion. Risky under the circumstances, but he was aware by now that alcohol can bestow a cavalier attitude towards social protocol. His hand moved from one breast to the other on a voyage of discovery. He was about to return the kiss when a voice called out.

'Alex. Son. It's your dad. Are you there? I've been looking all over for you,' George shouted as he entered the dogleg and walked toward them.

Hands on breasts and lips on lips had already parted. The two red faces went unnoticed by George, who'd been taking full advantage of the Singers' liquid hospitality.

'So good to see you, son. It's been too long. And who is this young lady? Is she your girlfriend? I seem to have upset your mother,' he continued, without taking a breath. 'I wanted us to be friends…' His words tailed off. It seemed to dawn on him that was never going to happen.

Mary was shaking as George approached. They hadn't met, so the moment was doubly embarrassing. Alex held the blush for a while but managed to control his body language – not that Father would pick up the subtlety.

The event was a wake-up call. But better the oblivious father than anyone else chancing across the scene. Taking such a risk in her parents' garden was lunacy, and Mary's drink problem could not be held responsible for all the blame. Alex had not been drinking, yet he'd been just as caught up in the moment as Mary.

They wouldn't have gone further, would they?

They walked, weak-legged, back with George as if they'd just stepped off a fairground switchback. But George was less interested in the emotional scene being played out in front of him, and more intent on talking about his 'new family' and the need to reconnect with Florence.

Now was the time for them to separate and mix with the other guests. After all, Mary was expected to be on duty.

The Singers hadn't missed much. They'd paid particular attention in some cases and concluded that Alex Brownlow was an exceptional child. *Science and evidence support the fact that* exceptionality *can be clearly observed not long after birth.* Plus, they'd experienced enough of the teenage population to allow them that opinion. They'd never seen Alex ruffled, not from their very first meeting right up until now. Anyone, let alone a child, would have been disturbed by the actions of his parents; the stricken mother and her lesbian relationship, the breakup of the family home, followed by his father's near-death experience.

They'd been updated concerning Alex's serious academic pursuits. Mary had to admit that he wasn't improving as far as school lessons were concerned, but he'd been studying his own interests with passion. How many fourteen-year-olds read deeply philosophical tomes like Viktor Frankl's *Man's Search for Meaning* and borrow sophisticated library books on how to interpret body language?

Gordon could easily imagine Alex as a stoic hero in a war zone, cool as a cucumber, while the rest of his mates shat themselves during battle. That said, Alex wasn't a cold person by any means, his friendly warmth was easily felt and the way he looked at Mary – so obviously a boy in love.

The lad didn't even panic when he saw his father lurching toward his mother. It might not have turned out to be a simple embrace! But Alex's instinct must have stopped him taking the wrong action, or the party would have been over in a flash and Picket and Sarge would have had to stop eating and drinking, allowing them to bring the full force of the law to bear on the scene. And maybe talk to the press about their latest arrest. Headline: *Top psychologists party turns into a nightmare: Brownlow attempts to kill his wife for the second time.*

They didn't make boys like that anymore, in fact he might even have been the last boy in his class – or would it be, of his class? Alex was a class act, class in the sense of decorum and resilience, someone they'd like their little girl to marry – one day.

The Singers continued to contemplate the various activities. They were taking an interest in Hawkins as he approached Alex and Mary. They'd both had issues with the Head, but in this pleasant garden drinking wine and eating tasty food in the sun, he appeared to be congratulating equally prized pupils. Hands were placed affectionately on his students' shoulders with Penny, Hawkins' young secretary, nodding approval throughout the exchange.

Jennifer Mayhew, the very teacher who had encouraged his interest in the brain and how it worked, smiled across the garden at Alex, raising her glass in a friendly invitation to join her. Alex poured himself a glass of lemonade, they swapped notes about who'd read what, and she suggested further study.

Gordon watched them with a smile on his face. He knew Jennifer – an ex-patient – would be a perfect guide for Alex. Her personal problems were about self-doubt, always needing to better herself. Not a bad trait. But she was one of the best teachers around. He had a special interest in all aspects of self-doubt.

George, disappointed with his efforts so far, steered Delroy toward the garden's dogleg which, having disturbed the two youngsters earlier, he'd earmarked as a quiet place to have a break.

Gordon and Imogen noticed the smoke rising from the hedge and as the wind changed direction took in the unmistakable smell of marijuana. Others sniffed the air. Picket and Sarge caught it too but decided to carry on drinking.

CHAPTER FIFTY-SEVEN

Alex and Mary helped clean up. Gordon sorted the barbecue, while Imogen said a long goodbye to the last of the guests; Picket, Sarge – followed by George, who'd decided to stick close to the lawmen for reasons he hadn't quite worked out.

Those cops could certainly hold their drink. They walked out from the party as easily as they'd entered it. Not so for George who could have done with a Zimmer frame. On the strength of his alcohol-induced confidence, he'd made a final attempt to embrace Florence who'd anticipated his approach and called out to Alex. All heads turned and George's plan was completely scuppered.

Imogen and Gordon eventually headed back to the house for a rest.

The two youngsters stacked the folding chairs and tables in the spare garage. There was tension in the air, a sexual energy above and beyond their experience so far, faces flushed from an uncontrollable string of emotions. They could barely look at each other. Once her parents had made it back to the house, Mary grabbed a blanket left on the lawn; someone must have felt a chill during the barbecue. Taking Alex's hand in a tight grip, she led him back to the dogleg and spread the blanket underneath an overhanging hedge. They lay facing each other, holding hands touching but holding back from the inevitable. Then they kissed for a long time before attempting the yet-to-be experienced sexual intimacy.

Intercourse was vigorous, brief – and painful. There was blood.

They lay on their backs now, silent for a while, listening. For the first time that day there were no unwelcome sounds to interrupt the precious moment. Their own heavy breathing, birdsong, the buzz of bees and the gentle hum of a light plane in the distance was the perfect soundtrack for their intimate scene.

They were shocked, rather than disappointed, at their less than satisfying attempt at intercourse. Mary felt the pain might be like childbirth – in reverse. And the ensuing relief from Alex's withdrawal, what a mother might feel once the final effort of giving birth, was over.

Alex regretted that Mary's sudden display of confidence was alcohol fuelled but needed no convincing that her desire was genuine. Plus, it might not have happened if she'd been sober. Left to him, it would probably have taken a bit longer to pick the right moment.

The birthday bash was over. Imogen dozed off in the lounge after unlocking the drinks cabinet and, having poured Gordon a finger of whisky, securing the bottle again.

'We got through it,' he said, raising his glass before taking a delicate sip. He always made this special treat last. Imogen knew the first drink was never a problem, it was what came after. But that was *once upon a time*; they'd sorted that, the system worked.

He examined his scribbled notes and the substantial remainder of his drink as if checking a precious artefact. 'Enough here to fill a book, never mind an academic paper,' he concluded. They'd sleep in the same room tonight, not in the same bed, but facing each other to review the day without having to finish it with a desperate alcohol-fuelled intimacy.

The obliging guests, with their antics, dialogue and revealing body language, gave Gordon more material than he'd hoped for.

Imogen stepped onto the patio to see how Alex and Mary were getting on with clearing up. She was surprised to see all the tables and chairs had been put away and wondered where the two teenagers were. Not that she was distraught. Gordon stepped out alongside her just as the two kids left the shelter of the dogleg. They weren't holding hands and made an obvious effort to keep their distance from each other – a sure sign to alert adults that something significant had happened.

'I think they've been incredibly stupid,' said Imogen.

'Let's hope not,' said Gordon.

The Singers had taken steps to make sure their past hadn't caught up with them – burying the reasons for her depression and his problems with alcohol. And in doing so, perpetuated a distorted sense of reality, not just of themselves but all those they touched.

Imogen was sleeping soundly now, her lips fluttering as she breathed.

Gordon twirled the whisky around in his glass. No hurry. He thought of Mary. She was a good girl. But her latent genes were already starting to exert their adult power. *The desire to get lost in alcohol gene; the tendency toward depression gene; the drive to succeed gene – academically and socially.* All fighting for prominence.

Gordon knew a great deal about everyone at the barbecue. But there were two people he didn't know inside and out. Mary and Alex. They were still mysteries, as all young people are.

For a moment, he considered the Brownlows; George's obvious desire to get back together with Florence and her opposition to it. Gordon was convinced that if Florence's scars had been hidden, and not such an obvious reminder every time she looked in the mirror, the relationship might have stood a chance. Who knows?

CHAPTER FIFTY-EIGHT

When you leave people alone – or let them go if you've become too attached in the first place – there's a chance they'll disappear out of your life. A good thing, a healthy thing because it will ensure mutual freedom and help one face reality.

The Brownlows had *let go*. All three of them. Like three souls waiting in an orphanage for separate guardians to adopt them.

George had a new family, Delroy's, people he wanted to spend time with and looked forward to going home to after a hard day's work. Individuals who'd no expectations, and didn't care if he smoked, drank or danced, though he was disinclined to move to music. Delroy was king in that department.

Florence had moved along nicely in the bakery business. The boss had bought another shop and put her in charge. Wages were up. Apart from meetings about supporting Alex and any financial issues, George had made no further attempts to befriend or embrace her. Business only.

Although Alex still lived with his ma, their relationship relied on collaboration with housework, cooking and the odd peck on the cheek or an arm around a shoulder to satisfy each other's physical connection.

Alex's life was more about his love for Mary, augmented by

the dramatically physical episode in her parents' garden. And the blood. He relived the experience day and night.

Not quite true. His interest in psychology and philosophy had taken over most of his study time. Gordon encouraged him, lent him books, redacted copies of clinic files, and talked about his patients. The thing that intrigued Alex was that Gordon never treated a person with the same presenting problems, in the same way. Simply because everyone's character and experiences were totally individual, he'd laboured. Words used for one didn't work for another. That was the art.

They talked at length about family, mainly Alex's. The lack of intimacy in particular, the buttoned lips which had led to such a calamitous end to his parents' relationship. Irreparable.

Gordon and Alex had bonded as the boy's interest in subjects of the mind intrigued him further. Buttoned lips were off limits. The psychologist couldn't resist a quote, explaining that a decent one could illustrate a complex lecture or concept in a line or two: *unexpressed emotions will never die. They are buried alive, and they will come forth later in uglier ways. Freud.*

Alex knew that.

Singer encouraged Alex to ask and answer difficult questions. *Have Dr or Mrs Singer ever suffered from depression or anxiety? Thoughts of suicide – in their darkest moments?* He questioned Gordon about anger and passion etc. Well, Dr Singer had encouraged it!

Alex was surprised to hear Gordon Singer admit to all of the above. He was open about it and went to some lengths to explain that people who take up disciplines involving the mind and mental health have usually experienced the spectrum of most emotions and experiences. Otherwise, how could they possibly understand the very cases they set out to help.

'People lie, of course they do, Alex. White lies – courtesy lies – I like to call them, are kind and considerate. *You didn't make the grade this time*, rather than *you're just not good enough*. But the big lies needed to keep some relationships going can only lead to disaster.

'Clinically it's how we work out the best approach for the individual; note the body language, facial expressions, the eye contact, words they use to describe their predicament. Then one's own judgment and gut instinct are used to sum up.'

The Singers were at a conference. Alex and May turned up at Number 12 after school, having skipped any bus that Eddie and Greg Smart might have been on.

Mary asked Alex to sit outside in the sunshine while she put the kettle on.

He felt at ease, taking in the scene; the well-kept garden, the birds flitting in and out of the trees and hedges before pecking at the lawn. The only time his heart skipped a beat was when he glimpsed the entrance to the dogleg where they'd lost their virginity. His colour rose as he recalled the event in detail.

Mary came out with tea and biscuits on a tray. Her colour was high too and he hoped she hadn't been at the bottle.

She put the tray on the wicker tabletop, adjusted her pleated skirt and knelt, knees bare, on the stone patio in front of him. Two pairs of burning cheeks faced each other. Alex felt excited but oddly anxious.

She looked directly into his eyes and, gripping both his hands as tightly as she could, delivered the bombshell.

'Will you marry me, Alex?' she asked, her voice unwavering as she produced a brass curtain ring from her pocket and slipped it onto his little finger.

'A perfect fit,' he said, looking down at the ring.

To reciprocate, he reached into his pocket for the only practical response available under the circumstances. Locating an elastic band, he removed the accumulated fluff, and wound it gently around her extended finger.

'How's yours?'

'Tight,' she smiled, displaying the slightly swollen finger.

They both stood ready to hug. Not a hint of alcohol when she kissed him.

'Yes! Of course, I'll marry you,' he replied, his answer more shakily delivered than the question. There was a long pause, the colour in their cheeks still high.

A key rattled in the lock. There was a swish as the front door opened. A draught worked its way along the hall and out to the terrace, toward the pink-faced pair.

'But not just yet,' added Alex, with a wry smile.

Gordon and Imogen shouted in unison, 'Anyone at home?'

ACKNOWLEDGEMENTS

I am so grateful to my wife Carol – reader, critic, and most patient friend – for her invaluable support. She has read, pencilled, and ploughed her way through several drafts, never doubting it would end up getting published.

Many thanks to my book production team, whom I have never met, but through the miracle of the internet and social media, produce the best results for my manuscripts: Julia Gibbs, copy editor and proof-reader, a great technician who always goes the extra mile and Cathy Helms at Avalon Graphics, who pulls out all the stops to design the cover and format my book ready for publishing.

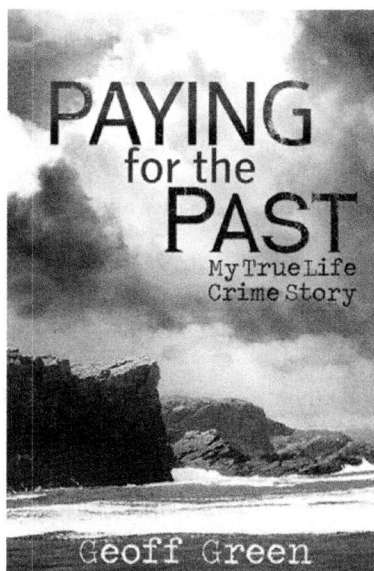

PAYING FOR THE PAST

My true-life crime story

Everyone knows the extent of their crime…but only one man knows where they are.

September 1975. Jim Miller and John Bellord, two wealthy men of impeccable character, fly to France and disappear without a trace. A blackmailed bishop, forgery, faked suicides, a multimillion-pound fraud and many lives ruined as police, Interpol, the media, and a psychic investigator join in a fruitless search for the two outlaws. Only Geoff Green knows where they are. He plans and executes their escape and finally gives them up following their hideaway year on remote Priest Island surviving a sub-zero winter. This is his account of what they did, how they did it, and why he confessed all. It is not only a crime adventure, but a personal story of total trust in a mesmerising mentor and his philosophy of life.

WHAT READERS SAY ABOUT, PAYING FOR THE PAST.

Ana Saldanha, author and translator.

I can't believe it's not fiction! It reads like the most engrossing adventure story I've read in a long time. But the honesty of a first-person account shines through. Compulsory reading.

Helen Holt, journalist, and author.

Here's a biography heading for the top. This is a crime adventure, mystery, thriller, – sure to make you think you're reading fiction. Fast moving and well written – you'll forget you're reading a true story.

Barry Winbolt, psychotherapist, and author.

A real page turner and a story of loyalty, compassion, learning, humility and self-awareness that most of us can only aspire to. The effects of reading it will stay with me.

Kenneth E. Lim, author of The North Korean.

What a fascinating narrative. The characterization is brilliant, supported gamely by believable dialogue. Everyone involved, including the miscreants, is viewed in a sympathetic light. Thank you so much for the intriguing read.

Available on: Amazon: https://mybook.to/PayingForPast

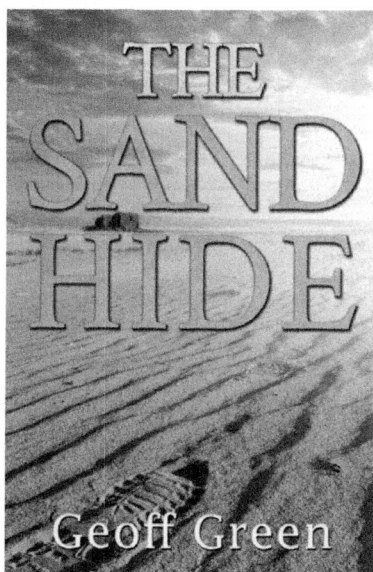

THE SAND HIDE

Alcoholism, abuse, betrayal and escape to the desert

Robert Dexter makes a lot of money before turning to alcohol and abuse. When he draws blood and puts his wife Laura in hospital, things have to change. Robert wants to win her back, but in a moment of madness he commits the ultimate betrayal. Nothing would stop Laura from leaving now. And where she was going, he'd never find her.

WHAT READERS SAY ABOUT, THE SAND HIDE

Andy Batkin's review on Amazon.

A hugely enjoyable second book from Geoff Green. But whilst his first is the jaw-dropping true-crime story of his own role in the Lucan-type disappearance and international manhunt for a pair of fraudsters in the 1970s, this is a gripping story of love and violence, loss and re-discovery.

Rosanna Ley, author of The Saffron Trail.

A sweeping and thought-provoking story of abuse and betrayal. Laura doesn't find it so easy to leave Robert, even after the way he has treated her – but some things are impossible to forgive. After what she has been through, the prospect of spending some time in a desert outpost in Morocco, far away from her old life, is too appealing to resist. But in this new life she may have taken on more than she bargained for. It seems that Laura's adventures are only just beginning.

Mike Lefroy, reader.

Will she, won't she escape her tormentor? A great holiday read as you are taken into the souks, medinas and desert villages of Morocco.

Available on Amazon: https://mybook.to/SandHide

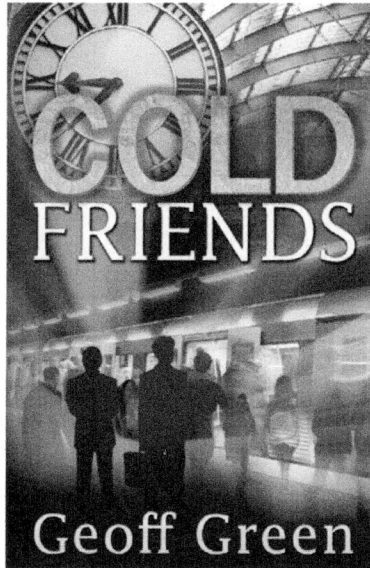

COLD FRIENDS

Someone is about to reveal your past.

Ben Taylor wants a quiet life. But when civil servant creep, Frank Carson, threatens his job and daughter Beth seems intent on wrecking her future, he thinks it's as bad as it gets, until he spots his old friend Craig Thomas, looking like a ghost on Victoria Station and knows he should have walked on. Past secrets threaten their comfortable suburban lives. From the moment they shake hands and exchange cards, Ben's life takes a downward spiral.

Available on Amazon: https://mybook.to/ColdFriends

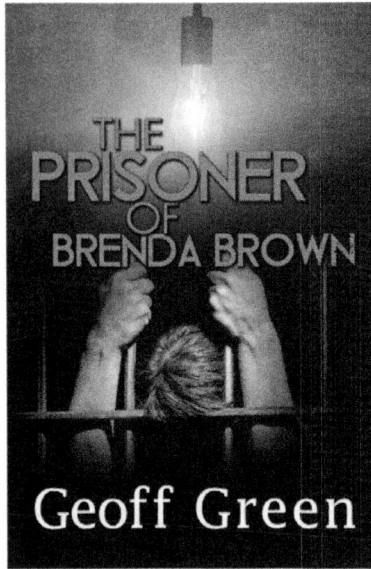

THE PRISONER OF BRENDA BROWN

Someone is about to reveal your past.

Kidnapping is a serious crime: a hostage is taken, demands are made, cash expected or, in some cases an exchange of prisoners. Kidnappers are usually men, but when Brenda Brown lures Melvin Greenstone into a basement cell, the case baffles everyone. No demands are made and there are no obvious reasons for his incarceration.

Available on Amazon: https://mybook.to/BrendaBrown

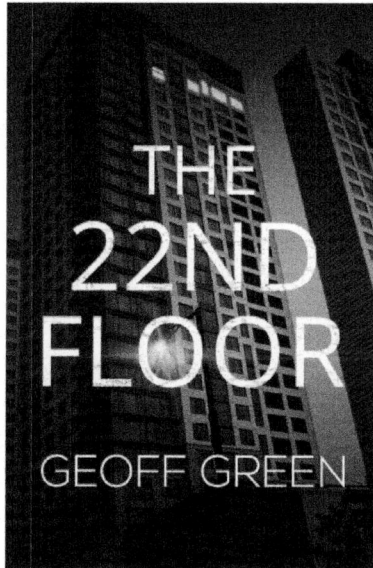

THE 22ND FLOOR

She'd been close enough to death to appreciate the true value of life.

Jeremiah Travers is super-rich. Zena Marshall knows how he made his money, his secrets, the collateral damage and why he'll live to regret it for the rest of his life. She intends to bring him down - and they're about to meet for the very first time.

Available on Amazon: https://mybook.to/22ndFloor

Printed in Great Britain
by Amazon